Something About Workmen

I let myself fall into his lap, and I feel his strong legs beneath me. I think about what he'll say when he lifts my skirt and sees the scarlet panties that I've chosen for just this moment. These naughty knickers are the most expensive item of lingerie I've ever purchased, and I want him to notice the extravagance. But he doesn't comment on the colour of them, or the silky fabric, or the way they hug my shapely ass.

Without a word, he slides them down my thighs and begins to spank me, slowly, steadily, until I'm squirming in his lap. He starts to go a little harder, and I realise that he's really smacking me now. I also realise that as I press myself against his leg, this is going to make me come.

Something About Workmen
Alison Tyler

BLACK LACE

Black Lace books contain sexual fantasies.
In real life, always practise safe sex.

First published in 2003 by
Black Lace
Thames Wharf Studios
Rainville Road
London W6 9HA

Design by Smith & Gilmour, London
Printed and bound by Mackays of Chatham PLC

ISBN 0 352 33847 4

For SAM

Until I met you, baby,
I didn't know what I was missing.

– Stevie Ray Vaughn

Prologue

EXT SHOT: CONSTRUCTION SITE: NIGHT

DANIKA ANDREWS, late twenties, tall, blonde, Amazonian in both stature and attitude, approaches the empty building site on foot. She's not appropriately dressed for the scene. No yellow plastic hard hat here. No scuffed workboots. The slick-looking European beauty is clad in a black, skintight dress and heels that click rhythmically on the concrete. Her long golden hair waves behind her in the light breeze.

DANIKA turns in a full circle, surveying the empty site. It's obvious from her expression that she's looking for someone. The scene is dark and ominous. Suddenly, lights burst on from all corners, and the broken ground is bathed in a warm amber glow. The change in atmosphere doesn't faze DANIKA. She continues to survey the scene, eyes roaming like a cat's.

> DANIKA
> You're late.

She speaks before another person enters her vision. Then, from behind her, footsteps steadily approach. A tall, broad-shouldered man walks up to her and encircles her slim waist with his hands. DANIKA leans back into his embrace, fitting her body into his in a sexy, feline manner. Although she doesn't turn around to face him, she continues to talk.

>   DANIKA
>   I hate waiting.

The man nuzzles his face against her neck, and his hand comes up under the gossamer-like straps of her thin dress. He is dark haired, but we cannot see his face yet.

>   DANIKA
>   (softly)
>   Hate it . . .

Her voice trails off. It's apparent from her change in tone that his kissing has gotten to her.

CLOSE SHOT:

DANIKA's face, eyes shut, lips parted. She sighs as the man continues to kiss her.

PULL BACK TO REVEAL:

The man spins her around and begins to methodically work his way into the low cleavage of her dress. He slides the top of the dress down from her shoulders, showing off DANIKA's perfect round breasts. Her naked skin shimmers beneath the lights. Her nipples are already fully erect. The man kisses her breasts hungrily and DANIKA moans at his caresses, but after a moment of giving in to this delicious sensation, she greedily wants more. In a dominant move, she puts her hands on his shoulders, pushing him down onto his knees. He presses his face against her dress, then slowly begins to slip the shiny fabric up to her hips. DANIKA has nothing on under the dress except for her garter and stockings.

The man has his face against the split of her body, kissing fiercely, so lost in the wonder of her that he doesn't notice as she slowly reaches behind her to pull a knife from a hidden sheath strapped high on her thigh, beneath her black garter. She easily takes control of the man before he understands what's happening; overpowering him in seconds with the finesse of a well-trained jujitsu artist, which is precisely what she is . . .

'You've got to be kidding.'

'What did you say, Cat?' my boss asks. Unfortunately for me, Trini has passed by my office at precisely the wrong time.

'Nothing,' I assure her, not wanting to go back to reading this script, but not wanting to talk to Trini right now about it, either. Up until Danika pulled the blade from her expensive hosiery, I'd been enjoying the sex scene, my mind tripping to find previous films that had employed the rarely shown man-going-down-on-the-woman scenario. *Betty Blue*. That was a good one. Leave it to the French to show lovers having a conversation while the man is dining on the woman's pussy.

'Tell me.' The diminutive Trini leans in the doorway, peering at me over her gem-encrusted spectacles. My boss fits Hollywood's show-off style. In a word, she *glitters*. From the rocks adorning her ring fingers to the metallic convertible she drives, Trini has an appetite for sparkle. Today she's clad in a black sweater shot through with silver strands accompanied by a choker made of multicoloured jewels.

I stare at her for a moment, not entirely sure how honest I'm going to be.

'Danika's a black belt,' I begin cautiously.

Trini nods.

'She's a jujitsu artist. She's a supermodel who works the runways in Milan as her cover. She can stride effortlessly in the type of heels that would trip a stripper.' I pause for breath, then continue. 'The girl is amazing in the kitchen, in bed, and apparently in deserted building sites. She knows how to speak eight languages, fluently. She's quite obviously the female James Bond. The only thing she isn't is part lizard, like that chick in *Species*. But at least that was sort of cool.'

'Danika's also a huge hit,' Trini reminds me. 'The sequel did better than the original. That doesn't happen too often.'

'But *this* one –'

'I know,' she sighs. 'Some of the dialogue is a little stilted.'

'It's not what she says, it's what she *does*.'

'That's why people like her. She acts in ways that normal folks can't.'

I understand the concept, but who can identify with a supermodel, Manolo-wearing jujitsu artist who gets her kicks having knife fights in empty construction sites without even bothering to get off first? Does your average middle-class American housewife really have those sorts of aspirations? Or was Danika created solely for the teenage boys who drool over the almost X-rated posters of her? I say none of this aloud, yet my boss seems to read my mind.

'Do what you can, all right, Cat?' Trini gestures to me to throw ideas at her. I'm drawing a blank, then suddenly –

'What if she fucks him before she kills him?'

'See?' Trini grins at me. 'That's why we pay you the big bucks.'

I nod. Right. Sure. But when I go back to reading the script, I no longer picture the half-Norwegian, half-South American movie star in the scene. It's me there at the building site, and I'm devilishly clad in my own style, although my hair is dark instead of blonde and I'm wearing zip-up boots rather than teetering sandals. When I look at the stranger, I can tell he's hungry for me, and that he wants to do it right up against one of those huge concrete tube things that you always see on job sites, but whose purpose has always escaped me.

But before we fuck, he has to take off my clothes. He lifts me in his arms and carries me to the back of his pick-up truck, which is conveniently parked on the dirt on the edge of the construction site. There is an old brown army blanket lying across the metal of the truck bed, creating a makeshift cushion. He sets me down on the rough-napped blanket, then starts to undo the tie on my scarlet silk blouse with a gentleness that comes as an unexpected and extremely arousing surprise.

I sigh as he unlaces the length of slim red ribbon and pulls the light fabric wide open. I'm not wearing a bra beneath, only a thin camisole edged in pale-pink lace. My nipples are dangerously hard already, tenting the delicate fabric, and my breasts feel larger than their usual mere handfuls of flesh. I want his hands everywhere at once, caressing me, stroking and touching, his fingers pressing up inside me, opening me up. I want far more than that: his lips on the under curve of my neck, his chest pressed to mine, his cock . . .

Oh, Christ, his cock.

He doesn't deny me. His large, strong hands pump my breasts through the diaphanous undergarment, and his thumbs firmly brush the tips of my nipples, making me arch my back and wordlessly beg him for more. The whole soft weight of my breasts radiates with the heat of his touch. I can feel how wet I am simply from this initial stroke, and I tighten my thighs together, but that only works to make me even more aware of how turned on I am. Wetness spills out of me, slicking the skin between my inner thighs.

'Open your eyes,' he demands. 'Look at me.'

I take a deep breath and then stare directly at him, at his cobalt-blue T-shirt and faded jeans. I look at his heavy, scuffed black workboots and then tilt my head to take in the battered leather gloves tossed near me on the floor of his truck bed. As soon as I see those casually discarded gloves, my heart beats even faster.

I want him to slide those gloves back on and finger me. I can see this easily: me bent over his lap and him finger-fucking me until the gloves are smeared and creamy-wet with my glossy juices. I imagine the feel of his fingers pinching my slippery lips between his gloved pointer and thumb, of him drawing the wetness up between my ass-cheeks and fluttering his thumb against my rear hole. My clit becomes swollen and hungry, and I know that as soon as he thrusts his gloved thumb in my ass I will come. I'm so turned on by this fantasy that I can't speak.

But maybe he already knows what I want. Maybe he can guess everything from the way I purr at him, moaning and arching my body as if I've become a yearning she-cat, desperate for a bit of attention. Urgently I spread my legs and he steps between them so that I can press my hips to his. I hope that he can feel my growing body heat. I am so ready for him. So needy.

'You like those?' he asks, lifting the gloves and slowly sliding them on, one at a time.

I nod, still speechless.

'Roll over, baby.'

I obey immediately, my feet on the ground, my body now pressed face down against the rough blanket. He slides my skirt up to my hips and pushes my knickers aside, using none of the gentleness he showed at the start. First, he thrusts two fingers into my pussy, and then he starts to rub my clit, using my own wetness as lubrication. My whole body tenses as I feel the leather of those gloves petting my clit. He uses his pointer and middle finger, and he rubs up and down, then captures my clit between his fingers and thumb, letting it slip free, over and over again.

The climax is so close I can feel the pressure of relief building within me, but he's not going to let me come before he's fucked me – I'm certain of this fact. As I stare at all the rubble of his daily grind, the battered silver tool box and the heavy machinery parts and reflective plastic cones, he unbuttons his fly, pulls out his cock and slides inside me. The truck rocks forcefully with our thrusts and, with each drive forward, everything about me and my normal daily life is stripped away.

His hands grip into my arms and I can feel the wetness on his gloved fingers; my own wetness. As his fingers work up and down, I am sure my naked skin must be growing marked and dirty. His callused fingers rough up the soft skin of my body so that I can imagine a road map of where he's touched me. Sex juices seep down my thighs, dripping onto the dirt between my spread legs. As I start to come, he leans forward and leaves bite marks on my neck. All the while he fucks me, and my body feels deliciously bruised inside from the intensity of his thrusts.

The cold chill of the night air complements the warmth of his skin and, just like Danika, I have no idea what his name is.

But sometimes names aren't important.

Not in situations like this.

lot is nearly full, half with cars the same style as Marilynn's – fancy fast sportsters in a rainbow of colours, heavy on the reds and turquoises – and half with more mundane vehicles – pick-up trucks and souped-up 70s automobiles including two vintage El Caminos nosed together in the corner. Our watering hole is considered old school, darkly wood panelled with a light-up jukebox in the corner. The place is upscale enough for the two of us, without being trendy with a capital T. I'd never come here with my other best friend, Janice Higgins, who prefers beach-view cafés that serve freshly squeezed guava juice and super-sized shots of recently mowed organic wheat grass.

'Come on, Cat,' Marilynn urges. 'What was going on with you back there?'

'I don't know what you're talking about,' I tell her, knowing that I'm not fooling her in the slightest. It's difficult to dupe someone who's known you since high school.

'You were making goo-goo eyes with that studly guy on the road crew. Admit it. Watching you watching *him* was like catching a scene fresh from a teen-flick. You'd find true love in a lazy summer afternoon, with a sky painted like cotton candy, and then you'd make out sweetly beneath the pier at the Santa Monica Boardwalk, sand in your hair, sea salt on your lips. His hands. Your breasts. If it were an R-rated movie, then his naked chest and your *naked* breasts . . .'

'Sounds like a teen movie, all right,' I agree. 'But in order to be in *your* type of movie, he'd have to have had two heads or something.'

'He *had* two heads,' Marilynn says matter-of-factly, holding the heavy wood door open for me. 'The handsome one with those amazing eyes . . .'

'They were amazing, weren't they?' I ask because I can't help myself.

'Yeah, sure,' Marilynn says brusquely. 'The head that was staring at you, and the rock-hard one tucked into his jeans that was yearning for a little something-something.'

We walk into the joint now, and I squint in the dim light, waiting for my eyes to grow accustomed to the dark atmosphere. Silently, I pray that the taunting will end as we pony up to the shiny chrome-edged bar. I smooth my hands over my slim polka-dotted rose-pink skirt, waiting for the bartender to make his way to our side. When he does I order quickly, my usual white-wine spritzer, and Marilynn requests a Tequila Sunrise. She has a broad appetite for liquor, likes to try different concoctions on different nights – sort of an 'If it's Tuesday, it must be bourbon' attitude towards getting drunk. There isn't a drink that Marilynn hasn't tried – from Zombie Mindblowers to Dirty Janes – and there are few that she doesn't know how to make herself. Janice thinks it's disturbing that Marilynn can't settle herself on one signature drink. To Janice, randomness is terrifying, but I find that confidence with alcohol incredibly sexy. It's a quality that bleeds into all aspects of Marilynn's life. She can't choose a favourite fragrance either; or, more importantly, a favourite man.

While we wait for our drinks to arrive, I make an effort to talk to her in a low voice about Declan, the barman she likes, who's too busy at the far end of the bar to come chat with us. Unfortunately, Marilynn's far too enthralled with the current topic to let this conversation go. 'Ever heard about someone named Logan?' she says. 'Someone named Logan Arthur Riley who is engaged to a pretty dark-eyed brunette named Catherine Esme Harrington?' She play-punches me on the arm. 'For Christ's sake, Cat, you're getting married soon.'

'I know,' I say, finally deciding to play this on the

level. 'But he really was *so* hot, wasn't he? Too hot to ignore.'

Marilynn fans herself in agreement.

'And I never look at guys,' I add.

'Not ever?'

'Not ever.'

She's quiet for a moment, and I can tell that she's recalling all the other girls' nights out we've had together over the years. The ones during which she effortlessly collects multiple numbers from potential bedmates, her red leather clutch purse spilling over with little slips of paper by the end of the night. The ones during which I sit placidly on a bar stool or in a booth, drinking my spritzers, choosing selections on the jukebox, and waiting for her to float herself down to me and get my opinion of her latest flame.

'Not even surreptitiously?' she asks, obviously not believing what I'm saying, because she would have noticed by now if this were true.

I shake my head.

'Like when nobody's looking. Or when some dreamboat accidentally bumps into you in line at the gourmet grocery store. Or when you're on the set, and a movie star walks by.'

'Never,' I tell her. 'And you know that movie stars don't do anything for me.'

'That's right,' she says. She knows. People who work in the movies rarely fixate on stars. We view their prima donna attitudes daily, and with their multiple quirks and odd decadent demands, the allure of a star-aura fades considerably.

'I just don't look at guys,' I continue. 'I've got Logan.'

'Yeah, you have Logan. So what was different this time?'

I can't explain. There was a connection. That's all I can think. And then I can't even think clearly any more, because I watch through the window as a golden-yellow truck slips into a parking space across the street. Who would ever have thought a yellow hue would turn me on? Like every woman who's fallen for Hallmark's version of romance, I've always believed red equalled true lust. Scarlet. Vermillion. Crimson. But not any more.

I watch, mesmerised, as the stranger gets out of his seat and heads towards the bar.

FLASH FORWARD:

Moving forward in time is a little Hollywood trick in which the action in a film progresses seamlessly from the current day to some time in the future. Often this happens when night falls, or a door closes, or an airplane departs. Once you know to look for this gimmick, you'll notice the use occurs repeatedly. Otherwise, all films would occur in real time, and outside of *Dinner with Andre*, most film-makers can't pull this off.

In my case, I'm jumping only about twelve hours forward in time. This type of move makes perfect sense to me, because I think in script format the way some people occasionally dream in a language that they've finally mastered, the way I've read that the most accomplished painters dream in colour, ranges of hues and palettes, swirls and designs. I even fantasise in script style, with my descriptions in the wides, dialogue in the centre.

This may seem seriously twisted to some, but after years of working in Hollywood, living with a movie mentality has become a way of life for me.

INT. POSITIVELY FOURTH STREET CAFE

JANICE and CAT sit at a café in Santa Monica, drinking freshly squeezed orange juice while waiting for their breakfasts to arrive. JANICE is a round-faced blonde, with thick, lustrous curls. Everything about her appears larger than life. Where Marilynn is lanky and lean, JANICE is all exaggerated curves and round features that she hides with tasteful, draping clothing. She never reveals her abundant cleavage or her delicious hourglass figure made by her small waist and sumptuous hips.

'In a film,' I tell Janice after bringing her up to speed, 'he would have walked right over to me, spun me around on the bar stool, and kissed me until I swooned against the bar. The rest of the patrons would have applauded our lust and made loud catcalls and whooping sounds.'

'I can see that,' Janice says, nodding. She's a movie reviewer for one of the few successful online magazines, and she has a mental category list of every movie she's ever seen, which is practically every movie that was ever made. Today, we're having breakfast at her favourite restaurant on Montana and Fourth, a white-walled, sunshiny room filled with colourful paintings by local folk artists and a message board in the back featuring advertisements for Yoga Therapy, Herbal-Infusion Colonics, and Intensive Nurturing Interpersonal Transcultural Psychoanalysis. I believe Janice has tried all of these services at least once.

'He would have wrapped one hand in my hair, caveman style, bent me back, and kissed me until I melted into his arms,' I say, creatively imagining the scene in technicolour brightness.

She twists one of her fat blonde curls around her fingers and stares into the distance as if she's right there with me, seeing the mental movie in my mind.

'And then Marilynn would have gone off with that bartender she likes,' Janice says, 'and the credits would have rolled.'

'No,' I shake my head, fervently disagreeing with her. 'No, this is the *start* of the film, not the end.'

'Did Marilynn go off with the bartender or not?' Janice wants to know.

'Sure, but –'

Janice smirks. She likes being right, and generally, when it comes to plot points, she is. But I don't let her get cocky on this one.

'They fuck, like, once a month. You know that. It was a gimme.'

'Make love,' she corrects me. 'Don't say the 'f' word.'

'But that's what they do.' I think about several sexy situations that Marilynn has told me about. There was the time that Declan put her right up on the bar after closing time and spilled expensive liquor in the valley between her breasts, then licked her clean. He took the whipped-cream canister used for topping decadent coffee-and-alcohol creations and spritzed her rock-hard nipples with the cold, whipped fluff, then licked her clean again. By the time he moved his mouth to the hot spot between her thighs, she was crying out his name, begging him to let her come.

Then there was the time they unintentionally wound up at a screening together, not on an official date, but not caring. She'd done special effects on the movie. He was there as a bartender with the catering crew. Both decided to pass on the flick in favour of a raunchy session in the men's room, with her holding on to the cold porcelain sink while he pounded into her from behind, the two able to watch every change in their actions in the fancy three-way mirrors. They only emerged from the rest room when the credits ran – he to serve drinks and she to down them.

In my book, those sorts of scenes define the idea of ferocious fucking. 'You have to admit it,' I continue to Janice. 'They really know how to f–'

Janice holds up a hand to stop me. Her skin is soft and well pampered. She gets manicures at least once a week, and it's obvious. This week's polish looks like gold lamé. Her fingertips positively glisten in a Midas-touch way.

'Maybe so,' she says. 'But in the movie, they'd finally realise that they were meant for each other. Two lost souls looking for love in all the wrong places, and at the bottom of all the wrong shot glasses, not under-standing that the right person was there all along, just at the end of the bar. For years, he's gritted his teeth when she's gone for other guys right in front of him. For years, she's hated every moment he mentioned his toxic ex-girlfriend. But now, at the end of this movie, they'd finally learn that their hearts belonged to one another. The film would be called *Happy Hour*.'

'It's not Marilynn's movie,' I remind her, sounding like a diva in spite of myself. How many times have I heard a starlet make a similar comment? Yet that doesn't mean I can stop myself from diving into the role of the superstar. 'It's mine,' I insist. 'I'm the lead.'

'Drama, comedy, or tragedy?' Janice says, thinking aloud. She bites her coral-slicked bottom lip as she regards me. 'With you, Cat, I'd have to say a farce.'

'Oh, thanks a whole hell of a lot.'

'In a farce, all the characters get scrambled, but everyone ends up with their original partner at the end.'

'I *know* that. Who's the script doctor here?'

She continues as if I haven't spoken. 'A good comedy always finishes with a wedding. That dates back to Shakespeare's time. A wedding makes the audience happy. So I guess some comedies can also be farces, if the partners marry each other before the credits.'

'Sure,' I nod. 'But I don't know why you're always so stuck on the genre of a situation.'

'It's how I work,' she reminds me. 'I need to know what I'm dealing with in order to figure out how the plot will unfold.' Another worry of her bottom lip before she nods as if she's satisfied with her detective work. 'I'm guessing he didn't kiss you.' Janice knows me just as well as she knows Marilynn. The three of us have been the strangest trio of buddies for years. I'm in the middle – the glue that keeps the others stuck in place – while Janice and Marilynn are on opposite edges of the spectrum. Our only similarity is our careers: we're all in movies, one way or the other. But isn't everybody in LA?

'And he didn't even talk to you. Maybe he didn't notice you were there at all. This was all in your head, from the very start. He was staring at the car, not you, because Marilynn drives such a cool ride. I mean, how many chicks have candy-apple red '67 Thunderbirds, right?' Occasionally, Janice can appreciate Marilynn's outrageous style, even if she'd never emulate it. 'That's a muscle car if I ever saw one. And then he happened to go to the same place you guys went because it's the closest beer joint to the job site. I don't know why you two like that place. It's so depressingly dark. You could have been out at the Juniper Beach Café, under an umbrella.'

I shrug. 'We like it.'

'OK,' she nods, although it's clear she can't understand this fascination with dark bars of ours. Janice likes hipper spots than Marilynn. She likes light and air and good clean fun, although she does always manage to put her personal preferences aside when it comes to writing reviews. 'Anyway, he was interested in the car, and if he did come over at all, it was to talk automobiles with Marilynn –' she snaps her fingers in a 'Eureka, I've found it' move that I find terribly annoying. 'Marilynn slept with him!' she announces gleefully.

'Sad sort of movie for me,' I say. 'I mean, a real fucking tragedy,' and Janice wrinkles her nose at me. Swearing is her number-one pet peeve, both in the movies and in real life. When the three of us are together, she consistently purses her lips when Marilynn swears. Once, she actually put her hands over her ears during a particularly X-rated moment in Marilynn's story, and I thought that Marilynn was going to slug her.

'So what happened, then?'

'He sat with a few of his buddies at the table by the window, and whenever I looked at him, he was looking at me.'

'Sounds kind of high school.'

It's the same thing Marilynn said last night. Teen-movie time. But I'm an adult. I don't want to be cast in a movie that features anyone who used to be on *Party of Five*.

'It wasn't,' I insist. 'At least, things like that didn't happen to *me* in high school.'

'You and Marilynn went to an all-girls' school, right?'

I nod, and now I'm the one to smirk. 'This would be a very different movie if it featured a cast from my alma mater.'

Janice ignores my light-hearted lesbian joke. 'So then he sent you over a drink with a note on the napkin that said you were the most beautiful woman he'd ever seen in his life.'

'No. I think Tom Hanks and Meg Ryan were in that one.'

'Email, not napkin,' she says. 'And the original was so much better than the remake, you wouldn't believe it. To me, it was almost as if the screenwriters hadn't even bothered to watch the original film.'

'They didn't have email in the original.'

'I know. But they had Jimmy Stewart.'

'You're losing me,' I tell her.

'OK. You sent him a drink with a note on the napkin that said *he* was the most beautiful –'

'No.'

'Then what?' Janice asks, 'What was the inciting incident?'

This is the point that changes the course of the film. Janice is as much a believer in life as art as I am. If something important happened to me, then it must have happened to me long before the end of Act One, right?

'I went to the ladies' room, and when I came out he was standing in the hallway, waiting for me.'

'And?'

'And he kissed me.'

'I don't fucking believe it.'

I picture my life playing out like a movie all the time. This is undoubtedly because I live in the land of the motion-picture mentality, and everyone I know has some connection with cinema. Even my fiancé, who is a well-paid senior civil engineer by trade, is a closet screenwriter, with deep, dark hopes of one day breaking into the big time. You'd think with my connections that I might be able to help him, but he's not interested in what he considers 'hand-outs'. He wants to do it on his own. He's not alone in his daydreams of stardom. As far as I can tell, everyone in LA-LA-land wants to be doing something else. Something aside from what currently pays the bills. One time, when I was pulled over for making a left turn against the light, the cop noticed my studio parking pass and actually whipped out a script for me to 'give a look-see'. I agreed, just to avoid the ticket.

And then there's me. I work as a script doctor, fixing the almost unfixable, righting the writing wrongs which spill over my desk in avalanches of paper every week. I'm an ace at knowing when a script is going haywire. I understand when characters do not behave characteristically and when a writer has forced something to happen simply because it's time for a transition.

My job requires a light hand and a sly way of behaving. I do everything in my power not to call attention to myself. In this way, I'm a little like a body double for a scriptwriter. I have a talent for getting inside the heads of characters and forcing plots to make sense. Unfortunately, I possess none of these skills in my own life. If I knew which scene would lead me directly to a happy ending, I'd take it in a minute. I don't need to experience a personal narrative arc before I find my resolution. I mean, as Marilynn would say, 'Who the fuck wouldn't take the easy way out?'

Instead, I plod through or flit through or fall through my days, piecing together the CinemaScope of my world. Some weeks, I star in the sappiest of dramas. Other times my life is pure comedy. But the scene with the man from the road crew? Well, for the first time ever, I found myself starring in an X-rated movie. Make that an *unrated* movie, the European cut of which has finally become available in the States. One with plenty of nudity, real-life fucking, and a plot that would confuse the best film buff. And although I don't spell out what happened to Janice, I relive the scene in my head:

He said, 'Couldn't take my eyes off you.'

I pressed myself against the wood panelling for support, feeling tremors start deep in my core. Was this man dangerous? Yes, and no. I had the distinct sensation that he wasn't dangerous in the sense that he could hurt me, only in the sense that he could turn my world around. Was I in trouble? Yes, and no again. In serious trouble because I didn't want to get away from him. Deeply in trouble, because I should have ignored him completely and stalked forcefully back to Marilynn, insisting that we leave the bar immediately.

'Just couldn't,' he said.

'Me, too,' I admitted, and I stared back at him again, as boldly as I could, working to memorise the lines at the edges of his green eyes, the burnished-gold colour of his skin, those amazing lips that somehow told me everything I needed to know without saying a single word aloud. He took a step closer and reached forward, then wrapped his hand forcefully around my delicate wrist, capturing me where I stood. I could easily imagine those hands holding my wrists over my head as he fucked me. The thought was sublime, being held in place solely by his power, submitting to the force of his thrusts. I could also imagine being led by the wrist down a long, narrow hallway, to a bedroom where unbelievable pleasures awaited me. From his eyes alone, I saw all those visions.

'What's your name?'

I didn't tell him. Not only because he was a stranger, but also because it was as if I didn't know myself any more. Who was I? Not Cat Harrington, she of the Cat and Logan duo, a pair who have been working the couples circuit for six years now. If he looked down, he would be able to see my extravagant diamond-and-pink-tourmaline engagement ring, sparkling even in this dim light. Would that have made him leave? It should have. But the best plots aren't made about people who do things that they should. Especially the ones in erotic art-house films.

'You're going to play it tight to the vest, aren't you?'

I smiled at that because he was right, then said, 'I have to.'

'What other things do you have to do?' As he spoke,

he took a step closer, and now we were almost chest to chest, with me looking up at him, and my wrist still caught in his forceful grip. I thought of every bit of clever dialogue I've ever written, but my brain was a complete blank.

'Do you have to turn around and place your hands flat against the wall?'

I trembled all over. I could smell the scent of his shaving cream, and I thought I'd never forget that aroma. Not ever.

'Do you have to let me pull your skirt up so that I can see what colour panties you're wearing?'

I couldn't – this wasn't me. But as he let go of my wrist, I found myself doing exactly what he'd suggested. Why? Because he was right: I had to. With my palms flat on the wood panelling, I thought only of what might happen if Marilynn came after me to see where I'd disappeared to for so long. She'd find me in such a strange position, one much more suited to her lifestyle than my own. Marilynn's known for being edgy. She pushes boundaries. She takes risks. I'm known for being normal. Just like in that Bowie song: 'I've never done good things. I've never done bad things.' It's the truth. I let Marilynn do the bad things and Janice do the good things, and I walk a line between them in what I realised suddenly was a place called 'Dullsville'. Above and beyond all else, I'm sweet, trustworthy, patient and normal.

Now, in a single instant, all that faded away, because here I was, facing the dark, oak wall by the payphone, as a complete stranger slowly lifted my pale-pink polkadot skirt, moving the silky fabric higher and higher up to my hips, revealing the fact that I had on a pair of simple white satin bikinis beneath. It was a hot day, and I didn't have on any nylons. Dressing is casually cool in California, regardless of the season.

'Pretty,' he said, smoothing his hand over the curve of my ass. 'So fucking pretty. Can I have these panties?'

I shook my head. My long curly hair brushed my cheeks. The whole world had slowed on its axis. We had all the time we'd ever need.

'You don't want to step out of them and let me take them home?'

Finally, I found my voice. 'Why do you want them?'

'Oh,' he sighed, 'that would be telling, wouldn't it?'

'Please,' I begged. 'Tell me.'

'I want to wrap them around my cock so that I can feel them.' He said these words softly, his mouth pressed against my ear, his breath tickling my hair. 'I want to drive hard into the fabric, let the softness overwhelm me. I want to come in them, knowing that you wore them, knowing they were on your body all day long, enveloping you, soaking up your scent. Don't you want to let me do that?'

I lowered my chin to my chest. Yes, I did. But I wanted so many other things, too. First, I wanted him to slide the panties off me himself. I wanted to feel his warm fingers touching my skin as intimately as possible. I wanted far more than that – wanted him to cup my naked pussy with his hand and see just how wet I was. I knew – oh, yes, I knew – but I wanted him to know, too.

'Do you?'

Yes, I thought. Oh, yes. Do that.

Although I said nothing, he took my silence for the affirmative. Without another word, he bent to the floor and slid my panties all the way down my legs, then waited for me to step out of them. I did so as carefully as possible, deeply aware of slipping the fabric over my fancy open-toed red sandals, and I closed my eyes as I heard him breathe in the aroma lingering on the fabric. I was extremely exposed, soft skirt bunched at my hips, ass naked to the world. I'd never been in a position like this before. Even when Logan and I first met, we never had the outrageous escapades that most couples experience before lust fades to familiar. We were sweet and soft from the very beginning. And what that ultimately faded into was an even respect for one another that never grew hot enough to sizzle. So different from what I felt right now.

The man stood and pressed against me, letting me understand how hard he was through his faded jeans. We were so close to fucking. All he had to do was pop the fly of his Levis and enter me. All he had to do was hold my wrists over my head as he slammed into me, letting my body contract on him, letting the two of us meld together into one moving, writhing being. And then all he had to do was brush my hair aside and bite my neck, let me feel his teeth sink into my skin, making me arch my back and moan, making me sob.

But that would be insane. Crazier even than this.

With our bodies sealed together, his clothed cock pressed against my naked bottom, he brought his mouth to my ear, and whispered, 'You know what you really need now, right?'

'No.'

'A good, hard spanking.'

'Oh, fuck,' I sighed. He'd found me out. So easily, so quickly, he'd found my secret.

'Don't you, baby? Isn't that exactly what you need? What you've needed all this time and nobody ever thought to give it to you.'

I nodded. In an instant, his hand was wrapped in my hair, and he'd pulled my head back so that I was looking up at him, tilted in an awkward embrace, but unable to keep my eyes off him.

'I'd use my hand the first time,' he said. 'Not a belt or a paddle or anything serious. Just my hand. But that would be enough, wouldn't it? That would give you just the kind of sting you're craving. The sweet pain that you deserve.'

'Oh, yes.'

'And *then* when you were all ripe and wet from the spanking, what you need next is a good, solid fucking.'

I was almost crying from desire. I could see everything he was suggesting in my mind: his rough, hard hands against my ass, my skin blushing the colour of ripe berries. How had he known to say those words? These were fantasies I'd never confessed to any lover before. I couldn't ask him how he knew. Didn't have time to respond at all, because right then we heard Marilynn's high heels click-clicking on the polished wood floor. I knew it was Marilynn and not some other Happy Hour floozy making her way to the ladies' room. I knew from her stride and from the way her heels met the floor that it was my friend, and I also knew that she must be wondering what in the name of Christ was taking me so long.

The stranger quickly lowered my skirt and pushed through the swinging door into the men's room, my panties still gripped in his fist, just as my best friend rounded the corner. I turned and grabbed the nearby receiver of the payphone, self-preservation taking over, then I lowered my hand slowly and looked over at her, like an actress caught in a corner, unable to get out.

'I was just calling Logan,' I said, breathlessly. 'But there's no answer.'

'Marilynn's eyes were suspicious. 'I've been out there forever, with all the other lonely-hearts, while you're fumbling with coins at a payphone. That's so fucking eighties, Cat. Why didn't you use your cell?'

'Battery's dead,' I said as I moved towards the light at the end of the hallway. 'Forgot to charge the thing last night.'

'Use mine,' Marilynn offered as she followed me to the bar stools. I had to work to sit right, knowing that my panties were gone, thinking that I was destined to leave a wet spot on the crimson leather bar stool as well as on the back of my pale-pink skirt. I knew he was going to walk past me when he left the men's room, and I prayed that he'd say nothing to me – but I knew that he would say something. I knew that as a fact.

Because, even though I didn't know his name, and even though we hadn't ever spoken to one another before, he wasn't so much a stranger to me after all.

2

INT. SMOKEY'S SALOON

CAT HARRINGTON, late twenties but could easily pass for younger, waits trembling as THE STRANGER lowers her innocent white panties and lets her step out of them. He holds the discarded knickers to his face for a moment, breathing in deeply before standing and leading CAT after him to the alley behind the bar.

> THE STRANGER
> (gruffly)
> This way.

EXT. SMOKEY'S SALOON

The alley is deserted. THE STRANGER lifts CAT in his arms and presses her against the chipped red brick wall of the bar. She can feel how hard he is in his jeans, and she sighs at the sensation. It is clear from the look on her face that she knows just how good it will be when he thrusts inside her for the first time. But it's not going to happen yet.

> THE STRANGER
> (in a husky tone)
> You know what comes first, right?

CAT shakes her head.

THE STRANGER
If you want me to fuck you, you know what
you have to do.

CAT nods, but THE STRANGER's expression lets her
know that he expects a verbal answer.

CAT
Yes, Sir.

THE STRANGER
Then assume the position, girl. Prepare
yourself.

Slowly, CAT extracts herself from his embrace. She
turns around and places her palms flat on the bricks.
She stares at her carefully manicured fingernails and
realises how different her life has suddenly become.
She's no longer a girl who would spend her lunch
hour getting a manicure. She's a girl who would let
a man she's never officially met, whose name she
doesn't even know, fuck her in an alley.

When THE STRANGER doesn't move, she realises he
wants even more from her. As gracefully as possible,
she gathers her skirt around her waist, offering her
naked ass to him. She holds her skirt with one hand,
and uses the other to support her weight against the
wall.

THE STRANGER
Such a pretty ass. It's going to be even prettier
when it's all blushing pink. And think about
this while I spank you, baby. You're going to
get so wet you'll be begging me to fuck you.
Begging. Do you understand?

CAT nods, then quickly catches herself in mid-motion
and stops.

CAT
Yes.

THE STRANGER
Yes, what?

CAT
Yes, Sir.

This is obviously the correct response. THE
STRANGER traces his fingertips over the ripe swell of
her ass, and the camera caresses her beautiful curves
along with the man's hand.

CLOSE UP: CAT'S FACE

She is very excited now, and the expression on her
face tells precisely how turned on she is. Her dark-
brown eyes are wide open, her raspberry-glossed lips
softly parted.

PULL BACK TO REVEAL:

THE STRANGER undoes the buckle on his belt and
pulls it free from the loops. He snaps the leather belt
in the air. The sound is loud, but CAT stays totally
still. Slowly, THE STRANGER begins to stroke CAT's
ass with the belt, not smacking her with the folded
leather, but letting her feel the gentle weight of it
against her skin.

THE STRANGER
Tell me when you're ready.

CAT
I'm . . .

'Cat!' Trini says, opening the door to my office with her
arms full of updated pages. Each new edit is printed on

a different colour of paper. By the end of a shooting, scripts can look like paper representations of rainbows.

'Is everything all right?' Trini asks, concerned.

I blink my eyes and nod, trying to erase the image that lingers. I gaze at the computer screen and see that I've actually typed in my fantasy. I quit the file without saving before Trini can come and read over my shoulder.

'Is the script going OK?'

'Yeah, fine.' I force a smile as I reach for the coffee mug on the edge of my desk.

'Are *you* OK?'

'Didn't get much sleep,' I say, hoping that I sound convincing. I realise my fantasies are blurring with the fictional life of Danika Andrews, and I'm not disturbed by that in the least. Maybe I should be. For God's sake, the woman is an international spy and an occasional assassin. She's a world-class martial artist while I've been known to fall off the treadmill. She can cook five-star meals, while I'm a pro at ordering out. The two of us should have nothing in common at all. Yet I've suddenly become one of those audience members our movies cater to, the type of patron who can lose herself in the movie, cast herself in the starring role. The type of person I've always been a little bit sceptical of. Why would someone happy with their own life need to live vicariously through someone else's? Isn't that a bit pathetic?

'You're sure that you're really OK?' Trini asks me kindly.

'Yeah,' I tell her. 'Just lost in a scene. You know how that can be.'

She stares at me suspiciously for another moment, and then she steps into the office and shuts the door behind her. I must be a lousy actress if my boss can so easily see through my lie. 'If you need to talk to someone, Cat...' she lets the sentence hang there, unfinished, and then finally adds, '...about anything. Logan. The wedding. Anything.'

I wonder if she believes that she knows what's going on. But there's no way she could. I've never acted like this before. And, as my boss – as *everyone* in the Hollywood family – knows, characters behave characteristically. That's the number one rule. Of course, it's when they break out of character that things become interesting. Thelma and Louise, for instance, changed their lives by changing their routine. (Although, I must say that on a repeat viewing of that film, I was left with the realisation that the true message was: 'If you're a woman who decides to change your way of life, you must drive off a cliff in a convertible.' Not really the female-empowerment movie everyone claimed.) But, in general, when characters decide to go against their daily routine, that's when their lives get interesting. Think *Desperately Seeking Susan*, *After Hours*, *Into the Night* and, my personal favourite, *Something Wild*.

'I'm fine,' I tell Trini, and she gives me a little shrug as if she can't force me to talk if I don't want to, and then she leaves me alone with my thoughts. And my thoughts are all about *him*, as they have been since I first laid eyes on him.

From the first time I caught sight of the workman, I thought of him as 'THE STRANGER', quotes and capitalisation definitely intentional. In my fantasies he was 'The Stranger'. In dialogue – and, as I've said, I do tend to think in script-style dialogue even when away from the office – he generally spoke gruffly. And from the very beginning, I saw him everywhere I went. That's what was so Hollywood, cute-meet about it.

Every time I turned a corner, there was his road crew, working on a new section of the city. Finally, I figured out that the road crews stayed in the same places, but that he was a manager, checking in at the different sites and that, for some inexplicable reason, the two of us were on the same schedule. In the morning, there he was at the intersection of Doheney and Third, where an oval concrete island with a new stoplight was being erected, one with even more possible signals to wait for.

When I went to lunch outside of the studio, I'd often catch a glimpse of him working with the guys on the earthquake-retro-fitting of an overpass in Culver City. At the end of the day, he'd generally be at the spot where Marilynn and I caught him. This is why it was no real surprise for me to see him there, even if I had the same reaction as always: dumbstruck awe and unspoken lust. But up until meeting him in the bar with Marilynn, I'd yet to hear him say a word. Now that I knew that his voice matched my fantasies, I felt certain that every other prescribed detail I'd given to him would match, as well. From his physical attributes – meaning his cock, of course – to his sexual appetite, both of which I supposed would be mammoth.

Until last night we'd only exchanged smiles and appraising looks. I never thought we'd go any farther than that because I'm not the type of girl to go any farther. I've got my man, my life, my schedule – all three are sorted out just fine, thank you. I'm not happy-go-lucky when it comes to anything, especially not love.

But Marilynn is. The phone rings, knocking me out of my fantasies once again. I know from the caller ID that it's Marilynn, calling me from her office, which is right across the lot from mine.

'Come see the new lust of my life,' she says over the phone. 'He's pretty fucking amazing.'

'He must be if you're talking about him in his presence. When did you meet him?'

'This morning.'

'After you left Declan?'

'I didn't go home with Deco. We did it at the bar.'

'You're the one who's amazing,' I say. 'You were with one guy last night and you already have someone with you now.' I can't figure this out in my head. 'And he's at the office, listening?'

'He's not paying any attention,' Marilynn says. 'He's that sort of a guy. Laid back. Comfortable in his own skin. Get your ass over here, and meet him for yourself.'

I hang up the phone, pick up my purse, then head outside into the California brightness. After considering walking over, I decide to take one of the little electronic golf carts across the studio to Marilynn's office. These are one of my favourite perks of working on a studio lot. The cars are adorable, easy to handle, and make everyone feel important.

Marilynn and I don't always work on the same lot. It depends on the project. But for the past few months we've both been located at the same studio, which is a thrill for us both. It's as if we're back in school again, able to hang out at recess or lunchtime. When I reach Marilynn's bungalow-style office, the door is open and I stroll right in.

'Here he is,' she announces. 'Don't you fucking love him?'

I find myself staring at a large glass aquarium-style cage from a pet store. I should have known not to be sucked in, but Marilynn is beaming. '"Comfortable in his own skin",' she repeats for me with a sly smile, 'get it? At least, until he sheds again.'

'I get it,' I say, 'but I don't understand it.'

'I'm on this new lizard movie,' Marilynn explains. 'So they sent over this purple gecko as inspiration.' She points to a tiny colourful reptile basking blissfully on a slim log.

The thing is cuter than I might have imagined, but I still feel sorry for Marilynn having to stare at it all day.

'I don't really mind,' she says. 'I've dealt with worse. You know that.'

'The rats,' I say, nodding.

'Yeah. That was *much* worse,' she agrees.

'So how was Declan?'

'Too good to believe,' she says, happy to recall the previous night. 'I drove back to the bar after I dropped you off, and we went back to the hallway. You know, where you were standing, by the phone.'

I blush as she says the words, but it's clear that Marilynn doesn't notice. She's far too intent to tell me about her tryst with the bartender. The two hook up sporadically, whenever Declan and his deeply disturbed wannabe-actress girlfriend are split, and whenever Marilynn's not busy banging one of her other beaus. I call his lady 'disturbed' only because of the information I've gleaned from Marilynn. But even the few facts she's shared have led me to believe the man would be far happier being celibate forever than continuing with his manic minx.

As Janice suggested, Marilynn and Declan would actually make a good team if they'd give themselves a real chance at romance instead of characterising their relationship as a series of one-night stands. Not only are both physically attractive and caustically witty, but they manage to bring out the best in each other. In Declan's presence, Marilynn shows off a little bit of her optimistic side, while he becomes all gentlemanly, shouldering away other possible suitors when they get too aggressive.

'He held me up against the wall,' Marilynn says, 'which I just love. Don't you just love that, Cat?' She's always goading me into sharing details about my bedroom antics with Logan. I rarely do, and not for the prissy reason I give Marilynn – which is that some private things ought to remain private – but because we really don't have the steamy encounters to share that she does.

Generally, I enjoy hearing her stories. Like the time a man shampooed her hair for her. That was a sexy scene I relive over and over. Or the time a date made an entire dinner for her, and the two of them let the food get cold while they fucked on the Spanish-tiled kitchen floor. But today, I don't hear anything Marilynn has to say about their surreal sex session back by the bathroom, because I'm lost in a vision of what could have been me. I drop the scene description and the dialogue for this fantasy. I simply start with the man taking my panties and placing them in his pocket, and then I work forward, imagining him bending me over a bar stool and spanking me, slowly, forcefully, before spreading my thighs wide apart and entering me with a long, deep thrust.

The more I visualise this picture, the more I want it to happen. I know this is selfish and not like me at all, but I try to convince myself that one little fling wouldn't hurt my current relationship. It might actually help it, right? If I give in to my desires, and feel guilty, then I'll know life with ... with ...

I want to smack myself when the name doesn't pop right into my head.

Logan!

. . . life with Logan was meant to be.

I think of Janice's reaction to the news that I kissed someone at a bar, which is all I actually shared with her. I left out the part about the impending spanking, the hot dialogue, and the fact that he took my panties away. I remember her unusual burst of swearing followed by utter disbelief. 'You're kidding. God, Cat, you had me for a second there.'

And me smiling at her and allowing her to think that she knows everything there is to know about me.

But nobody knows everything. Nobody knows what I want this man to do to me, except maybe for the man himself.

FLASH FORWARD:

He says, 'Bend over and lift your skirt for me.'

I do so automatically, even with my fingers trembling. The light fabric rustles against my naked skin. I've never been so aware of every tiny sensation.

'That's a good girl. Now count. I want you to count every blow, and don't mess up. I'll have to start all over again if you skip.'

'Yes, Sir.'

His hand connects with my naked ass, and I let out a shuddering sigh, followed by a whispered, 'One.'

'Louder!'

'One!'

He lands a matching blow on my left cheek, and then the stinging spanks begin to rain down faster and faster, and I have to work to keep up with him, frightened of failing. I don't know what will happen if I let him down, and I don't want to find out. Or maybe I do. I don't dare think like that. Not yet.

When I ultimately stumble and forget where we are in the number game, he doesn't start over as he assured me he would. Instead, he pushes me forward even further, so that my hands slip off the wall and move down to the ground, and he nudges my feet apart and grips on to my hips. I close my eyes and revel in the way he manhandles me, the rough embrace of his fingers digging into my skin.

With one firm thrust, he drives inside of me. I feel his hot skin against my hotter backside, and I moan fiercely at the connection.

RETURN TO PRESENT:

Did that happen? Did he spank me until I creamed? Ah, that would be telling, wouldn't it? And yes, I will tell. I'll tell all. But not yet. Because I must confess that my all-time favourite movies are the ones that skip around in sequencing. They're the hardest to pull off successfully, to create in a way that won't annoy the audience, but they're the most fun to watch. High on my list is *Memento*, a tour-de-force of mindfucking the audience. Then *Sunset Boulevard*, classic of all classics, which serves up the end at the beginning, but you forget during the movie what you've been told at the start. *The Usual Suspects* comes next, with its shuffling of scenes that leaves you believing you know what's going on when you haven't got a clue. *Pulp Fiction* – now, there's a mind-warp for you. *American Beauty* – an *homage*, perhaps, to *Sunset Boulevard*, but with a starting twist that you don't even think about until later on. Oh, and *The Secretary*, which is a favourite for any spanking aficionado, and starts in the middle, goes back to the beginning, and then ultimately takes you to the end.

But where was I? At the start, in the middle? Or just fantasising as Marilynn sighs, 'He just knew exactly what I wanted. Has that ever happened to you, Cat?'

And I'm lost again. What I can't figure out is how he knew I wanted to be spanked. I've never told anyone that. I never thought I could. From the start of my relationship with Logan, he made it clear what he considered 'acceptable' sexual relations. We have sex at night, when we're both cleaned up, with the lights out. On special occasions, we sometimes light a candle or even incense. The thought of confessing to Logan that I want to be bad with him, that I want to be dirty, is an impossibility.

Yet I didn't have to confess to the stranger at all. He

knew. From the way I looked at him, or the way I dressed, or the fact that I let him abscond with my panties. He knew precisely what to say.

I think about what might have happened if I'd been in the bar without Marilynn, if she'd gone home early with Declan, leaving me to phone Logan for a ride. The stranger and I might have found ourselves for real in the alley behind the bar. And maybe, just maybe, he would have made all of my fantasies come true.

FLASH FORWARD:
After he spanks me, he fucks me. Simple as that. I wrap my long legs around his flat waist and feel the ridge of his cock pressing against the inner walls of my pussy. He slides back and forth at a languid pace and, as he works me, he stares directly into my eyes, making me feel incredibly naked – more naked than I already am. His hands are under me, cradling my ass as he rocks me at his set pace, and I realise how strong he is. My weight doesn't faze him. It's as if I weigh nothing at all as he lifts me up and down, sliding his rod deep into my pussy and then lifting me up again. I lean my head back, feeling my long hair flowing across my back, feeling the way my muscles squeeze down on him automatically as he continues to take me on the most decadent of rides.

I could come like this, I realise. From the way my clit gets stroked each time he pulls me in close to his body. I could come solely from being taken like this, even though that's never happened for me before.

I know that some men are simply better lovers than others, but I never knew exactly how good a man could be. Every move he makes fits me, fills me, sends me reeling. He knows how to touch me with his hands, his mouth and his cock. Even better than that, he knows how to talk to me. His voice is low, so that I have to lean even closer to him to hear it, and he whispers the most filthy secrets to me as he continues to drive inside of me.

RETURN TO PRESENT:
God, if I'd only had the fucking nerve.

3

When I pull up alongside the road crew the following morning, there he is, waiting for me. He's tall with a steel-like posture, and I admire the way he looks as if he'd be as comfortable in a boardroom as he is by the side of the road. Although we've been playing a flirtatious game for a bit, our encounter at the bar the other night has changed the rules. The stakes are much more serious now, and I think from the way he gazes at me that we both know that.

While I watch him, he peels out of his reflective orange vest, discards his hard hat and then stares fiercely at me as he slowly takes off his shirt. Muscles glide when he flexes his arms. In an instant I undergo an amazing transformation, from mindful to mindless. Lust pulses through my whole body. I want to get out of the car, walk over to him and throw myself into his arms. I think of all those romance bodice-ripper covers I've sneered at while in line at the grocery store. Suddenly, I wish I could star in one myself.

He poses, in a completely unselfconscious manner, letting me admire all there is to admire. His strong, flat chest. His biceps, his abs, and all of those other muscles whose names I don't even know. I just know that he has them.

My heart pounds as I gaze at his amazing body, the flatness of his stomach, the trail of dark hair that runs towards the fly of his jeans. I want to lick along that trail until it disappears beneath the waistband of his jeans, and then I want to rip open his button fly and follow it down, lower, lower, until his cock is out and in my mouth, pulsing between my lips, thrusting forward against the back of my throat –

He knows I'm watching every move, and he juts his chin towards me, in a gesture that I sense is a dare, and then the cacophony of horns blares behind me, and I have to go. I don't want to. In fact, this is just another thing on my list that I don't want to do. But I have to. Before I do, he mouths two words at me:

Your turn.

My turn?

I shake my head at him, flushing the colour of the fuchsia convertible in front of me. No way. No how.

Your turn. He lips the words again to me with another slow wink and, as I drive away, I know that I will obey. I don't know how I know, but I do.

I make it to work, yearning to come. Without considering exactly what I'm doing, I hurry to the final stall in the bathroom, ripping my skirt waist high and pawing at my nylons, desperate for relief. I don't care if I rip the fine fabric, don't care about anything except coming. I'm so wet that my fingers make a squishy sound in my juices as they finally connect with my clit. I have no idea how this has happened to me. I'm not the kind of person who touches herself at work. I'm not the type of person who touches herself much anywhere.

But here I am, a mess of wet panties and drenched nylons, my fingers squeezing and teasing my swollen clit, my eyes closed, breath coming faster and faster. I make random circles up and over that hot little button, my fingers pressing harder than ever before as I see him in my head, naked to the waist, watching me watch him.

God, did he look amazing standing there, not caring what other people thought, not having a fear at all as he let me and every other commuter drink in his amazing body.

In my sultry fantasy, I see myself naked all the way, leaving my car and rushing into his arms. It's easy for me to imagine him lifting me into his arms, letting my legs come around his waist, pushing up by locking my feet on the backs of his calves and striving forward.

Your turn.

And then I come, so hard that I actually moan out loud, visualising my stranger fucking me on that road site in front of all the other commuters, ripping my clothes off for me and fucking me naked on Doheney.

Not a bad name for a film, I decide, as I work to put myself back together in front of the line of sinks. *Naked on Doheney*. It's got a good ring to it. And then I laugh, seeing a different woman looking back at me from the bathroom mirror. Who is this girl who would give her panties to a stranger?

Not Cat Harrington, that's for sure.

Maybe I've transformed into Danika.

I get through the rest of the day in a daze, feeling as if I'm listening to conversations while underwater, making decisions with a brain heavy with sand. I only have memory available for my construction worker, and for the thought of his lips offering that solitary dare:

Your turn.

I don't have time for this, I tell myself on the ride home. I'm getting married sooner than I dare to admit. I'm supposed to be planning the minute details of our honeymoon, checking the final registry for our gifts to make sure that we don't wind up with eight espresso-makers like Janice did. There are dress fittings and cake tastings and champagne to be ordered, but I can no longer be bothered with any of those details.

At least, not tonight.

This evening finds me standing despondently in front of my full-length bedroom mirror, faced with a situation that's brand-new to me: I'm trying to figure out what outfit I could wear that would allow me to take off my shirt while driving. I chastise myself for not owning any easy-access clothing. Marilynn would have the right kind of outfits in her closet. There's no doubt in my mind that she'd have something stashed away from her years as a rock'n'roll groupie up on Sunset Boulevard, some skintight lizard-patterned creation that I could borrow in order to flash him so that he could see my bra and my breasts and a peek at my naked body – and then allow me to get dressed again without having an accident or cluing any of my fellow commuters into the show. But even though I'm sure she'd have an outfit to lend, I can't imagine calling her and explaining my predicament.

And what about Janice? She wouldn't have anything suitable, but she *would* have certain specific questions to ask me, such as 'What colour is today?' That's one of Janice's shticks. She always thinks about what colour she's 'feeling' before she gets dressed. Is today a blue day, or a pink day, or a black day? She likes to point out pedestrians passing by when we're sitting in her favourite café. 'See,' she'll say knowingly. 'It wasn't only me who was feeling lavender today. Look at his tie, and her skirt, and that old woman's scarf. Today was lavender for *everyone*.' I try not to get too involved in this type of conversation, because I think there are enough people in LA for her to prove her point with any colour she chooses. Janice likes to see only what she wants to.

But now I find myself trying to remember her advice from days past. Blue is calming. Green is healing. Yellow energetic. Black gives you power when you're feeling afraid. But what does 'naked' equal? What about the colour of my flesh, that pale, almost translucent shade, so different from the airbrushed San Tropez-style glamazons prevalent in Los Angeles? This hue has never come up in our colour-coded conversations. And, more importantly, here I am back again at the big problem of the day: what can I wear that will let me do what he asks without getting myself into real trouble?

I can't believe I'm actually considering going through with this. Maybe the spirit of Danika really is rubbing off on me. Maybe in my heart of hearts, I *am* a six-foot-tall supermodel, half-Norwegian, half-South American, with steel-blue almond-shaped eyes and blonde hair that's as straight and thick as an Aztec's. I'm someone who leads a double life, partly on the runway, partly as an international spy. Or maybe not. Danika wouldn't be nearly as confused about her attire as I am.

What the hell should I wear?

Not any one of the many black suits crowding my closet. Not my favourite peach-coloured lace shirt with the adorable Johnny collar. It would be impossible to unfasten all those tiny pearl buttons while driving, even an automatic like mine.

A sweater, then, I decide. I have a sweet little grey-and-black leopard-print silk cardigan sweater that I pair with a pencil skirt and spectator pumps straight out of the 50s. It's a form-fitting sweater with a row of five shiny black buttons down the front. What I decide I'll do is button only the one in the middle. Then, when I get to eye-level with my Stranger, I'll whip that one open, so he can see the turquoise satin bra beneath. If I manage to snag the red light, I can even pop the clasp on the bra. If not, he'll at least see plenty of skin above the demi-cups.

Who am I? Planning a show like this one. Just doesn't seem like me at all.

But I like this new me.
I like her a lot.

Before I leave in the morning, Logan slips behind me. He puts his arms around my waist, and I'm flustered by the closeness of him, especially when I've been lost in daydreams of showing off my tits to another man.

'I have this fantasy,' Logan starts. Now my eyes go wide. I can see our reflection in the mirror over his dresser, and I look aroused and intrigued as well as guilty as hell. Maybe all I needed was for Logan to treat me sexy in order to feel sexy. Maybe I don't need to flirt with a stranger in order to get excited. Slowly, I button a few more buttons on my sweater.

'Tell me,' I whisper to Logan.

'I don't think I've ever shared this with you before,' he continues, still embracing me, although not doing the things that I'd like him to, like kissing the back of my neck or stroking my breasts or squeezing them firmly until I let out a little whimper of pain-mixed-with-pleasure. 'I've always wanted . . .'

I realise that I'm holding my breath, waiting.

'. . . to open a little B&B somewhere up the coast.'

I sigh dramatically at the letdown.

'Nothing big,' he continues, moving away from me. 'I know that it sounds absurd. But I think I'd be good at it. I could write in one of the rooms when nobody rented it. You could keep doing your job from anywhere. You wouldn't have to be on location all the time. And if we were only a few hours away, you could always drive in to the city when you needed to take a meeting.'

I don't say a thing.

'Just something to keep in the back of your mind,' he says, oblivious to my disappointment. Then he grabs his wallet from the top of his dresser. 'For the future.'

But I'm back to living in my fantasy future, my thoughts returning to my sexy stranger as I lift my purse from the chair and gather my keys.

He's there again.

Thank god, I think, as soon as I see him. His presence transforms the corner of Doheney and Third from an asphalt jungle into a real live jungle. I catch sight of his yellow truck first, as shiny as if it were wet, adorned with paint the bright golden colour of a sunflower in bloom. The truck is insolently parked half on the kerb, half in the road, surrounded by a gathering of neon-orange cones. I know it is his truck, because I memorised the plates. Just repeating the combination of letters and numbers to myself can make me wet. NZ3 462. My own secret sexual code.

Several workers hunker down around a deep dangerous-looking crater in the centre of the road. Expensive cars slow in angry huffs as they putter past. Everyone in LA is in a perpetual hurry. That's the rule: look busy and people will think you're important. But I take my time, inching as slowly as possible by the road site, hoping that he'll be facing my way.

Each day I've learned more about him. Now I know what he looks like without a shirt, and I can only imagine what he might look like without those faded jeans and heavy, kick-ass workboots. Without anything on his body but me.

But where did he go?

He was standing there a moment ago; now he's gone.

Just as the light in front of me flickers to red, forcing me to stay put, I see him. My heart races, and I have to swallow hard, internally on fire simply at the mental recall of fantasies I've engaged in with him and of the very real memory of losing my panties to him. He quick-steps his way towards my car, and when he is right alongside me, I do the trick I practised over and over again in front of the bedroom mirror: I flip open my sweater, showing him the dreamy cups of my satin underwire bra, the one truly racy item of lingerie in my top dresser drawer. He looks as if he expected nothing less of me, and his eyes take on a warm, heated glow.

Then, before I can do anything except blush, he slides a note under my windshield wiper. I lower my eyes as I fasten the top button on my shirt then quickly look back at him. The light turns green and he waves almost in a salute as cars sound their angry melody of horns behind me.

Time to go.

I do my best to drive safely to the nearest parking spot. Well out of sight of the road crew, I pull over, power down my window, reach forward, and slip his note free. My hands tremble as I get ready to crack the seal. Right as one of my French-manicured nails flicks under the crest of the envelope, my cellphone rings.

Could be work. Could be an emergency. I am a doctor, after all, I remind myself with an insane giggle. A *script* doctor. What sort of emergency could there possibly be?

'The character isn't following her orders, doctor. Give her a new monologue and then send her on her way!'

'Nurse, I don't think this patient will pull through . . . we'll have to cut the –'

'The cord, doctor?'

'No, the scene.'

Another insane giggle fills my head. Out of habit, I reach for the phone and automatically check to see the incoming number. Here is another code I have embedded in my memory, but these numbers no longer make me wet. Did they ever? From the seven digits, I understand instantly that this is my fiancé calling. Will he know from my voice how guilty I suddenly feel?

'*Hello,*' I practise to myself. '*He-llo.*' Does that sound normal? Doesn't it?

'Hey there, Logan.' I sound like a phone-sex operator.

'Hey, Kit-Cat,' Logan greets me with his standard salutation. He makes no comment on the sexy quality of my voice. 'Meetings all day, hon,' he says, sounding half-apologetic. 'Don't know if I'll be home in time for dinner so you'll probably be on your own.'

'No problem,' I assure him, staring at the envelope in my hand. What secret message waits for me?

'We'll do late drinks if you'd like,' Logan promises. 'Buzz me.'

'Right,' I tell him. 'I'll do that.'

I hang up on his 'Goodbye', then pull out the hand-written note from the white envelope emblazoned with the County logo.

Beauty – it says. I stop reading for a moment. I like that, and I say the word aloud, imagining him saying the word with me. Naming me. 'Beauty.'

We've got to start meeting like this.

Drinks at 6?

Then Jo-Jo's, which is the name of a bar in Hollywood.

I've named the place. I've named the time.

Meet me there and tell me your name.

My eyes scan his manly handwriting to the very bottom of the page. The letter's signed simply 'Brock', with his phone number. It couldn't have been more perfect.

We have to start meeting like this.

If I'd read that in a script, I would have edited the hell out of that line. It sounds too cocky. Too confident. Because Brock wrote it to me, I love every single word and not one feels clichéd. I know the bar where he wants to meet, and I can guess from the outside what the interior looks like. Maybe I'm calling up notes from scripts I've read in the past. Still, I see it clearly in my mind: a bartender who has been there for years – if female, then surgically buxom with a bad red-dye job. If male, then goateed and risqué with a ribald joke for every pretty lady. Smoking patrons at each table, even though it's been illegal in LA to light up a cigarette anywhere for years. Secretive smoking, I guess.

I have to go, don't I?

I mean, I've given the man my panties after all. As unusual as that action was for someone like me, I feel that the gift has created some form of commitment from me to him. Probably in some distant tribal community we'd be married by that action, destined for a life together of untold bliss.

'Do you live your life like a normal person?' That's what Danika, the lead of the movie, is supposed to ask her friend. And her friend says 'yes' but Danika knows better. Of course she does. This is her movie. She has to push the boundaries or else there wouldn't be anything interesting for the audience to watch. So Danika knows better.

I can't say the same thing for myself.

EXT. SHOT: JO-JO'S PLACE

Late afternoon light filters through the circular-leaved eucalyptus trees standing in a row on the sidewalk. A few cars decorate the parking lot. One lemon-yellow truck stands out boldly from the rest of the vehicles.

CAT HARRINGTON, stunning in a subdued manner, stunning even though she doesn't seem sure of her beauty herself, parks her silver sportster, top down, in the far corner. After a moment of obvious reluctance, CAT exits the car, shakes out her dark-brown mane of hair, and stares at the truck. She's visibly conflicted, and she hesitates with her fingertips resting on the door of the car. After a minute, she slides back into her convertible and pulls out.

CAT
(under her breath)
Don't have the guts for this.

I live my life like a normal person, and a normal person doesn't meet a complete stranger for drinks at a bar. Not even a stranger as good-looking as Brock. A normal person goes home at the end of the day and has a frozen gourmet dinner (an oxymoron if there ever was one) while waiting for her boyfriend.

Logan promised late drinks, as if that were some kind of consolation prize for making it through an entire day without him. I push around the unappetising frozen 'gourmet' dinner while watching entertainment news coverage on cable. My mind, however, is on Brock. I play games with my food, using the prongs of my fork to draw designs in the leftover pasta sauce, until Logan calls and says that sorry, hon, he won't be home until much later than he'd thought, and when I call Janice and she says that sorry, love, she can't break away from her plans either, I go to bed early and dream of Brock.

But that's not exactly true, now, is it?

No, it's not. Because I have his number. And I can't turn out the light and fall easily into peaceful slumber. Logan won't be home for hours. I can get away with a phone call to Brock, to tell him that yes, he totally turns me on, but that I'm committed – or maybe I *should* be committed – and that I simply can't see myself playing a role that comes equipped with a Scarlet A. But somehow I don't manage to make the call.

* * *

The next day, I pass the road crew to find the six muscular guys in their normal positions and a new foreman staring from the work spread in front of him to a clipboard, then talking animatedly into a cellphone. I glance around as much as possible without ploughing my car into the Humvee in front of me, but he's nowhere in sight.

I stood him up last night, maybe he's doing the same to me by withholding his presence. I should have gone, I tell myself. But why? We couldn't possibly go further than we went the other day. I still can't believe I actually did what I did. Can't believe I split up a set of La Perla lingerie without a moment of thought.

Where is he?

Distracted, I drive the rest of the commute without seeing anything around me, telling myself that I should be grateful that I got away without damaging my relationship with Brock –

Oh, God, with Logan. *With Logan.*

I should be pleased he wasn't there this morning to make me want him even more. Another thought occurs to me, one that feels truer than any of the others: What can I possibly do now that I've stood him up? It's effectively over. I've ended the thing with a whimper, not a bang. That doesn't help my thoughts to dissipate.

I cruise in my car past several of the sites I know that he oversees, and at the end of the day, when I drive back to Santa Monica, he's not in any of the locations where I normally find him. My whole mood is heavy by the time I get back home. I'm sure Logan will be able to sense my sadness, but he's off in his own little world.

Logan says marijuana makes him think more clearly. When I walk into his office, I wave my hand in front of my face. I can't imagine how the fragrant smoke could possibly clear his head. Just a second-hand hit makes me forget what it was I came in to discuss with him.

At first I think he hasn't heard me approach since he doesn't acknowledge my entrance. Finally, he says, 'Working,' in a way that lets me know he does not want to be disturbed.

'Dining,' I say, seeing as how we're conversing in one-word sentences.

'Pizza,' he responds, indicating the empty box on the floor emblazoned with the insignia of a local delivery restaurant.

Cautiously, I look over his shoulder at his computer. He looks up at me, then shields the screen with both hands. He will *not* have people read his work before it's finished. 'Would you taste an uncooked omelette?' he likes to ask. 'Would you view a half-completed painting? Would you live in a house without a roof?'

'Go out with Janice, or Marilynn, or something,' he says, lifting the marijuana roach from the Vegas ashtray on the corner of his desk and relighting it with a gold-tipped match. His wheat-coloured hair falls past his brow and he tosses it away from his forehead with an impatient flick of his head.

I used to think that move was sexy. The quick jerkiness of it, as if he couldn't even be bothered to use his fingers to move his hair. Now I know that the impatience spreads to every part of his life in which I'm concerned. Logan doesn't have time to discuss the wedding – he leaves the details to me and his mother. He doesn't have time to talk to me about the honeymoon. Between his day job – with the increasing pressure of an impending promotion – and his quest for success via night-time writing, he doesn't have much time at all. I used to try to discuss things with him, but the discussions always wound up building into fights.

And Logan refuses to fight fair. If I get angry, he strokes my hair away from my face and says, 'You're so pretty.' If I scream at him, he just grins and says, 'Silly girl,' as if he knows that soon I'll come around to his way of thinking.

'I'm going to be at this pretty late,' he tells me now. The match flame glows in his eyes, and I can see how bloodshot they are. I turn to leave the office, but he calls me back. To say he loves me? To share a quick romp on his walnut desk – something we've never actually done before, but I've fantasised about every once in a while. I glance at him, willing him to step into the emptiness left by missing Brock. This is Logan's moment. He could change how I feel about him, about myself, about a workman, with a single action.

Come on, I urge silently. Step up to bat, Logan. Take me where I need to go.

I wonder if he can sense my desperation from my body language. Apparently, it's a language that he's not well versed in.

'Get me another beer before you go, will you, Kit-Cat?' he asks, handing me over his empty.

CLOSE SHOT:

DANIKA's face, eyes shut, lips parted. She sighs as the man continues to kiss her.

PULL BACK TO REVEAL:

The man spins her around and begins to kiss into the low cleavage of her dress. He pulls the top of the dress down, showing off DANIKA's perfect, round breasts. Her skin seems to shimmer beneath the lights. The man kisses her breasts hungrily and DANIKA moans at the sensation. She puts her hands on his shoulders, pushing him down onto his knees. He presses his face against her dress, then slowly begins to slide the dress up to her hips. Under her dress, DANIKA has garters and stockings and a pair of fire-engine-red lace panties.

The man looks up at the beautiful supermodel. He could speak in one of eight languages, and she'd understand him. He chooses English. Oddly, he sounds just like Brock.

>THE MAN
>What do you want?

>DANIKA
>I think you know.

>THE MAN
>We're playing it like that, are we?

DANIKA smirks.

>THE MAN
>I think you want to take these off and give them to me.

>DANIKA
>Why would I want to do that?

>THE MAN
>Because once you slide them down those beautiful legs of yours, I'm going to give your amazing ass the spanking it deserves.

For once, DANIKA loses the smug expression. She gazes down at THE MAN.

>DANIKA
>What did you say to me?

>THE MAN
>You heard me. Don't make me repeat myself, Dani.

Very slowly, she begins to slide her panties down her awesome legs. THE MAN waits patiently. It's obvious that he's going to enjoy the show.

THE MAN
You're not as tough as you act, are you?

DANIKA says nothing. It's as if the man has found out her secret fantasies, the ones she's never been able to reveal to any of her previous lovers. DANIKA always has to be in charge. She always has to be the one on top. But not now. Not with him. Not any more . . .

When she gets the panties completely off, she hands them to the man, who brings them to his face and breathes in deeply. He then grabs on to DANIKA, spins her around, and pushes her forward, roughly.

THE MAN
Place your palms flat on the ground.

DANIKA works to obey as gracefully as possible, but the man is interested in her ass, not her grace. He strokes her naked derrière with one hand, then raises his palm high in the air.

THE MAN
Are you ready, Dani? Then count for me,
baby –

PULL BACK TO REVEAL:

Me. Laughing to myself as I quickly delete the previous scene. I don't think Trini would approve. This isn't an Adrian Lynne production, after all. Mickey Rourke and Kim Basinger won't be featured in the lead roles. I've gotten myself in trouble by saying I want to make the movie racier. Trini likes the idea. In the previous two movies, Danika proved just how outrageous she could be in every scenario outside of the bedroom. Yes, men wanted her, but she was far too tough for them to handle.

Now I've suggested that we show how dominant Danika can be between the sheets as well. (Or on a construction site, as would befit the opening of the film.) But with my current mental state, Danika has lost her dominant stature, transforming strikingly into a much more subservient lover. I place Brock in every scene and, with me starring as Danika, the situations become more and more familiar.

And ever more racy.

4

The next day, I drive by the site to find that he's still gone. Gone, as in vanished, like in a Hitchcock film. Maybe he never existed in the first place. Or is that more in the style of the master surrealist David Lynch? I think about every place I've run into him and how I might be taking it for granted that he'll be there. Now I fear that I'm never going to see him again, and all because I don't have the confidence to act the way I want to. That's precisely when I notice a bright yellow truck out the window of my office.

Couldn't be, I tell myself.

'There's no fucking way,' I say, even as I'm walking closer to the window to peer outside.

But yeah. It's him. Of course it's him. It had to be him. He's not looking my way. He's talking to one of the lot supervisors, and I recall something in the studio newsletter about road construction taking place during this month on part of the studio lot that the County owns an easement for. I hardly paid attention to the article, focusing instead on the information about a studio-wide costume-party event coming up soon. I only skimmed the road construction piece to make sure that the activity wouldn't impact on my parking space. There were other facts which I immediately forgot because they were simply too inconsequential for me to pay attention to. The tiny write-up ended with apologies for inconvenience.

No need to apologize, I think, as I glance at my

reflection in the glass of my shelving unit. No need to apologise at all.

I watch him through the window until I see him nod and head back to his truck. Then I fumble in my desk drawer for the note with his phone number and dial him up before I can stop myself. He answers immediately, and from the moment I say 'Hello,' I can tell he knows who I am. That doesn't stop him from asking.

'Tell me your name.'

I look at the open script on my desk. There it is, in inky black Courier font, the answer to his question. 'Dani,' I say automatically. I don't have the nerve to say 'Danika,' because he'd know without a doubt that it was a lie. Will he guess that this is one, too? Maybe, but he doesn't call me on it.

'You didn't come, Dani.'

Oh, he has no idea. I've come so many times to thoughts of him. So often that I've actually lost count.

'I know.'

'Why not?'

For some reason, I can't make myself say that I'm engaged. Because if he knows that, there's a good chance that he won't meet me. So I simply say, 'I promise that I won't let you down again.'

'Why should I believe you this time?'

'I have to see you.'

'What else do you have to do?'

I think instantly of our interaction at Smokey's. 'I can't say it on the phone.' I am still staring through the window at him in his truck. I wonder if he can feel my eyes on him.

He laughs. 'When?'

I look at my electronic calendar. Two days before we make our final decision on the wedding-cake frosting. How inappropriate is that? I name the time, and Brock says that he'll be there.

'Don't keep me waiting, Dani,' he says. 'I hate to wait.'

'See ya later,' Logan calls out to me from his office in our second bedroom.

'About ten,' I tell him, my standard goodbye, before grabbing my briefcase and heading to the door. Just when my hand touches the knob, the phone rings. I sprint to catch it, for some reason guessing that this will be Brock cancelling on me. That would serve me right, but it's also an impossibility. I haven't given him my home number, only my cell and work. Guilt waves through me, but all of the inner turmoil is only a false build-up because it's Janice on the other end.

'Thought you taught tonight,' she says, obviously surprised to catch me.

'I'm late,' I tell her. 'Running out the door right now.' Then I realise it's a bit strange that she's calling if she thought I wouldn't be here. 'Why did you call if you thought I'd be out?' I ask.

'I was just going to leave you a message,' she says, 'about lunch tomorrow.'

'Let me call you from the office in the morning,' I tell her, and then I yell out goodbye once more to Logan and head out the door before the phone can ring again.

Every Wednesday night, I teach a college extension class on screenwriting. But tonight I've called in a substitute for my class in favour of another learning experience entirely. I'm not planning on being the teacher tonight, but the student, and I relish the change in roles. In order to keep up the charade I've dressed in my usual, businesslike manner. I always wear suits when I teach, because the outfit makes me feel more professional.

As I drive to the bar in Los Feliz, I think about the type of outfit I'd like to have on, a slinky little red dress in a style made for Rita Hayworth. Or that extremely outrageous outfit Patricia Arquette wore in *True Romance*, a turquoise, off-the-shoulder top, cow-printed mini-skirt, shiny metallic sunglasses bought, she explains, in Las Vegas. I realise that in my fantasies I must have an overworked costume designer. I hope that Brock isn't disappointed by my dark skirt-suit, patterned scarf and black power-loafers with the no-nonsense stacked heels.

Before I leave my car, I check my reflection in the rear-view mirror. This is my last chance to back out. Once I enter the bar, all bets are off. All promises broken. Of course, maybe when I see him, I'll come to my senses. I'll tell him that I have to take a different route to work from now on. Maybe I'll say, 'Hey, Brock. Wrong place. Wrong time.'

But somehow I know that I won't.

With that little pep talk, I add a final coat of mascara, slide on a darker shade of lipstick than I usually favour, and then pull the handle on the door, sealing my fate.

Brock is my fantasy. But I have learned from years of living in Los Angeles that when you meet fantasies face to face, they have a tendency to disappoint. I hope that this isn't the case tonight. I don't have time to worry about the concept, because he's there when I walk in. This saves me all those awkward moments of wondering whether or not he'd show up, a situation I thought about way too much before coming. He's comfortably ensconced in the back of the bar, kicked back at a burgundy leather booth, and he's looking both relaxed and excited as I make my way to his side.

'Didn't stand me up this time,' he says, motioning with his head for me to take a seat next to him.

I know precisely how wet I am, and my legs are so weak that I have to work not to collapse against the leather or fall right into his arms. In my mind, I see the script, and that's what helps me to behave like a normal person. A normal person who's cheating on her fiancé, anyway. And how normal is that outside of the talk-show-trash world of *The Jerry Springer Show*? I glance to the right and left, surreptitiously scanning the rest of the patrons just to make sure that I don't know anyone here.

'You expecting company?' Brock asks, noting my surveillance.

I shake my head, and I do my very best to sit down in a ladylike manner, but all of that is apparently lost on Brock, who immediately moves as close as possible to me and then slides one hand up under my skirt to test for himself how aroused I've gotten on the drive over.

He sighs when his fingers meet my wetness. I feel my cheeks turn strawberry-red, but I'm not ashamed, only aroused. I like the fact that this man has no qualms about fingering me in public. I've never been with some-one like him before. Hell, I've never been with someone like *me* before, someone who would let a veritable stranger finger her under a bar table during Happy Hour. And yes indeed, this hour has just gotten much, much happier. I close my eyes as I feel him tracing over the split between my pussy lips, and then I draw in a deep breath as two of his fingers slide inside me.

'Here's the question,' Brock says, 'should we stay or should we go?'

'You're just singing along with the jukebox.'

'No, I'm asking you to chart the course.'

'For tonight.'

'For however long you say.'

'You'll do anything I want?' It makes him sound like a genie. If I rub him in the right manner, like in that Christina Aguilera song, will he make my fantasies come true?

'I don't think that's the way things will go,' he says.

'Meaning?' I actually relish the challenge in my voice. I stand up to him in a way I never do with Logan. Why is that?

'I think *you're* going to do everything I want.'

'And why do you think that?' I ask.

'You're going to want to behave for me, that's all.'

'You sound so sure about that.'

'I am,' he says, 'because your bottom will be so sore you won't know what else to do. You'll simply *have* to obey.'

'Oh, God –' The words escape before I can do anything to stop them. I realise that the evening may throw up greater sexual challenges than I had bargained for. I haven't told him that we can't see each other. That this is all too out-of-control for me. In fact, I haven't given him any inclination at all that I'm far too good a girl to behave like this. Not me, with a boyfriend – excuse me, 'fiancé' – at home, and a whole different lifestyle than one of a cheat.

'That's the truth,' he continues into my silence. 'Your poor cherry-coloured bottom will make you behave.'

I tense up at his words, trying to pull back from him, but his fingers are way up inside me now, and he knows exactly how turned on I am, and he also knows that I've just gotten a great deal wetter. I've become a flash flood, and all because of the way he's speaking to me and touching me.

'You stood me up,' he continues. 'Am I right?'

I nod. I did.

'I can't just let that slide, can I?'

Now I shake my head automatically. He can't.

'Do you understand why?'

From his tone of voice, I can tell that he expects an answer, but none of the possible statements I can think of make any sense. So I wait for him to tell me.

'I'm not that sort of a guy.'

'What sort of guy are you?' The words come out in a breathless rush.

'The kind who has to take care of business when it happens, before we can move on. You and I both know that we have to deal with that before we can go any further, don't we?'

Now I nod because, as he says the words, I realise they're true. Even though I didn't want to, I stood him up. He can't let that go. I'm only wondering how he was able to read me so well. I don't even have to ask, because he seems to understand the question pulsing in my eyes.

'Only bad girls behave the way you do. Flashing a stranger simply because he told you to. Letting a man whose name you didn't even know take your panties away from you in broad daylight. I can spot bad girls easily. You were the easiest ever.'

I reach for his drink and take a sip, grimacing at the strong taste of gin.

'So the real question isn't "Should we stay or should we go?" I guess. The real question I need to ask you is "Are you ready?"'

'For what?' I whisper.

'Everything you've ever wanted.'

'I thought you said I'd do anything *you* wanted.'

His hand is on my wrist as he stands and then easily pulls me to my feet. I follow him away from the booth, stumbling as we exit the place, trying to straighten my skirt as I trip along next to him.

'Don't you get it, sweetheart?' he asks, his face against my thick hair as we stand out in the parking lot, staring at the cars. 'Don't you understand yet, Dani?'

I flinch inwardly at the false name, but I don't correct him. Instead, I turn and look at him, my eyes open wide, waiting.

'Those two things are one and the same.'

But now I have to stop him. Now is the last possible moment for me to save myself. 'Here's the thing,' I say, in my not-very-script-doctor-esque dialogue. 'I'm not exactly free.'

'You're a call girl? I'd never have guessed.'

I can't help but laugh, because even though I know he's teasing me, I understand that if that were really my problem, I'd have the kind of movie on my hands that I'm always stuck working on. Hard-working prostitute with a heart of gold (or at least good Mexican silver) unable to convince anyone she should be taken seriously until she meets her match in a down-on-his-luck cop.

'Not a call girl,' I say, 'script doctor. Very taken script doctor.'

'Taken,' he says, nodding, and then he lifts my hand and admires my engagement ring.

'Yeah.'

'But the man's not right for you.'

'You sound so confident,' I say, and I feel myself starting to relax, even though I shouldn't. 'And you don't know anything about me or him. Not really.'

'He's not right for you. If he were right, you wouldn't be here. That's an easy solution to deduce.'

'But you are right for me?'

He doesn't answer. He takes my hand and turns it so my wrist is upright, and he brings his lips to the fine tracing of veins and kisses me there. I feel his kiss in every part of my body and I no longer remember what's right or wrong. I simply follow him into the inevitable.

Or, in plain English, to the golden-yellow County truck of my dreams.

He spanks me slowly and steadily, his hand connecting firmly with my panty-clad ass. I feel a slight sting, but nothing serious, nothing to make me cry out, or to make me beg him to stop. Truthfully, I don't want him to stop. I want him to give me more, much more, as much as he thinks I can handle. I have no idea what my limits are in this situation. I've never been in a scenario like this before – at least, not outside of my fantasies. So I just don't know. But I think he does. I have put all of my faith into the simple fact that he says he knows me, knows what I want, and what I need, and that he plans on giving me all of those things.

I'm held firmly over his lap, and I'm aware of every single sensation that ripples through me. I know that we are in a deserted alley several blocks away from the bar and that if someone were to drive past the mouth of the alley, they could look our way and see me receiving my well-deserved punishment. But I don't care about any of that. All I care about is the fact that I want him to pull my panties down and do the job properly. I want him to make me feel this punishment deep inside myself. I want his large palm to slap repeatedly against my bare skin loud enough to echo, hard enough to really hurt because I know somehow that the harder he spanks my naked ass, the wetter I'll become. Instead, he's teasing me. Light little blows rain down on me, and I squirm forcefully against him in order to let him know what I want. But I don't have the words in me to tell him.

'Bad girl,' he says, softly, 'such a bad girl.'

Am I? Yes, without a doubt. Have I ever been before? Not in this way. Not on this level. Not to this extreme.

'You know it,' he continues, 'don't you? You've always known what you were capable of, even if you were scared to admit the fact to yourself.'

'Yes,' I whisper.

'Tell me what you want, Dani.'

Oh, God, I want so many things I can't even think,

can't number them or keep track of them in my mind. But first and foremost I realise exactly what I want, what I need him to do in order for me to come.

'Keep talking like that,' I beg. He's been turning me on all evening with his sexy talk. Now I want more. I want him to call me names. I never thought that concept would arouse me before. Logan and I haven't even considered dabbling in the art of 'aural' sex, aside from occasional 'ohs' and 'yeses'. But hearing Brock say what he wants to do to me, and what he wants me to do to him, excites me to the extreme. Now I want him to push the boundaries. I want him to verbally put me in my place, to call me a cock-tease, to tell me that I'm a naughty girl, that I'm a slut. I don't know why I want him to say these things, but I desperately do.

'You know I'm telling you the truth,' he says, 'you're all a big show. Pretending to be such a sweet and angelic thing on the surface. Pretending you have everything together for all of your business associates and your clean-cut friends. But that's only the way you are on the outside, isn't it? Inside, you're a completely different person. Inside, you'll do anything I tell you. Anything at all. I don't even have to sweet-talk you. I just tell you: take off your shirt. And you do it. Or give me a pair of your sopping-wet panties. And you do it. You're a little tart, and you didn't even know it.'

I can't stand it. I'm so close. 'Spank me harder!'

'Can't,' he tells me. 'Your beau would notice the marks, don't you think?'

I sigh, because I realise that he's right. When this is over, I have to get back in my car and go home to Logan. Home. The concept feels alien, as if my fiancé lives a million miles from the back alley I'm in right now.

'He's not blind, is he?'

'Not in that way,' I say, thinking that he's blind in

many others. Suddenly, I feel a pulse of freedom throb through me. 'I don't care,' I tell him, my breath a rush as I work to get the words out. 'Spank me harder. God, please. Mark me up, Brock. Let me feel it. I don't care.'

'That's a lie,' he says. 'Don't lie to me again. Not ever.'

I start to say that I'm sorry, but he cuts me off. Even as I start to speak, I realise I've lied to him already. He thinks my name is Dani. How am I ever going to come clean about that? Again, I say, 'I'm sorry, Brock,' but he silences me with a violent command to hold my tongue.

'Do not lie to me,' he says, and his tone is menacing. 'Because you *would* care. Later. When you got home to your safe little world. You'd care a whole hell of a lot. You're not sure that you're going to commit to me yet. And that's OK. It's more than OK. It's completely understandable. I don't blame you for being cautious.'

Cautious, I think. How cautious is this? I'm bent over the lap of a man whose last name I don't know. None of my friends knows where I am. If he turned out to be dangerous, nobody would know what happened to me. Brock phrases these fears in a simple sentence.

'You don't even know me yet.'

'I know you,' I start.

'Sh, Dani. Quiet for a minute. You don't know me at all. But you will. Slowly, as slow as it takes. I'm a patient man. That doesn't mean I'm not going to punish you, because I am. But only when you're really ready –'

'I'm ready –' I interrupt, but once again he cuts me off.

'Look down at your hand,' he says, and I understand what he's talking about even before gazing down at my finger. The ring. Its shine blurs in the tears that slowly fall from my eyes.

'When that ring comes off, *then* you'll be ready.'

5

'I'll bet even Mark Anthony and Cleopatra had cold feet,' Janice says emphatically after I've confessed several – but not all – of my recent transgressions. I don't dare tell her everything. She'd ignite with indignation.

'Did they actually get married?' I ask her.

'Napoleon and Josephine,' she offers next.

'He left her when she couldn't bear him children.'

'Samson and Delilah?'

I shake my head – can't picture Logan with long hair, can't picture me with a set of shears cutting off his 'power'. It's far too Lorena Bobbitt for someone cultured like me.

'Daffy and Daisy Duck,' Janice says finally, glaring defiantly to see if I'll challenge this one. I don't, although I mentally wonder whether ducks *can* get cold feet, what with being submerged in water all the time. They must have some type of mechanism to keep themselves warm.

'It happens to everyone,' Janice continues.

'I think about this guy constantly,' I tell her seriously, my voice low. We're seated in a rear corner of a high-end industry restaurant, and I don't want any snooping customers to overhear. Logan's mother Bernie has invited three hundred people to the wedding. I know fewer than a quarter of them. An attendee could be seated at any table, spying.

'Relax, Cat. Fantasising is simply your way of dealing with stress,' Janice explains. 'Logan's mother is constantly after you with questions about the layout of the tables and the positioning of the guests. The caterers call you. The florists are in a bidding war. Your parents phone every other day to check up on what's going on.' She ticks these items off with her fingers. 'Something's gotta give, right? Of course your mind is going to take you on some wild trip, creating a fictional romance with a beautiful boy.'

Man, not boy, I think. Truth, not fiction, I think, but I don't interrupt.

'Fantasies are free,' Janice says, 'instead of paying astronomical travel prices, you can use your mind to visit a faraway land –'

'Not that far away, actually.' Doheney and Third. I could be there in ten minutes.

'I mean, how long has this been going on?'

I shrug.

'It's a brand-new thing, right?'

I consider the question. 'About a week since I first caught sight of him.'

Janice says, 'Exactly,' as if I've proved her point. 'It started when you felt the wedding really approaching. This is your way of making sure that other men still find you attractive. That other men want you. You're going to be Mrs Logan Riley,' she continues grandly. 'Brock's going to be a passing fancy, someone you once almost met. In two years, you won't even be able to remember his name or what he looked like.'

'Did you have cold feet?' I ask, hoping that my face doesn't show disbelief. I'll always know what Brock looks like.

'Both times.' She hesitates. 'Maybe I should have paid attention the first time.' She shakes her head like a dog with fleas in a dramatic way to demonstrate that she's getting rid of bad thoughts. 'But Logan is perfect for you. He's smart. You're smart. He's gorgeous. You're stunning. Fantasies are simply a way to escape stress.' I watch as Janice twirls the heavy white-gold wedding band on her finger. Sometimes, I think she simply wants me to join the herd of married women, to be her confidante when she and Allan have their little spats. And they do have their little spats. Logan has taken to calling them 'the Bickersons'.

Now, as if she's done her duty in advising me, Janice lowers her voice, switching subjects with finesse. 'But is he cute, Cat? Is he totally handsome like Marilynn said? I mean, purely for conversation sake, what does he look like?'

'He has this straight dark hair,' I tell her, 'that's long in front. His face is slightly angular, so that when he's not smiling he looks sort of like a statue.' I don't pay any attention to the fact that she's giving me a thoroughly disgusted look. I just keep talking, because I've wanted to tell someone about him for what seems such a long time, and it feels so good to say the words out loud. Maybe this was all I needed, an opportunity to talk. Maybe this venting process will cure me of my overwhelming desires. 'There's something in the shape of his lips, the line of his jaw, that reminds me of a tiger –'

'A tiger?' Janice interrupts with a sour expression.

'It's true.' But now I'm suddenly glad I didn't tell her the rest. The way his green eyes are spun with golden flecks. The fact that the mere brush of his fingers against mine sends sparks that flare through my entire body.

'It's a crush,' she says, shaking her head. 'You should hear yourself. You're like some love-struck kid.' I'm about to disagree, but then she leans forward across the table in a way that lets me know she's about to reveal a great secret. I know Janice well enough to have memorised all of her little traits. 'I still fantasise about other guys,' she admits. 'One at my gym, in particular. That's why I know what you're going through. It's natural. Just part of the whole deal.'

'What deal?'

'The growing up deal. You didn't think you were going to escape into adulthood without any of the soap-opera problems, did you?'

I look at her incredulously, waiting for her to explain.

'There wouldn't *be* soap operas if people didn't have affairs, or think about having them. All normal, healthy adults are constantly confronted by decisions. "Should I work on my marriage, or have a fling with the guy at the grocery store?" This is your true indoctrination into the life of an adult.'

I consider this, weighing her statement to see if it makes sense. 'Did you fuck someone at the grocery store?'

Janice gives me an exasperated look. 'If you weren't having second thoughts, you wouldn't be being honest with yourself. If you didn't find yourself looking at other guys – lots of other guys – and wondering if Logan is the right one for you, you would be lying.'

'I can't remember the last time Logan and I had sex,' I blurt out. Maybe this is sharing too much personal stuff (or as Marilynn says giving 'TMI' or 'Too Much Information'), but it's the truth.

Janice fans away my concern as if it were a bad smell, the way she waves her fingers in the air when-ever Marilynn lights up a Marlboro Red. 'You have to remember that getting married is difficult for guys, too. Maybe more so. He's worried about his masculinity, his bravado.'

'Bravado?' I ask suspiciously. She knows Logan. 'Bra-vado' isn't a word that one would generally use to describe him. Not even in the best of times. He's an engineer. A *civil* engineer. By days, he plans roads and bridges. By night, he tries to write screenplays, because like almost everyone else in Hollywood he wants to be something he's not. I used to find that ambitious. Now I find it sad.

'Logan is worried that his friends won't take him seriously once he gets married, that they'll think he's tied to you. That old-fashioned ball and chain business, right?'

'Everyone at his office is married. All of his friends are, except Paul.'

'He's worried that you're going to be the last girl he'll ever get to sleep with, and that scares the daylights out of him.'

My eyes widen. I guess that makes some sense. Even though I know that Logan had fairly limited experiences before me, it does compute that he might occasionally play 'best offer' the way that his friend Paul does. Paul always tries to keep his calendar open, in case something better comes along.

'Believe me, Cat, on your honeymoon you two will be bouncing like bunnies.'

I take a sip of coffee and consider what she's said. Cold feet. It sounds right, but I'm not convinced. So this is what I decide – despite what Janice has told me, I'm going to go see Brock again. I don't have to do anything. *We* don't have to do anything. We can just talk. I can explain to him why this can't continue. Why I've been forced to choose a new route to work. And then we can shake hands and part company, knowing like in that old sappy Olivia Newton-John song that things might have worked out in another place and time. But not here. Not now.

That's the plan, anyway.

And you know what people say about the best laid plans . . .

DISSOLVE TO:

I won't see him, but I do call him. He says that he's fine talking to me about what he'd like to do. Over several days, the phone calls get hotter and hotter. For some unexplainable reason, standing out at a payphone adds to the intensity of our connection. I can't call from work, because the proximity of my co-workers makes it impossible for me to carry on any sexually explicit conversation, and those are the only kind of conversations I need to carry on with Brock.

I don't dare dial from my cellphone, because Logan could track those calls if he wanted to, if he ever got suspicious and needed to check up on me. How do I know that? I've worked on enough screenplays about jealous lovers to know that you hide your tracks. Who would have guessed that my job skills would come in handy in such a way? I know all the tricks of the sly lover, even if this whole affair is a first time for me.

Brock answers my calls immediately, and he always seems to know it's me on the other end of the line. His voice caresses me, and I have to close my eyes when we talk, so that I can pretend he's right next to me, touching me while he describes each thing he wants to do to me.

It's just phone sex, right? I try to tell that to myself. This whole fantasy world I've created around him boils down to sex. But what's wrong with that? For some reason, the thought of having sex with Brock makes me feel as if all my problems will disappear. Just by letting him fuck me.

Of course, I want him to spank me first. To give me a real, solid spanking, first with his hand, then with something more serious – a paddle of some sort. This is what brings me to a sex-toy store in the middle of the afternoon. And I'm not there by myself. I've got Marilynn in tow. She knows her way around the store the way Janice knows her way around every bakery in town. Marilynn points out her favourite dildo, and then she shows me which lube she prefers out of the multitude lined up near the counter. I can't possibly blush any harder than I am, until Marilynn says, 'I never would have thought Logan would go in for kink like this.'

When I don't immediately respond, she punches me in the arm, a little harder than simply a playful punch. 'You dog,' she says.

'I didn't. I mean, I'm not —'

'You bet you're not. You're not buying this stuff for Logan at all, are you?'

I shake my head.

'So, spill it all.'

'Not here.'

'Then let's go.' she sets down her purchases on the counter. 'Hold these, please, Cherie,' she tells the nubile blonde, and I have enough of my wits about me to realise that she's on a first-name basis with the cashier. 'We'll be back in an hour. We're going to get wasted first.'

'We don't have to go anywhere,' I tell her. 'I'll come clean.'

Still, even though Marilynn is my best friend, I don't tell her about Brock. I just can't. Maybe I know that she will approve of my actions as much as Janice disapproves. So all I end up doing is saying that I wanted to surprise Logan.

Marilynn grins widely. She enjoys my new bad-girl persona, and she tries to get me to do things that cross even more of my mental boundaries. Later that evening, after we finish shopping at Pleasures R Us, she takes me to Smokey's.

'Come on,' she urges. 'Do a shot.'

'No thanks.'

'You don't want to do one?'

'Nope.'

'Then do six of them. The guys will line 'em up for you.'

'No thanks,' I tell her.

'Then let's go out and get burgers and greasy fries,' she says, 'we'll do a drive-through and get all juicy and messy in the car.' But Logan knows me as a vegetarian. It's almost as if my name equals one. Cat = vegetarian. And I think that my car will then smell like meat and Logan will know something's up. He'll know that I cheated, even if it's only with Marilynn and a hamburger and I can't do it.

EXT. SHOT. MANN'S CHINESE THEATER – DAY

This world-famous theatre is a favourite spot for tourists. Amid the hustle and bustle, the camera finds DANIKA and CHELSEA, DANIKA's long-time best friend.

DANIKA places her hands in the prints left long ago by the sultry starlet Marilyn Monroe. Perfect fit. She smiles charmingly at a foreign tourist, who snaps her picture, then she stands and runs her fingers along her skirt. Her best friend stands at her side, looking uncomfortable.

CHELSEA
I don't understand why we're here.

DANIKA
I'm meeting someone.

CHELSEA
Who?

DANIKA
I don't know yet.

> CHELSEA
> I don't get you, Danika. Sometimes you make
> no sense.

I understand Chelsea's confusion. She isn't aware of the fact that her gorgeous best friend is also a world-famous spy. I guess Chelsea didn't see *Danika's Adventure*, the first in the series, or *Danika's Folly*, the sequel. The poor girl thinks her old college buddy has become a first-class flight attendant, and that is why she travels so often and why, at a moment's notice, she is able to order in French at fancy restaurants, and why she's never bothered to settle down and have a family.

Danika enjoys playing the normal person when she's not working. She likes being a tourist and hanging out with her friends, which is why it's so awkward for her when she has to kill the foreign tourist who took her photograph without letting Chelsea know. She does this effortlessly, before moving on to a steamy fuck-session in the bathroom stall with a fellow spy who has been hanging around in case she needed any added assistance. Danika is like *La Femme Nikita* meets Traci Lords. At least, she is with my help.

Thing is, despite what I told Trini on my first read through of the script, I'm starting to like her. Even though I refused to tell Marilynn what was going on, I actually imagine asking for advice from Danika. What would she do in my situation? She'd probably kill Logan and then eat Brock for breakfast. Why am I always like the Chelseas in the movies? That's what I don't know. That's what I'd like to change. But things are moving too fast in my world. The caterer has brought the final samples of the foods for us to taste. The RSVPs to our hand-lettered invitations are arriving daily. Logan's mother has become my constant companion.

If only I *were* Danika. I'd definitely know what to do.

'When the ring comes off.'

I twirl it around on my finger. I tease it up and off, then put it immediately back on. I remember that once, several months ago, when Janice and I were out walking on the Palisades, a brightly coloured ladybug landed directly on the pink tourmaline in the centre. 'Oh, look!' Janice yelled out, extremely excited. 'A ladybug! That's good luck!'

Even as she spoke, I had a sick feeling in my stomach, as if I'd been suddenly found out. As if the ladybug knew I needed all the help I could get, and that's why it landed on my stone, to impart as much good luck as it possibly could. As if it were saying to me, 'Good luck, kiddo. You're going to need it.'

At night, I climb into bed with Logan long after he's crashed. He sleeps hard when he's coming off a high. It takes me much longer to fall asleep and, even after I do, I wake in the middle of the night, start from a dream in which I've married Brock. He has said 'I do' and lifted the pure white lace veil from my face, leaning in for a kiss.

With my breath held, I push up in bed and peer over the lump next to me, hoping against hope that I'll see long dark hair, tan skin, sharp features. That I'll see a broad, muscled chest, strong arms, an awesome ass. Instead, I see Logan's tousled blond hair, his jaw slack, snoring.

I roll over and face the window, thinking only of escaping. I'm like Rapunzel, except in my case I'm already living in a tower with the prince, and I've chosen the wrong prince, after all.

'Cold feet,' Janice said. If this is cold feet, I've got a monster case of it. I've got hypothermia, as far as I can tell.

6

The responses to our invitations arrive each day in the mail. Of the three hundred people invited, two hundred are coming so far. Logan stays as removed from the situation as possible. He doesn't nod when I come in, my arms filled with response cards. He doesn't ask who has said 'yes' and who has said 'no'. He simply shrugs his shoulders and goes back to typing.

'Your Auntie Eunice can't make it,' I tell him one day, deciding to see if he's listening.

'Too bad,' he mutters.

'Neither can Uncle Zebediah.'

He makes a tsk noise, but doesn't take his fingers off the keyboard.

He doesn't have an Auntie Eunice or Uncle Zebediah.

Janice says I should go easy on him. That he loves me, has asked me to marry him, has done his duty. I wish he would give me a reason to stay. I wish he would kiss me at night, hold me in the dark, whisper my name over and over.

Janice says that I don't have enough patience, that real relationships require hard work. I know they do. But I feel as if I'm the only one working. Janice says to give it time. I give it a week before I decide to meet Brock again. Then I pull the ring off again, look at it, and slide it into the coin part of my wallet. It's off. Maybe not for good. But it's off enough for the moment. I drive to the nearest payphone and call Brock's number. Is it a sign that I already know it by heart?

'It's off,' I say.

That statement could be interpreted more than one way. As a scriptwriter, I know this full well. 'It's off' could so easily mean that our blossoming relationship is finished. But Brock understands. In a low voice, he asks simply, 'Where did you put it?'

'Change purse.'

'Not ready to give it back yet.'

He's not asking a question. But I answer him, anyway. I stammer over the word, 'No.'

'That's OK,' he assures me, and I can tell from his voice that he means it. 'You will be.'

'How do you know me so well?'

'I told you before. You're an easy read.'

'But Logan doesn't –' I begin, feeling even more unfaithful because I'm being critical of my man. I shouldn't do that. I should take responsibility for my own actions without bringing Logan into this. In fact, I feel guilty even for saying Logan's name out loud to Brock. This isn't about Logan at all. It's about me. Me and Brock. The words come out anyway. 'He just doesn't –'

'Of course he doesn't.'

So he understands. From the little I've told Brock, he knows what Logan is all about. That simple sentence sums it all up. The way he says the words 'Of course.'

'So?' I say, waiting.

'I can't play with you the way I want until you're really free.'

Tears are already forming in my eyes. I can feel them.

'But we can start.'

Now relief washes through me. I lean back against the plate glass of the phone booth, and I feel how hot my cheeks are, how ready I am. The transformation is unbelievable to me, how quickly I've accepted the fact that I will do what Brock says, when he says it, and that everything we do together will fulfil me in a way I've never been completed before. If I were to slow down long enough to think about the repercussions, I might reconsider. But lust has distorted my logic.

'Where?' I beg. 'When?'

'My house,' he tells me, giving me an address high up in the Hollywood Hills. 'Now. Be here in twenty minutes.'

'Twenty,' I echo, thinking about the distance and realising that he's giving me an impossible task.

'Twenty,' he repeats. 'Be on time. Every minute you're late will be an extra strike against you. And I mean that quite literally.'

'I can't get there in twenty.'

'Can't isn't in your vocabulary any more,' he says, sounding a bit like Danika. 'You do what I say, whatever I say, if you know what's good for you.'

Oh, it will be good for me. I'm sure of it. I hurry to my car, and I do my best to make the drive in the time he says, but I know all along I'm not going to make it.

And I guess he knows this, too.

'Strip,' Brock says when I take my first step into his place. I hardly have the time to take in my surroundings, the dark maroon carpet, deeply creased brown leather sofa, clean lines of the lamps and tables, the fact that there is framed artwork hanging on the wall that looks like original works rather than reproductions. He has style. That's obvious from even the quick glimpse I've taken of his decorations. He doesn't live in a standard bachelor-style pad, but then I guess on some level that I knew he wouldn't.

'Here?'

'Don't question me, Dani. Do as I say.'

Once again, I find myself freezing up inside at the name of the character I've given him. I should tell him my real name, but I can't. Not yet. I have to play the part of someone else. Otherwise, I won't be able to go through with this. I'm lying to Logan and I'm lying to Brock. Can't come clean to anybody all the way. That wouldn't be fair. I fumble uselessly for a moment with the buttons on my blazer, before finally ripping the jacket open and off, then looking around for a place to put it neatly. This is habit.

'Drop your clothes on the floor.'

Following this command goes against everything in my body. This is a seven-hundred-dollar suit jacket, after all, my very best item of clothing that I wear whenever I have a big meeting or if I need an extra boost of confidence, but I manage to obey. First my jacket, then shirt, then skirt, then shoes, then hose, then . . .

'Everything.'

. . . bra and panties. I stand, shyly, one hand over my small breasts, the other crossed over my lower body, uselessly trying to hide myself from his probing gaze. I feel intensely naked, and my thoughts race through my head at a ferocious pace. I don't know why I want to cover up before him. Maybe a part of me believes that at any moment he might reject me. Or maybe I feel virginal with him, as if I've never done this before, which I suppose is true, in a way. With Brock, everything is new. Did I ever feel that way about Logan? I don't think so, but the truth is, I can't really remember. Our start was so long ago. But I don't believe I ever had butterflies with Logan.

'Move your arms. I want you open to me. I want to see everything without hindrance.'

I place my arms at my sides and immediately stare down at the floor.

'Look at me.'

As soon as I obey one request, I seem to disobey an unspoken one. I feel as if I'm destined to do everything wrong. Now I tilt my head to the side, looking up at him from under my long dark lashes, and I bite on my full bottom lip as I gaze at him. I've never felt more exposed in my life. Strange thing is that I like the feeling. I don't want to hide from Brock. I want him to see all of me, just as he said. I want him to climb inside my head and discover each and every filthy fantasy I've ever had. Somehow, I think that he won't find them filthy. Or that even if he does, he'll be thrilled to make them come true.

'I'm going to take your picture.'

'No!'

He actually smiles as he starts to unbuckle his belt. 'Don't tell me no. I mean that. That's rule number one. Don't ever tell me no.' The belt snaps between his hands and I jump at the crackling sound.

'Sorry.'

'Don't apologise. That's rule number two. If you don't fuck up in the first place, then you won't have to say that you're sorry. Pretty simple concept, isn't it? Someone as smart as you are should be able to follow a rule like that.' His voice is hard as he talks to me, hard and almost clinical. For some reason, every statement he says makes me wetter. I want him to tell me all of the rules. I want to obey every single one for him.

'I'm going to take your picture,' Brock says again. 'Don't worry so much, Dani. I'm not going to abuse my power. I won't hurt you with it. But you have to learn to let me do what we both know I need to do.'

My mind is spinning. I find that I'm mesmerised by the way he's slowly coiling and uncoiling his belt. What's he going to do with it? I think of my purse, and in my purse, my wallet, and in my wallet, my ring.

'Bad girls are punished,' Brock says simply. 'Does that make sense to you? Does that sound right?'

Now I nod. From the look in his eyes, I realise that

I've failed him already, or again, and we haven't even started. Not yet. Not really. Except that maybe we started the very first time I saw him. Maybe I knew then – that somehow it would all come down to this: with me naked and exposed in a room I'd never been to before, waiting for everything he had to give. Maybe I clearly understood in my subconscious that he would be clothed and commanding, ready to impart the delicious concoction of pain and pleasure I've longed for my whole life. Maybe I knew. Maybe . . .

'Answer me verbally when I ask you a question.'

'Yes,' I say. And then, for some reason, I don't say, 'Yes, Brock,' I say, 'Yes, Sir.'

Brock smiles at that, as if I've given him some unexpected compliment. His smile makes me feel suddenly warm inside. I realise that I am on a quest to please him. 'Here are a few more things for you to remember,' he says, and as he talks, he grabs hold of my wrists and binds them behind my back using his belt. 'I can't mark you. I know that. And I won't. Don't worry about that at all. Let that thought vanish from your mind.'

My body relaxes in relief.

'But that doesn't mean I won't punish you, because I will. In many ways, many forms.'

I nod, then say, 'Yes, Sir,' and he smiles again.

'There are more rules,' he says, and now he has one hand on my pussy and his fingers work their way up and down, searching out the wetness that shows us both how excited I really am. So very excited, and we've only just begun. 'Many more,' he continues, 'but we'll learn them all together. Over time, you'll understand everything I want from you.'

As he speaks, he moves to grab my colourful scarf from the pile of my discarded clothing, and he uses this as a gag, tying it across my lips and beneath my heavy mane of hair. I've never been gagged before, never really considered the concept. I test the shiny fabric with my tongue, consider how I must look with this new adornment. Brock doesn't let me guess. He tells me.

'Beautiful,' he says. 'I knew you'd be beautiful like this when I first saw you. Now, let's finish the job.'

I stare at him, curious. I don't know what he means.

'I'm going to fuck you, Dani,' he says, and I shudder all over. I want him to, more than anything I can remember ever wanting before. My whole body opens itself to him. I can feel how my pussy lips seem to expand, how I am ready to welcome him with every part of my being. I know exactly how serious this is, how important. I know that I will remember this forever, no matter what happens with me and Logan, or ultimately with me and Brock. This moment is important because this is the first time we will fuck.

And I mean that exactly as it sounds. Fuck. In fact, I mentally devour the word. Marilynn uses it as a constant shocker. Janice hates the way it sounds. I've never cared much either way. In fact, I always felt that I could take or leave four-letter words. But now I see this word's power. I test it by repeating the word over and over in my head:

We are going to fuck. Fuck. F-U-C-K. We won't make love. I've always been irritated by that euphemism, anyway. When I see the phrase in a movie script, my nose wrinkles up in distaste. People who truly plunge themselves into pleasure don't need to skirt the issue. Besides, 'making love' conjures images of grassy fields and rainbows. Images that have no business being in any sort of room with me and Brock.

'The picture is a before shot,' he says. 'I want to see the difference. I want you to be able to as well.'

What was it that I felt guilty about two weeks ago? Staring at him through my windshield? Dreaming about being across his lap while he spanked my naked ass? Now I'm letting him take my picture, and I have no desire to stop him.

He raises a slim digital camera from a nearby table and takes one single shot. Then he lifts me in his arms and carries me down a hall to the master bedroom. The focus in this room is the bed. It's obviously a king-size, I can tell that from a single glance, and it stands against the far wall, stretching towards us. Brock sets me down in the centre of the mattress, then has me spread my legs wide. He undoes the belt from my wrists and has me reach my hands over my head. In moments, I'm bound, captured by leather thongs fastened with heavy silver chains on my wrists and heavy leather cuffs on my ankles. Along with being a stellar road-crew chief, Brock is apparently a master of bondage; he has me tied so completely and easily that I can hardly move at all except to lift my hips up off the mattress, which I do, insisting with my body that he care for my basic, hungry need.

Desperately, I want him to fuck me. To make me feel it down to the centre of my body. To make me cry out against the gag as I buck and writhe against him. Brock has other plans, as I might have guessed he would. With me so well captured, he can take his time, admiring me as he moves around the bed, slowly taking in the way I look. I know that the camera is just in the other room, but I try not to think about that right now. What would it mean for him to take pictures of me? Could mean nothing at all. Could be an entirely harmless fetishistic hobby. Or it could mean the end of my relationship with Logan, my standing in the community. I could be the next big Hollywood scandal: *Screenwriter casts herself as*

Danika Andrews, tests the pleasures of bondage with a randy construction worker...

Brock silences my worries with his mouth. Not by uttering another word, or reassuring me with tender kisses, but by sealing his mouth firmly to the split of my body. Now I have a reason to test my bonds seriously, squirming with deep, untold pleasure at the way he licks and laps against my pussy lips. Brock ignores my thrashing, and he uses the flat of his tongue in long, slow licks over the most tender part of my body.

Christ, it feels amazing. As he works me, slowly, gently, I realise that it has been months since Logan last visited the region between my legs. For some reason I didn't realise I missed this satisfying treat. Perhaps this is because Logan always seems to approach the concept as a job, a task to keep me happy and willing to bestow the matching diversion on his own organ. But the way Brock eats me let's me know that he is a man who lives to give a woman pleasure. He uses his whole mouth, his lips and tongue, his fingers to spread me open. He breathes on me, once, twice, so I can feel that rush of air against my clit, and then he suckles from me, ringing my clit with his lips and kissing it firmly.

I make moaning, murmuring noises against the gag. I suddenly realise how captured I am because of all the things I *can't* do. I want to stroke his thick, dark hair, to touch his warm skin, to feel him all over with the flat palms of my hands. But I am unable.

Brock seems to know that I crave even more contact. He must sense that I want something else, something more, because he moves away from me and quickly strips, discarding his clothes as haphazardly as he had told me to lose mine in the living room. He moves the scarf gag away from my mouth, and I realise suddenly that I miss it. I like being completely trussed, my legs and arms and mouth forced to obey his commands. I like being bound and gagged. But Brock has other ideas. Ideas that necessitate the use of my willing mouth and parted lips.

'Trust me,' he says, and then he climbs back onto the mattress. 'Trust me, Dani.'

I realise that I do. I *must* trust him in order to have let him bind me up so seriously and securely. I force myself to believe that he has my own best interests at heart – and he proves in a moment that he does, but this time he positions his body above my own, and I am honoured by the sight of his majestic cock for the very first time.

This is like a dream, I realise. Because even if I felt guilt at cheating on Logan, I could tell myself that I can't do anything about it. I'm captured, after all. I'm a love slave, a bad girl in bondage, I have no recourse except to part my lips and take the rounded head of Brock's cock into my mouth, sucking it with abandon. What else is there for me to do? I can't play coy and ignore it, not something as big and hard as this is. I don't want to disobey, but I couldn't say no even if I did want to, because, as soon as I part my lips, his cock slides inside, and I begin to trick my tongue along the length, losing myself in the taste of his skin, and the warmth and silkiness of his hard rod.

'Get it all nice and wet,' Brock instructs, 'because I'm going to fuck you hard as soon as you're ready. So hard. As hard as you need.'

I do exactly as he says. I'm a machine, a magical sucking machine, working my lips up and down his shaft as Brock continues to play his own sweet tricks between my legs. He gets two of his fingers damp with my pussy juices and he reaches underneath my body to trace his fingertips against my asshole as he puckers his lips around my clit and starts to drink from me again. His fingers are forceful and probing. He presses hard with the tips of them inside of me, and I groan and suck him even harder as I squeeze against his hand. I am very aware of the intrusion of his fingers, of the way that he demands I let him inside me, and I am also aware of how much I like it.

Everything Brock does makes me feel dizzy with pleasure. I buck against him, still sucking him, and I am sure that, unlike Logan, he understands my body language. I want him to let me come, to let me reach that flickering finish line, but seconds before I can climax, he pulls away. Quickly he moves on the bed again, so that he can undo the bindings that are tight on my ankles. He flips me so that the chains on my wrists make an almost crunching sound as he positions me onto my stomach. He leaves the wrist cuffs on me, redoes the gag between my lips, and then slides his cock into me from behind, doggy-style.

As he fucks me, he brings one hand under my body to strum slowly on my clit. He works me with a knowledgeable pressure, as if he understands exactly what I need in order to reach my limits. I'm so excited at this point that I feel I will come at any second. Unlike the rare sex sessions I experience with Logan, today it's only a matter of when, not *if*, I'm going to climax. Brock thrusts hard into me, fucking me fiercely. With my haunches raised up to him, I try to tell him something else with my body: I want him to spank me as he fucks me. I want him to leave glowing plum-hued handprints on my ass-cheeks that match each thrust. Instead, Brock lets one hand lightly play a game of pat-a-cake against my left cheek.

'I know what you want,' he says. 'I do, Dani. I can tell by the way you're showing me your ass that you want me to give you a proper spanking. The kind of spanking a girl like you really needs. Trust me on this. I know exactly what you want me to do, and I'd be more than happy to make that wish come true for you.'

I make a mewling sound against the gag, urging him onward.

'But not today. I won't mark you. Not today. If your Logan –'

I hear the condescending tone in his voice when he names my fiancé, but I try not to pay it any attention. He can't help his tone. I understand that. The way I can't help having given him a fake name, he can't help feeling superior to the man I've committed to spending the rest of my life with – the man I've betrayed with someone I hardly know.

'If your Logan goes out of town, you're going to tell me. If there's a time when your body can be truly mine, even for twenty-four hours, you'll tell me immediately.'

I think about the business trip that Logan has planned just before our wedding, and I nod again, blinking. What would that mean, to be truly alone with Brock for hours at a time? The thought terrifies me and excites me, and I say nothing about the trip, and not only because of the gag in my mouth.

Do I look different afterwards?

I should. I know that. I should have a huge Scarlet A burned into my skin to show my shame. Or at the very least, I should have a scarlet-coloured blush on my cheeks to show my so-recent arousal. Instead, I look the same as always. I move closer, staring at my reflection in the mirror, trying to determine the answer to that question, then asking a different question entirely:

Do I look like a cheater?

I can't tell. I feel different, but I think that I look exactly the same. How can that possibly be? My whole world has been altered, but I haven't changed my appearance in the slightest.

Do characters in movies look different? It seems that people are always able to tell a cheater by one quick look. 'I knew you were different when I walked in here.' Or one smell. 'You have her perfume all over your body.' Or a single false move. A receipt left carelessly on a bedside table. A new pair of satin panties to replace the cotton granny-style favoured for years.

I try my best to remember actual scenes from films. I remember that in *Fatal Attraction*, Michael Douglas looked virtually the same all the way through. Maybe men are different from women in that respect. In *Unfaithful*, the central female transforms herself, but only when she's going to see her lover. The happiness that she feels doesn't blur into her daily life. That seems to be part of the point. She could have her lover, and a happy montage with her family. But that movie was different from my life. She and her husband appeared to be made for each other. She simply fell in lust with someone else who showed an interest in her.

But shouldn't I look different, if only because I've just been so well fucked? After a long, thorough shower, I decide to try myself out on Marilynn before confronting Logan. She's up for meeting at a bar, as I'd somehow known she would be. I tell her nothing. I just say that it's been a day, that I deserve a drink.

Why? For coming three times? Hell, I deserve a whole bottle.

Marilynn doesn't even sit down before she starts in.

'You did it.'

'Oh, God, how did you know?'

'Jesus, Cat. You're positively glowing. I've never seen you glow before. I didn't know you could. End it now.'

'With Brock? I can't.' As soon as I say the word, I feel

a shudder rush through me. 'Never say can't.' It's as if he's with me even when we're apart, as if he's watching from some corner of the room, taking notes, remembering my transgressions for the future.

'Not with Brock, you moron. With Logan. You'll never be able to go back to him. Not now. And why would you want to? You have that amazing sexy look radiating from you. Don't you feel different? Alive and awake? How could you give that up?'

'I –' I start to say that I can't, but stop myself. 'I don't know.' That's fair. That's honest. 'I don't know what to do.'

'You're being silly. You need to get out, now, while you still have a little dignity and before people really get hurt. Remember what happened to me.'

'So you *did* learn something.'

'It was all wrong with us and I didn't know how to escape. I was too young to know that you could just take the front door and leave. So instead I dragged both of us through all that fucking garbage. You remember all of that. You must. You were right by my side for it, holding my hand when I let you.'

I nod. She's right. The end of Marilynn's marriage wasn't pretty.

'Get out now, Cat. You're worth more than that.'

'The wedding –'

Marilynn snorts. 'God, you're going to have to learn for yourself, aren't you? I'm offering you this amazing advice for free, from a first-hand experience, and you're going to have to burn all those bridges down yourself.' She puts one hand on top of mine, and I know that the gesture is meant to soften the blow of her words.

'Leave when it's right for you then,' she says. 'When you can be sure that you know what you're doing and when your head isn't all clouded by that good-sex vibe. But trust me,' and she pats my hand now. 'You will leave. You're going to have to. You'll never be able to live with yourself if you don't.'

But, of course, that's not what happens at all. Because Marilynn doesn't know anything about Brock, and I don't tell her.

CUT TO: INT. DARK BAR

MARILYNN approaches the table. She says nothing about CAT's appearance. She's far too intent on telling CAT about what's been going on with her and Declan. The rest of the conversation is an imaginary one that takes place in CAT's head, her own nerves and guilt playing out a scene of her own creation.

While MARILYNN tells of the delightful new way that Declan likes to fuck her – in a sex swing suspended from the ceiling of his apartment! – CAT realises that the guilt is too much. She's got to fix her life. Starting with Logan, she has to come clean.

But not yet.

7

The next day, the road crew is in the same place as always. Brock stands at the side, scanning the traffic instead of paying attention to his boys. He must have memorised my schedule by now, the way I've memorised his, knows to look for me right before seven-thirty every Monday through Friday.

I see him, and I know he sees me from the smile that instantly lights his face, and then I watch in my rearview as he climbs into his truck and pulls out right behind me. We drive out to Will Rogers Park, with him following behind me, choosing a spot in the corner of the dirt lot where nobody can see us, where nobody can find us.

As soon as we get there, and I walk out of my car, he sits on the edge of his truck bed and waits. When I reach his side he lifts my skirt, lowers my panties, and puts me directly over his lap. He doesn't say a word as he spanks my naked bottom with his heavy hand until I think I might come just from that sensation. My cunt is pressed against the rough fabric of his well-faded Levis, and I rock my body on this fulcrum as he punishes my ass for me. When he thinks I'm ready – and only then – he whips me around and bends me over, my hands pressed into the dirt, and he undoes the fly on his jeans and pulls out his hard cock. He slides in with one hard thrust, then grips my hips and takes me on a ride.

I squeeze him easily, effortlessly, my body automatically taking over from my mind. I'm so wet and relaxed inside that the pleasure radiates through me with each forward thrust. I feel the sensations in my fingertips, in the tips of my toes, in my breasts, in my flat belly.

I feel Brock everywhere.

Suddenly, he moves me, so that I'm across the back of his truck bed, and my hips are raised even higher for his pounding thrusts. I've never fucked in the back of a truck before. I've never even had sex in a car before. The encounter is enlightening. I understand the appeal of outdoor romps, of doing it where someone might see you.

And it's good.

That's an understatement.

Without even having to pause for thought, I can say that this is the best sex I've ever had. Despite the fact that the metal of the truck bed is hard below me, that his hands are dirty and my clothes get torn. Despite the fact that he bruises my lips when he kisses me afterwards, that he's bruised my bum with his hearty spanks, and I know that there is no way I'll ever make it back to my real life again. That door is permanently closed to me, because here I am, ravaged in the back of a virtual stranger's truck, and all I know about him is his first name.

FADE OUT with shimmering waves letting the audience know that this was a fantasy.

The vision follows me to the tailor's, and I stand there, gazing at my pristine reflection in the mirror, seeing without really seeing the girl looking back at me. Here's something I'm pretty sure most people would consider taboo. I'm fantasising about a recent sexual encounter with someone other than my fiancé while getting fitted for my wedding dress. This is more than taboo, I'm fairly sure. On a scale of moral goodness, this is out-and-out unacceptable.

Is that why I'm so wet in my pretty finery? Is that why, when the seamstress bends down at my knees to check the folds of fabric rippling delicately by my ankles, I lock myself into a frozen position, hoping desperately that she won't sense my arousal from her proximity to my sex? The mortifying thought ought to still my straining libido, but it doesn't.

No matter how hard I work to push the ferocious fantasies from my head, all I see is me and Brock fucking. Here I am, in a sleek-fitted ivory silk gown, looking as if I should be photographed for the pages of *Beautiful Bride*, while in my mind, all I can see is him ripping my clothes off me, tearing my skirt to shreds, demolishing my blouse and my bra, taking me so hard that my entire body vibrates with the power of his passion.

'You must be so excited,' the seamstress says, pinning a bit of the hem into place now that I've finally found the heels to wear with the dress.

'Excited?' I echo. Oh, God, she knows. She knows that I'm turned on, and she guesses, somehow, that I'm thinking about a man other than my chosen groom, and she's going to tell Logan –

'You look just gorgeous, and the shoes are so perfect.' She's in full-on gush mode, the way so many women get around anything wedding related, and all I can do is nod in answer, relieved that she hasn't stumbled upon my secret shame.

'A spring bride,' she trills, 'all the flowers will be in bloom and the weather is sure to co-operate.'

I nod again.

'This time of year is such fun for a wedding. Do you know where the ceremony will be?' Then she giggles, joyously. 'Oh, you must, by this point. We're getting so close now, aren't we?'

'Yes,' I say. 'So close.'

'You don't have cold feet, do you?' And now I understand that she is teasing, and that she must have this type of conversation with every bride who crosses her threshold. I mumble some response and she winks at me, then leaves me alone to change back into my street clothes.

Carefully, I remove the dress and then stand there, in the garters and corset, pure white confections that I bought several weeks ago with Janice. Maybe all brides fantasise about other people as the wedding day approaches. Maybe some of them even engage in brief but passionate flings. The seamstress even mentioned the concept of 'cold feet'. So maybe I'm normal. I try to convince myself.

But somehow I know that I'm not.

When I can't wait any longer to see him, I call again. We decide to rendezvous at the mall in Century City. 'Come on,' he says, as soon as I walk towards him at the designated meeting spot. 'Just come on.'

We hurry down the escalator together to the multi-level underground parking garage, and when I spot his County truck, I feel as if I am going to faint. He rushes me towards it, then opens the door and boosts me up onto the seat. I wait as he shuts the door and heads around to the driver's side. I wonder if he's going to take me somewhere else, but it's as if he understands that we don't have time. We fall into each other in fast-motion. I see everything that happens as if I'm watching the action on the screen. I see his muscular body, strong hands on mine. And I think: This is right. It has to be right. To feel this good, it has to be right.

I'm not captured this time, so I have the ability to take control of my actions. I use my hands to stroke him through his jeans. He is wearing black jeans on his tight body. I've dreamed about him in his black jeans and nothing else. In seconds his white shirt is up and off, tossed somewhere on the floor, and I can feel his skin. It's only been a few days since we were last together, but I feel as if it's been months. I drink in his skin with the palms of my hands. My nails dig into him, because even if he has to be careful not to mark me, I don't have the same constraints with his body. He groans and pushes against me as I rake my nails along his arms, then down his strong, naked chest. He leans his head back against the seat and lets me touch him all over.

We're in a blur of motion, but I register every single second. I pop the fly on his jeans and bend at the waist, releasing his hard-on and locking my lips around it. I bob my head, getting his cock nice and wet with my mouth. I revel in the way he tastes. His cock presses hard against the back of my throat, and his fingers twirl through my dark hair, messing up my tresses, tangling and untangling the long, soft ribbons of my curls.

And then he needs more. His hands on me are quick to lift my semi-sheer blue floral sundress. He doesn't say a word as he pulls the dress up and over my head to reveal my underwire strapless bra and white thong panties. I put so much thought in what to wear under the dress, and now his hands roughly rip the bra open and let it fall away from my body. For a moment he stares at me, and then he grabs me and lifts me forward so that he can suck on my tits, first one and then the other, his mouth hot and raw on my nipples. I realise that I'm making noises that I can't decipher. Moans and sighs, nonsense words strung together in odd disjointed sentences. 'Please. Oh, God. Yes, that. Do that.'

Then I am up on his lap, astride him. His hands grip into me, and I have to think about it. No marks. We can't leave marks. His mouth opens on mine, then moves down my neck, lips sliding on my skin in a line down my body. As he kisses my neck, his hands move to cradle my ass.

Yes, do that, that bad thing, pull them down. Pull my panties all the way down and take them off. Now, yes, now. As I feel his warm fingertips slide the barrier of the panties away from my pussy, I help guide his cock inside of me. His hard cock, still wet from my mouth, slides easily in and, from that very first thrust, I am breathless.

I pump myself up and down on him, gripping into the cold silver metal of the headrest behind him, rocking my body to get as close to his as I possibly can. He lets me fuck him, and I can't believe how good it feels.

'You're going to come from this,' he whispers, bringing his lips to the curve of my throat and kissing me. His fingertips move to the space between our bodies and his hand rests in the perfect place, his thumb right on my clit as I continue to drive up and down.

'Aren't you?' he teases. 'Aren't you going to come, my dirty girl?'

Can't think. Can't talk.

Windows steamed up from our heat.

'So you slept with him,' Janice says when I finally confess what has been going on in my world. After meeting Brock in the mall, I decide that I need someone else's opinion of all this. But I don't expect Janice to say what she says. It's far more of a Marilynn concept, and I stare at her with my mouth open, like a character in a cartoon. If I could, I'd bug out my eyes. After a moment, I make myself ask, 'What do you mean "so"?'

'You had a fling. You had sex with him in the back of his truck.'

The *front*, I think, but don't say, because I'm sure that it won't make any difference to Janice. But it does make a difference to me. We were in the front of his truck, and we didn't have enough room, but we made do. And he fucked me so hard, Janice, that I thought I saw stars. I was sure I'd scream his name, that people would come running, but I managed to be silent. We stared into each other's eyes while we did it, and I've never felt –

'People have done worse,' Janice continues, oblivious to my mental ramblings. 'Much worse than screwing in a pick-up.'

That's all she has to say to send my mind spinning all over again. Is that what we did? Screwed in a pick-up? That's not what it felt like. It felt like diving into something – something without an end, without a start, without walls or limits. It felt like his skin on my skin and his mouth on my mouth, and Janice interrupts me before I make a pool of sex juices on the vinyl booth beneath me.

'Don't you think things like that happen every day?'

'Not when you're engaged.'

'Sure they do. It's not even worthy of a soap-opera plot. In order for it to be on TV, you would have had to sleep with his brother. Or his father. Or his sister. Or all three in a single day. This is par for the course, Cat. You had to get it out of your system. I would even have recommended it, if I didn't think you'd go crazy at the thought.'

'I can't continue with the wedding, Janice. You're not suggesting that, are you?'

Now *she's* the one with the incredulous expression. 'Of course I am. Love and lust are entirely different things. You love Logan. You'll be with him forever. One last fling with a pretty boy doesn't change that.'

'It does,' I say, but she's starting to confuse me with what I can only think of as her illogical logic.

'Do you think Logan's been faithful to you the whole time? For six years?'

That stops me. Do I? I never really considered it. We don't have sex very often. Could it be because he's sleeping with someone else? The thought seems impossible to me. Logan keeps everything so compartmentalised in his life. He has a place for work, a place for writing, a place for me. Is there a section in his life devoted to somebody else?

'Have *you* ever cheated?' I ask.

Janice doesn't answer me immediately. I can tell from her expression that she wishes she could change the subject.

'The guy from your gym,' I say, feeling very Miss Marple-like in my deductions.

'Sure, once,' she says. 'It doesn't mean I don't love Allan. It just means I had a bit of extra sexual steam to blow off.'

'Aren't you worried he'll find out?'

'We didn't have an affair,' Janice explains. 'We had a fling. A one-timer. I think they're healthy. People only catch on to cheaters when the sexual heat crosses over into a relationship.'

I can't believe what I'm hearing.

'Read the magazines, Cat. You're living in a dream world if you don't think people do stuff like this.'

'Does Allan?' I ask now.

'I'm sure he has. He's always away on business. Haven't you ever read the studies? More than seventy per cent of people have cheated at some point in their life. More than eighty per cent of people fantasise about cheating. And those numbers are probably higher in Los Angeles.'

'But more than fifty per cent get divorced,' I remind her.

She raises her eyebrows at me as if the percentages don't have anything to do with each other.

'Don't you feel jealous?'

'Not of a one-night stand,' she says, but her expression is closed and unreadable.

'Look, kiddo. I'm not recommending you sleep with every guy you like. I'm not even telling you to sleep with Brock again. I'm just saying that in all honesty, monogamy doesn't always work. That doesn't mean you should scrap your relationship. Read the papers. You're right that divorces consume half the marriages. If you want to stay together, you sometimes have to turn a blind eye to what's going on. You have to forgive your partner, and yourself. You have to learn not to dig too deeply.'

'So you're saying I should go forward with the marriage,' I say, just to hear the way it sounds.

'That's exactly what I'm saying. In five years, you'll understand better. You'll thank me for this advice.' She takes my left hand in hers and turns it so my ring catches the light. Rainbows shoot across the table. 'I promise.'

Once I begin cheating, strange things happen to me. It's as if I become someone else, like a star in one of the movies I've spent months of my working life rewriting. Or as if I uncover a part of myself that I didn't know previously existed. I've always been confounded by my Gemini sign, but now that Zodiac character makes perfect sense for me. I'm the twins: two individual people, the person Logan knows and the person Brock knows – and those two people couldn't be more dissimilar. For instance, with Brock, I eat meat. Not just any meat. The best they have. The top sirloin, rare, please. Bloody rare. If Logan ever caught me with so much as a cocktail wiener in my hand, he'd have a fit.

With Logan, I'm a light drinker. An occasional white-wine spritzer at an event will tide me over. I'm so unsophisticated with alcohol that I don't even care if I'm drinking Chardonnay or house wine. I don't know the differences between the names of some of the reds and some of the whites. Syrah? Not sure. I even drink rosé, which offends most knowledgeable wine connoisseurs.

With Brock, I drink Tanqueray Martinis, straight up, with an olive. I know how to order my drink at our bar, and I feel oddly pleased with my new vices. In fact, when I'm not dreaming about fucking Brock, I'm dreaming about eating with him and drinking with him, diving into all those previously forbidden pleasures. Ones that I, as a good girl, was so desperate to avoid.

So maybe I'm two people, but the one I've been for so long always seems to win out – except, that is, when I'm in Brock's presence. Then the bad girl stifles the good girl, ties her up and throws her in the back seat where she can't make any noise, and all she can do is watch.

And, oh boy, does she like to watch.

When I tell my latest theories on life to Brock, he just grins. 'You want me to tie you up and make you watch, is that it, bad girl? What precisely would you like to watch me do?'

My breathing stops. Just stops. I have to force myself to take the next breath, and when I do, I shudder all over. Even though I'm a script doctor, and it's my job to know what's going to happen next in any movie, I didn't see that one coming.

'You can't tell me?' he teases, running one hand

under my chin to force me to face him. The good girl is already tied up and gagged in the back seat, right? So why not add the bad girl to that list? Why not tell him my steamiest fantasies and let him take me where he wants to, take me where I want to go, too.

I nod, but that's not enough. *This* script calls for dialogue.

'Tie you up and take advantage of you. That's what you'd like, isn't it? But we've already done that, so you're thinking about something else, aren't you? Something more serious. More sexy.'

I swallow hard, but I say nothing.

'I want you to tell me, baby.'

'There's nothing specific,' I lie.

'No,' he says, 'you tell me. You tell me exactly what you want, Dani.' He's like a sex genie. Anything I say, he'll make come true. I decide to test that out on him.

'A threesome,' I say, not giving any more detail at the moment, just letting Brock run with it.

'Oh, you are a bad girl, aren't you? You want me to share you, is that right?'

'Yes,' I say, realising as I say the word that 'yes' is exactly what I want. Brock puts one hand on my thigh and squeezes. He doesn't seem surprised by my fantasy in the slightest. In fact, I decide, he was expecting this all along; if I hadn't suggested it, he'd be the one to tell me that was on his plans next. Then he starts the engine and off we go to his apartment, high up in the hills, where the bougainvillea is plentiful and cactus flower in every yard.

Up here it's like a completely different world from the black-top-covered land down below. The area where he works all day. Up here, high in the hills, almost above the smog line, it's like coming into paradise. But I hardly see the view today, because Brock is going to tie me up again when we get to his place. Yes, he is.

He's going to throw me down on his bed, take off his belt, and bind my wrists over my head. And then, when I'm captured, and can't do anything about it, he will fuck me. I know this as I know my own name. I like being tied, and he knows it. And when he ties me down, he'll tell me what it will be like when he brings a third person to join us. He'll describe every dirty detail as he spreads my legs wide apart and fucks me, and I'll scream because nobody can hear us at all. And because that's what bad girls do.

They scream.

'Sure,' Marilynn says later that evening. 'That's just what bad girls do.'

'Come on,' I urge. 'Are *you* vocal in bed? Do you make noise?' I haven't told her about Brock yet, but I know that she knows something's going on with me. I appreciate the fact that Marilynn never pushes. She lets me take my own time to share the secrets on those rare occasions when I actually have secrets to share.

'How can you even ask that? Just look at me.'

I do. I take in her lovely rich-brown hair. Her huge kohl-ringed eyes. Her lips, so full and red no matter how many times she brings the cigarette between them. I think, yes, she is a screamer, but her sounds are different from mine. She is low and husky, even when she's loud. She's Bacall at climax. She's so rich and deep a man could get lost in her voice. Then she winks at me, and says, 'Bacall's what they called me in college anyway,' and we both laugh our way out of that.

Still, I don't end up telling her about what happened today. I don't tell her that Brock tied me down to his bed and blindfolded me, as I knew that he would, and then he left me alone while he made a phone call from the other room. I don't tell her that ten minutes later his doorbell rang and that, after a moment of hushed conversation in the other room, I heard two sets of footsteps approaching. I don't tell Marilynn that I was so wet I could hardly stand it, that when four hands started to touch my breasts I cried out, begging for more.

Brock said, 'Sh, baby. You'll get what you want. You'll get everything that's coming to you.' And he was right.

I go home and think once again about how to break up with Logan. I'll never be able to live with Logan as man and wife now that I've tasted how good sex can be with someone else. I thought I might be able to, when Brock and I had only engaged in a single romp. But now that I'm seeing him whenever I can, I simply can't imagine stopping.

Oh, man, does that sound shallow. Sex isn't everything. Isn't that one of Janice's favourite lines? Sex isn't important – companionship is. Trusting your partner. Living with someone you love.

But all that is bullshit, I realise. Even if things don't work out with Brock – even if he breaks up with me when he learns that I've been lying to him about my name – I won't be able to return to the rut of a life I share with Logan.

But how do you quit someone you've been with for six years? I've never broken up with anyone before. My college relationship simply dissolved when we both found other people. We parted on good, if vague, terms at the end of a semester, knowing that the vacation before school started up again would somehow wipe the past clean. I have no reference for this kind of situation. Nothing except what I've seen in movies, and not one scenario seems appropriate to me.

Write a letter, I decide. I'll write a letter and let him read it. If he wants to talk to me afterwards, he can.

But then, I think, what if this is just a fling? What if

Brock likes the idea of a conquest, and now that he has me craving him all the time, he will lose interest? What might I be throwing away? A secure lifetime with someone I genuinely love, even if I'm no longer really *in love* with him.

What should I do?

At the very moment I'm thinking that, the phone by the bed starts to ring, scaring me half to death. I answer breathlessly, 'He-hello?', my voice all trembly like some heroine in one of those teen slasher films, only to be greeted by the sound of Logan's deep baritone fighting to be heard amid a background melody of a neighbourhood bar.

'Baby,' Logan says, 'You won't believe it –'

'Believe what?' I ask, trying to get my wits together. Would *he* believe that I was trying my best to think of the perfect way to get out of the wedding? Would he drive home immediately to star in a five-alarm fight, or would he laugh it off in his usual casual way, unconcerned. He knows his Cat, after all.

Silly girl. You're so pretty. Come to your senses, Cat.

He knows all about me. No need to worry that I'd be wooed away by another man. But what about spanked away? What about all tied down and screwed away? What about offered up to another man and fucked away? These thoughts could never cross Logan's busy or drug-hazed brain. They would be too shocking in a do-not-compute manner.

'That's just it. Just what you won't believe.'

Are we in a David Mamet play? Is Logan trying out new dialogue on me?

'Come on down to Bar Fly,' he says, 'I've got news. Big news.'

'Big fucking news!' someone yells.

'You tell her,' I hear in the background.

'Who all is there?'

'The office crowd,' he says, 'and some others.'

'I'm not really dressed –'

'So get dressed.'

'She's naked!' I hear in the background. 'Have her come naked!' 'Yeah, Catherine! Come on down!' There are catcalls and wolf whistles and I know that this social event is going to be like all of the other get-togethers with Logan and his workforce: almost entirely made up of men, with a scattering of the token lesbian engineers who round out the office where he works.

'This is big,' Logan says, ignoring his friends. 'I mean, really big. Don't be too long, Cat. Come join us.'

So I do what he says. I push my worries out of my mind, put on something slinky and silver, and muss my hair in a sexy manner rather than try to comb it into a decent style. I hurry out of the apartment, wondering what could possibly be this important, and why he wouldn't have just told me on the phone.

In the elevator I adjust my outfit, do my lipstick in the reflection in the glass and, mind still racing, exit into the hippest bar in Santa Monica. Logan and I know the bouncers. My studio does plenty of business here, and the County hosts the biggest corporate shindigs here as well. So I breeze in past the burly bouncer and the sleek, model-like hostess, and find Logan amid a group of men in suits and men in jeans, and butch girls in cargo pants, and then suddenly I get it. The *big* promotion. The one he's been talking about for a while. It's here. And there's been an impromptu celebration. Don't know why I can't figure out the rest of it – the fact that Brock would be here, too. Of course, he would.

Because there he is.

Logan rushes to my side and whispers the news in my ear. 'Got it, baby,' he says, his voice rich with barely concealed excitement.

'It,' I repeat, bewildered. The sight of Brock so close by makes me feel as if I have tunnel vision, as if my visual scope contains only his presence. I force myself to look at Logan, to try to make sense of what he's telling me, but Brock remains directly in my sight. Just staring at me. I wonder for a moment if I've actually gone over the edge, entering a magic mental state in which my dream man will suddenly appear everywhere I go. That wouldn't be so bad, would it? Happens in films and good TV shows all the time. I believe, according to one of Janice's columns on the movies, this trick is known as 'magical realism'. Think about *Like Water for Chocolate* or *Dona Flor and her Two Husbands* or even some of the artsier episodes of *The Sopranos*.

'The promotion. I'm in charge of –'

'Everything!' This is an interruption that comes from someone behind him who butts into the conversation with a widespread reach. 'He's in charge of the whole fucking city, Cat.'

'All right,' Logan says, holding up his hands. 'That's exaggerating, now, isn't it, Chet? Let's all be honest here, shall we.'

'Seriously,' Chet disagrees, 'you're the Senior Engineer in charge of capital projects. Capital projects with a capital C for "C-notes". For moolah, baby. The bridges. The largest overpasses. Anything that the city is forced to spend a lot of money on, you're in charge of. From design to completion. That's amazing, man. Especially for an idiot like you.'

Logan socks him playfully, and I realise that what I'm witnessing is a flagrant example of men being men, so I hardly pay attention. Out of habit, I tilt my head towards the talkers as if I'm listening intently to all of this, but in reality, I'm focused on the whereabouts of my lover. I realise with a jolt that Brock has moved from my line of vision. Now I don't know where he is.

Has he left the building upon seeing that I've arrived? Is he planning on confronting me and Logan, of showing Logan the pictures he took of me on his digital camera, of telling Logan about what he and I and an unnamed third party did this very afternoon?

Insecurity waves through me.

Another man pounds Logan on the back in a congratulatory way. I feel my face frozen into a smile, as I keep my eyes scanning the room for Brock. I saw him before; I know he's here somewhere. There's Paul, Logan's best friend, arguing in a corner with his girlfriend Kim. I turn away from them before they can make eye contact with me. I'm not in the mood for one of their battles. I'm far too consumed by thoughts of Brock.

Then I feel a strong hand in the small of my back, and I know without turning to see him that it's Brock. The feeling of his fingers against my skin, even through the filmy material of my dress, makes me want to melt. I think about the way he touched me so recently, the way his mouth felt on the split of my body, parting my nether lips, opening me up so that he could drive inside with his fingers crossed over one another. I think about the belt he had in his hands, and the description he gave me of how that belt would ultimately feel on my naked hide when he finally was given the freedom to treat me the way he wanted to. I think about the future stripes that will line my ass, and the way that I'll feel when I stare at my punished reflection in the mirror. I realise that I'm getting wet again, or that I'm wet still, and I also realise how incredibly inappropriate this is.

He takes another step so that he's right at my side, so close I find myself staring at him, wide-eyed.

'You look familiar,' he says softly, a famous Hollywood pick-up line. 'You look familiar' could be an easy lead into 'Haven't I seen you before?' Which can just as easily lead into 'Haven't I seen you up on the screen?

Aren't you an actress? Oh, yes –' accompanied by a sharp finger-snap of recognition '– that actress, Jesus, what's your name? It's right on the tip of my tongue.' But with Brock, the pick-up line works, because I truly should look familiar, and what was on the tip of his tongue was my throbbing clit. Christ, he fucked me only hours ago. My pussy still feels swollen from his thrusts.

'Have we had the pleasure of meeting previously?' he asks next.

The pleasure, I think. Oh, yes. Yes, definitely. We have had the pleasure. All the pleasure and more.

But I don't say that. Not here. Not with Logan standing at my side. I don't say anything like that at all.

My breath catches in my throat and I work to find something appropriate, some response that will make sense and that won't come out like, 'That's because you came in my mouth twice this afternoon. And if you're anything like me, then you've been lost in lustful visions since we parted. You've been envisioning me on my knees sucking your hard cock until you shoot. You might not realise this, but I've actually been writing pages of a script in which you go down on your knees and lick my pussy until right before I come, and then, when I'm teetering on the brink, you bend me across your lap and give me a quick spanking, and then – when I really am on the very, very edge – you fuck me. God, you probably have my panties in your pocket right now, which you finger at all the most inappropriate moments of the day, like when you're talking with your boss or giving orders to your crew, or congratulating my fiancé on his promotion.'

Logan, only half-paying attention, thrusts his hand out. 'Good to see you, Brock,' he says, before adding proudly, 'this is my fiancé Catherine Harrington. I don't think you two have been introduced before.' So I'm revealed like that. In a single beat, and by my own man. I feel as if I've been placed on display, nude and exposed, as if Logan has not only said my name, but taken off my clothes and put me on a pedestal for all to see. Would that be so bad? To be revealed? If I were really stripped down, would Logan realise that I'm not meant for him, but that I'm really meant for Brock. Would everyone in the crowd realise that as well and start to chant our names, cheering us on à la *An Officer and a Gentleman*. What would our movie be called? *The Workman and the Slut*, perhaps?

'Cat,' I say, as Brock squeezes my hand for one beat too long and one level too tight. He's letting me know how he feels about being lied to.

'My friends call me Cat,' I say, because for some reason I can't be quiet. I want to apologise. I want to beg his forgiveness and tell him that it wasn't really my fault for lying to him. I had that damned script in front of me. I wanted to be the star in the movie, not the sidekick Chelsea-type I've been all my life. Brock says nothing to alleviate my worries that he's truly angry with me.

'Cat,' he repeats simply, dark eyes gleaming at me as if he's just uncovered a precious treasure. 'Charmed.'

I must say something back. Something other than what I most want to say, which is 'Now that you know my name, what are you waiting for? Fuck me again. Just fuck me. Right here. In front of Logan and his boss and all the other people whose names I forget as soon as I'm introduced. Spread me out on the hard wooden floor, lift the filmy silver skirt of my seriously over-priced dress, and fuck me until I scream. I've never been one to scream during sex before, Brock. I'm not the type of girl who makes a lot of noise. I remain contained, focused on every action, thinking about what I'll do after the sex takes place. But I know that I will scream when you take me again. I know that things will be different now that you know my name. You can call out "Cat!" when you come, and hearing you voice my name will make me come. And when I come, I'll scream.

'After we gather ourselves together, I want you to fuck me again, to fuck me ever harder. Until I cry. Until I liquefy into a puddle of sweet satiny sex juices. Oh, but first, spank me. Come on, Brock, just spank me. Put me over your knee and make me pay for being such a bad girl. Because I am, Brock. I'm a bad girl. I'm *your* bad girl. You can use your belt now, like you wanted to. You can make me pay for lying to you.'

In script format, I'd have a huge monologue right about now. I'd explain every deviant little fantasy I've ever had, and then, because I'm the one writing the script, Brock would respond by making all my daydreams come true. Every last one of them. I think of *Too Beautiful for You*, my favourite French film starring the luminous Carole Bouquet and Gerard Depardieu (OK, so don't *all* French films star Monsieur Depardieu?). In particular, I remember the fantasy scene at the dinner table, when the guests simply say exactly what's on their minds. Things along the lines of: 'I want to eat your pussy. I want to taste you.' But outside of films, French films to be precise, when do things like that actually happen?

Never.

So instead of babbling incoherently like a mental patient on an X-rated verbal bender, I manage to make some banal chitchat that basically fits the situation. Brock takes it all in, nodding patiently before Logan says he'll see Brock later and then steers me over to the bar and orders me my standard white-wine spritzer. I'm not an adventurous drinker, but when I see Brock at the other end of the bar ordering a Martini, I realise that's exactly what I want, too. I push my spritzer aside and ask the bartender for a Tanqueray Martini, straight up, with an olive, while Logan looks at me, baffled.

'You *never* drink those.'

'We're celebrating,' I explain, trying to adopt a light note in my voice. 'Aren't we? Isn't that what people do during celebrations? Order fancy drinks?' I'm overcompensating. I ought to shut up now, but I find that I can't control myself.

'You'll be passed out on the floor in ten minutes.'

'Just don't take advantage of me,' I wink.

'Remember ski weekend at Mammoth?' Logan counters, his handsome blond brow furrowed, and at his words I do have a flash of the last time I experimented with alcohol while Logan was present. I lost my inhibitions for the evening, which was a liberating event for me and a startling one for my man. No, the night wasn't what one would call pretty, wasn't what Logan expected from me at all. Unfortunately, Logan's least favourite encounters are with the unexpected. *Any* unexpected. He doesn't like going to improvisational comedy shows for this reason. He hates it when I talk about changing my hair colour, or my standard choice of perfume, or when I discuss the possibility of cancelling out my vegetarian lifestyle and returning to the pleasures of being a meat-eater. So watching me play dangerously with a new drink sends a visible shudder through my routine-loving man.

What Logan doesn't know is that my first few trysts with festive substances occurred way back when in college, and while the memories may be a bit blurred at the edges, all were extremely pleasant. In fact, I'd like to employ a technique called 'the flashback' right now. Yes, I know full well that some film-makers frown on this kind of movie-making trick, calling it a gimmick and considering the concept to be dated. But I've always been a fan of learning more about a character or scenario through an actual peek into history. Of course, I also occasionally like 'the wash', that 70s groovy way of making a scene disappear sideways or upside down into the screen, so maybe I'm a little dated in my cinema tricks.

Regardless, bear with me.

FLASHBACK:

The first time I ever got drunk was with two male buddies, freshman year at college. Mike, Todd and I became fast friends in the dorms. The boys were both juniors, and they'd fully figured out how to have fun with the collegiate system. While I was floundering, confounded by a roommate who constantly had her boyfriend in for 'sleepovers', demanding I vacate the premises or listen to (and watch) the two humping aerobically on her skinny twin bed, Mike and Todd were experts. They knew how to smuggle alcohol back into the dorms in suitcases, had set their room up to look like a bachelor pad, complete with multimedia centre and mood lighting, and they always had other places to be if one 'got lucky'.

I never realised that they were both going to get lucky with me until the night that it happened. But maybe that's because I wasn't on the same page of the script as they were. One evening, right after finals, the three of us did shots of tequila until the wee hours of the morning, and then our smashed little trio ended up in bed together, in a sweet sexual-sandwich situation. I guess that it didn't happen accidentally. The three of us had been flirting around the concept for quite some time. Todd would mention something one evening – Mike would echo the fantasy the next day. The sexual tension bled into our viewpoints, our senses, until every time I was with them, my body tingled in anticipation.

In this case, reality was worlds better than any fantasy. Tall, dark Mike took the position behind me. Slim, blond Todd chose the front. At some points during the night, I was upside down, I think. Other times, sand-wiched so tightly with them, I was aware that Todd's hands were roaming up and down over Mike's bulging muscles, that in some way I was the catalyst that freed up their interest in one another. An interest that could never be spoken aloud. Not with Mike an active member of the ROTC programme and Todd a much-hunted bach-elor who would find different girls' panties draped over his computer terminal if he left the dorm-room door open while running down to the cafeteria to get a snack. Todd was like a rock star, like slim-hipped Bowie or lithe Gavin Rossdale. Mike was like every girl's fireman fan-tasy: strong, handsome, well built, powerful. Together they took me places that I've never visited again. Or, at least, that I hadn't until meeting Brock.

Mike used his hands to part the cheeks of my ass. He pressed the length of his cock between my two rounded cheeks just as Todd slid his rod into me in front. I groaned and arched, feeling myself being filled in front, paying attention when Mike reached forward to grab a bottle of lube that just happened to be sitting on the table by the bed – more indication that this accidental romping had been well planned by the boys in advance. He oiled himself, then lubed me up, and he slid inside of my ass as Todd continued to fuck my pussy. We got into a steady rhythm, the three of us. Todd thrust forwards, Mike countered, and I let my body be pressed back and forth, rocking, rolling, and finally coming. And coming.

And coming.

I woke up between the two of them, feeling a sense of euphoria I'd never felt before – but that was such a long time ago . . .

RETURN TO PRESENT DAY:
While Logan looks on in only partial mock-horror, I swallow the first large sip of the Martini. It's sharp and

strong, and I lock eyes with Brock while I flick out my tongue to lick my top lip. He smiles disarmingly at me. Maybe Danika would stalk around to his side of the bar and toast glasses. I'm sure she would. But I don't. When Logan turns to talk to a fellow co-worker, I raise my glass slightly, ever so slightly, in his direction.

At the sound of his name being called from across the room, Logan grabs me by the elbow and hurries me over to meet yet more people. Some I've talked with before, at various office functions and New Year's parties. Some are brand new, and as always I immediately forget their names as soon as I'm introduced. I feel Brock nearby. I don't know how, but I know when his eyes are on me, and I'm glad that I took the time to choose a pretty dress. Although I had no idea I'd see him here, he was definitely on my mind when I slipped into my clothes. I imagine that he's doing to me what I'm doing to him – that he's mentally undressing me at every possible chance. I know the public-speaking trick of envisioning an audience naked. Now I only think about him naked and me naked and the rest of these partiers dressed in their hippest finery, watching us fuck as if we were a sporting event put on for their pleasure.

That's not what I tell Brock when he corners me by the bathroom. I just look at him, look around quickly to make sure that nobody is watching us, and say, softly, 'I couldn't tell you before.'

He puts his finger to his lips, letting me know that he doesn't want to discuss our other relationship here. Not any part of it. Instead he smiles as he says, 'Nice to be properly introduced.'

I shake my head. I have no words.

'You look stunning,' he says next, eyeing me up and down.

All of my cares and worries about getting caught or

saying the wrong thing disappear from my head, and instead I tell him the truth, which is this: 'I thought of you as I chose my panties.' Then I hurry into the ladies' room and collapse against the mirror for support.

What am I doing?

I haven't the faintest idea.

The door pushes open slightly. I stand up straight, smoothing my hair and trying my best to make myself look appropriate in case the woman entering is someone I know. Turns out, it is someone I know, but not a woman.

Brock looks around cautiously and then walks in. 'Why were you thinking of me? You didn't know I would be here.'

'But you were on my mind,' I confess. 'You're always on my mind now. Always. I was picturing what you might say if you saw me in these.'

'And what did you imagine?'

'Can't tell you –'

'Never say can't.' I look at him, startled as always by the utterly delicious strictness of his voice. He continues speaking, without any explanation. 'I need those.'

'You already have one pair.'

'But not those,' he says. 'You put them on thinking about me. You said so yourself. To my way of thinking, they belong to me. So let's have them.'

My legs are trembling. My hands are shaking. What if someone walks in? Logan's boss's wife. Logan's boss. Kim. Logan himself, worried that I've already managed to drink myself into a stupor, that I'm holed up in the bathroom making snow-angels on the tiled floor. Brock doesn't seem to have a single worry. He leans against the turquoise-shellacked wall and waits. I should be incredulous. I should slam right out of the bathroom and find Logan. I should *not* do what it is that I do, which is lift my skirt so he can see the filmy satin panties, then slowly, so slowly, slide them down my legs, making sure that he can see everything – my cleanly waxed pussy, the shiny wetness adorning my most private regions, the fancy garters that I slid into while imagining Brock admiring them. I step out of the frilly lingerie and Brock bends down and snatches the panties in his hand.

'Didn't even hesitate,' he says, bringing the soft fabric to his face and inhaling with a luxurious languor. My dress slowly falls back into place, but Brock shakes his head. 'Uh-uh, baby. I want to see. Lift that up again.'

I immediately obey, all thoughts on hold as I do what he says. I lift my dress all the way to my waist and let him look at me as if I were a private girlie show put on for his sole enjoyment.

'God, are you beautiful.'

I sigh, my body shaking now.

'I want to lick that pretty pussy of yours. Can I do that?'

I shake my head.

'Come on, Cat. Can't I just get a taste of you on my tongue. All I want is one little taste before we go back to the party.'

Again I shake my head, and I press back against the mirror, feeling the cold polished glass against my ass.

'Can I tell you about it, then? Can I tell you what I want to do?'

Now, I nod. I'm desperate to hear him tell me all of the salacious details. Every last one of them.

'OK, but here's what you have to do for me. You have to stay just like that, with your dress up at your waist. You can't let it fall down, not even the slightest bit. If you do, I'll have to punish you. Do you understand?'

I nod again.

'Will you do that for me? Will you be a good girl?'

I manage to say the word 'Yes' in a voice that sounds nothing like my own.

'Now, I want you to spread your legs a little bit more. I need to see everything.'

I slide my feet apart, thinking that the juices from my body will start raining down on the floor any minute. That I will make a lake of pleasure juices right here, and Brock will know exactly what he does to me. But maybe he does already. Maybe he's an expert in what makes me wet.

'This is what I want to do,' he says, my panties still tight in his fist. 'I want to run my tongue up and down that silky slit of yours. Lick each drop away. Ring your clit with my lips.'

I moan, my eyes open wide, my body on display for him.

'I want to French-kiss that pretty pussy of yours, slide my tongue way up inside you, flick it over your clit again and again. And I want you to think about this while I make you come. I want you to know that as soon as you climax, I'm going to have to give you a spanking. The sort of spanking that you deserve. Even before I fuck you, I'm going to spank you. I'll use my hand firmly on your naked bottom and make it a blushing pink all over. Cherry pink. Pure, ripe and perfect.'

I suck in my breath, and I hear the tremble of fear and desire vibrate deep inside my throat.

'You would *have* to get a spanking, wouldn't you?' Brock says, and he's closer to me now. So close.

I say nothing.

'Answer me, Cat. When I ask you a question, I want you to answer me. Do you understand that?'

I nod, yes. Then I say, 'Yes,' because nodding is obviously not enough. Not for a situation like this.

'You'd need a good spanking, wouldn't you? A good

hard one that you could really feel. Especially after the way you behaved today. God, did you look lovely with my cock in your pussy and his cock in your mouth. So now you'd really need a spanking, wouldn't you?'

'Yes,' I say again.

'Tell me why.'

I can't think. How can I talk?

'Tell me why.'

I shake my head, even though I know what he wants me to say.

'Tell me.'

'Because I lied to you.' I feel as if I'm a second away from crying and a flicker of time away from coming.

Brock says, 'Not even close, baby. I knew that was a stage name from the very start. I heard your friend call you by your real name at the bar. I always knew you were Cat. So that's not why at all.'

'Then I don't know,' I say, and I sound as if I'm begging.

'Only a very, very bad girl who needed her bottom thoroughly spanked would let her lover make her come right here, in the ladies' room, with her fiancé just outside the door.'

And those are the words that manage to break the spell. My fiancé.

I lower the dress and hurry out of the bathroom, this evening's last image of Brock holding my panties up to his face, grinning. I think about his smile as I make my way through the crowd to find Logan. It's as if he knows all the rules and he's deadly certain that I'll be back again soon to play his game.

I will not see him again.

That is what I decide when I get into bed with Logan. He snuggles up to me, his face pressed against my cheek, and he says, 'Thank you, baby.'

'For what?'

'Your support. I know how much you hate get-togethers like that. But it was important for me that you be there.'

I murmur something; I don't know what. I wonder if Logan is going to fuck me, and I wonder whether he'll be able to tell that another man was inside me today.

Jesus, two men.

Logan and I don't fuck that much any more. Every once in a while, I read an article in a ladies' magazine about how often is 'right' in your relationship. There are always examples of people who have sex several times a day, and always a few sad souls who have sex a few times a year. Most couples fall somewhere in the middle. Lately, Logan and I fall in the outer reaches. Occasionally we have a burst of sexual energy, and we'll do it a few times in a row for several days. Just when I begin to feel elated by our new-found interest in one another, the flare will fade out, and we'll go back to our cuddling in the evenings, and safe nonsexual kisses in the mornings. To the life that we've shared for the past six years.

People can adapt to anything. I've adapted to this. It's wrong to think that Brock can fix me. It's probably wrong to think that I need fixing at all. I'm scared about the wedding – that's what this is all about. Being with Brock was a last-ditch effort to change my world. But I don't want it to be changed.

That's what I tell myself. That's what I assure myself.

I will not see him again.

But I lie.

8

'Not that colour, honey,' Bernie snorts, tearing the pale, sky-coloured swatch of fabric from my hand. 'You don't want your girlfriends dressed in blue.' She makes it sound as if I've suggested they wear plaid, or drape themselves in cream-coloured togas, or parade down the aisle in nothing but their birthday suits. It's difficult to believe that, this close to the wedding, I still don't have dresses for my bridesmaids, but with Bernie's constant meddling, decision-making has been an impossibility.

'Why?' I ask, knowing that I sound naive, but unable to stop myself. Sometimes arguing with Bernie comes naturally to me. She and I have such different tastes in everything, from food to fashion.

'Blue is for boys.' She says it as if it's one of the unwritten commandments, then shakes her head violently as if I ought to have known better. Her scarlet beehive doesn't move, sprayed as always into a hardened shell of obedience, but she pats the back of it lightly with her hand just to make sure.

'What colour, then?' I ask, looking over the vibrant squares of shiny cloth. Displayed on the Formica 50s-style kitchen table before us are a variety of pastels, several tasteful florals, and a rainbow of solid colours.

'You ready?' she asks, then cocks her head and waits, as if listening to an imaginary drum roll.

I nod.

'Black.' She says the word slowly, perfectly enunciating it, speaking with both extra volume and clarity as if talking to a foreigner. Her tongue hits the roof of her mouth to stretch it out. Blaaack. Orange-toned lipstick has smeared to her two front teeth, but I don't bother to tell her.

'For bridesmaids?'

'It's the new rage,' she explains, handing over a section of material that looks as if it's been ripped from a plastic garbage bag. Bernie takes a bite out of one of the finger sandwiches on the platter before us, watching closely for my reaction.

'Black?' I ask, thinking I might have misunderstood. I *must* have misunderstood.

'It will make you stand out so much more,' she says after swallowing. 'It's the hip colour for post-millennium weddings.'

Exactly what I've always dreamed of: a post-millennium wedding, with me at the front, leading the way, the bride of the century.

'Besides, black's slimming,' she adds. 'If you insist on including that fat friend of yours in the line-up.'

'Janice is not fat,' I lie, out of my outrageous sense of loyalty. 'She's voluptuous. Like Mae West.'

'Black will help camouflage the horsey girl, too,' Bernie adds. 'Make her look a little more feminine.'

'Marilynn's lanky,' I tell her forcefully, pushing the cloth samples into a colourful pile and standing up. It's enough for one day. No one could expect more of me. Except, apparently, Bernie. Before I manage to make my escape, she places one heavily jewelled hand on mine.

'We haven't talked centrepieces yet, and I can't believe it. Your wedding is around the corner, and you have refused to make so many of the important decisions. If you don't watch out, you're going to be left with daisies in a tin can on the centre of every table.' The whine in her voice has power. That tone alone makes me sit back down, however perched to fly I might be. While I settle uncomfortably on the edge of the sparkly vinyl chair, she takes a bite out of another sandwich. The platter is filled with small squares, each missing one bite and coloured around the edges with neon lipstick. Bernie points to a kiss-decorated pumpernickel square with cream-cheese and black-caviar filling, and says, 'Delicious.' She offers it to me, but I shake my head. 'Even better than the salmon-caviar hearts,' she assures me. I'm not a fan of either. As far as I'm concerned, fish eggs is fish eggs.

'What are you working on, hon?' Bernie asks me as she pulls an envelope out of her overflowing handbag. I can see that the envelope is filled with glossy photographs. I gaze at them with trepidation, only half-paying attention to my own answer. 'You know,' I say, 'the new Danika movie. It's not really as good as the first one was.'

'Sequels never are,' Bernie announces in her end-the-argument style. She has amazingly defined opinions and she rarely strays from them once her mind is made up. I used to think this was oddly charming. That was before she turned her take-no-prisoners style on me and my wedding. 'It's my theory,' Bernie continues, 'that screenwriters really only have one good movie in them. Once they make that movie, they're done. They might as well go write for TV.'

I know that it never makes sense to do battle with Bernie, as Logan is fond of reminding me. 'Why throw yourself repeatedly against a brick wall?' he always asks after I come home, battered, from one of my useless confrontations. But now she's talking about something I know, something I live with all the time: the movies. And I can't help myself.

'Only one?' I ask, watching Bernie begin to fan out the photos that I have yet to glimpse.

'Definitely. Look at *Usual Suspects*. Those writers never did another thing.'

'But how about Tarantino?'

'*Reservoir Dogs* was all he had in him.'

My eyes bug out. It's as if she's never heard of *Pulp Fiction*, or my personal favourite *True Romance*. In my opinion, writing doesn't get much stronger than the dialogue in that movie. Marilynn and I are always quoting it to each other: 'I'd fuck Elvis,' has got to be one of the best lines in history. That, as well as Brad Pitt's stoner line: 'Don't condenscend to me, man.' This is the one I'd love to use right now.

'I feel the same way about books,' Bernie says. 'Just because an author wrote one good novel doesn't mean you're going to like anything else they ever do.' I know now that I have to shut up, because authors' names are racing through my head like a literary tickertape: Raymond Chandler, Dashiell Hammett, Elmore Leonard, Roddy Doyle, Bill Bryson. The list of all my favourites goes on and on, and I've read and enjoyed every one of their books, including Leonard's Westerns, and I'm not generally big on that genre. But why am I holding back? For who? For Logan, so that his mother will like me. Just as I start to think 'fuck it', preparing to launch my argument, Bernie says simply, 'Of course, Danielle Steele's the exception,' and then she spreads out the last of the pictures and my mind reels at the ugliness displayed in front of me.

Quickly, before she can share any of her ideas, I say, 'I was thinking white roses arranged in silver bowls.' This is something I've always imagined for my wedding, a simple, tasteful arrangement of flowers. How can she argue with that?

Bernie shakes her head, then quickly pats the back again. 'Old news,' she says dismissively. 'Once you see these, you'll want them.' She hands me the first of the Polaroids. I squint at it.

'Twigs?' I ask, bringing it closer to my eyes. 'Sticks?'

'They're olive branches, symbolising peace. They'll be tied with those adorable little red bows that all the celebrities are wearing these days.'

'The AIDS ribbons?'

'Very chic,' she says. She pronounces it 'chick'.

'Instead of flowers?'

'Flowers wilt.' Bernie tries to make a face. It's difficult for her to do after her most recent plastic surgery. The skin from her hairline to her jaw is anchored so tightly that when she attempts to wrinkle her forehead, it only ripples slightly. 'Is that the way you want to start your marriage? With wilting centrepieces? What will people say?'

Shrugging, I stand up again. I don't know what people will say. I only know what I will say. And I know I have to get out of the room fast, before I say it out loud.

I tell myself that after something as horrific as that encounter, I deserve more than a little pleasure. This is how I justify seeing Brock again. It's how I make peace with the fact that I want another fix of him, despite all the assurances I made myself last night that I'd end it. End things before they started to get really out of hand.

But when I arrive at the site, I find that the workers are gone for the day. The dismay that wells through me lets me know that this is something I want. An undeniable urge. I've always had a difficult time with scripts in which people cheat. The ones who act like they couldn't help themselves always baffle me. Why not end a relationship neatly before moving on to the next?

You know things aren't working, you can save all those hard feelings and damaged egos.

Right?

Wrong.

Now that I'm enmeshed in this situation, I feel empathy for all those fictional characters I've been so hard on all these years. The conflicting sensations are right here, pulsing through me. The desire to do the impossible – to make everything work out for everybody. And the selfish yearning to just track Brock down and let him fuck me again, repercussions be damned.

Of course, that's just when Logan does something unexpected and sweet. We have a little tradition, a dinner out when we're distracted, when one of us becomes too preoccupied with work to pay attention to the other. The way we let each other know we're feeling neglected is to place a take-out menu on the bed. Not just any take-out menu, but one from the first restaurant we ever went to. It's a silly little Thai food place with the most wonderful mistranslations of items on the menu, accompanied by write-ups for dishes like 'My Favourite Munchies' and 'Love You Tender Crab Cakes'. We both know how saccharine sweet it is to go out on an anniversary and order platefuls of overly cute dishes, but that's what we do. And we've been doing it for years, now.

When I see the pink paper on my pillow, guilt floods through me. I've neglected him. That's what the menu says. I've neglected him more than he can possibly know, with my thoughts, fantasies, desires and my body. I hold the menu in my hand and look at the different love-struck items and then I sigh. I have to give this a go, don't I? Logan deserves that much. At the very least, he deserves dinner, doesn't he? I can't deny him that.

Especially with our wedding so close now.

But after our meal, I decide, if I want something seriously, I mean I crave something, I ought to give

Logan a shot at giving it to me. Does that make sense? I'm so sure that Brock can fulfil my desires, why not put *them* out on the mattress in place of the pink paper menu where Logan can look at Column A and Column B and take his pick. We're a little buzzed from the wine at dinner, and I whisper in Logan's ear that I have a surprise for him.

Logan doesn't like surprises. He wants to know everything ahead of time, so that he can plan his moves. That's what makes him such a good engineer, I suppose. But it makes him no fucking fun as a lover.

'Just tell me, Cat,' he insists. 'I don't want to wait until we get home.'

'Trust me,' I say in my most sultry voice.

He won't play along.

'Why can't you just tell me now?'

'Because it's a surprise.'

'Come on, Cat. I hate surprises. You know that.'

The silence between us grows larger until we get home. Sadly, I realise we're not even speaking to each other now. How could that have happened so quickly? From being at ease and having fun at the restaurant to rolling over without even a goodnight kiss back at home. Depression rushes over me as strong as the guilt that assailed me when I saw the paper menu.

When Logan falls asleep quickly at my side – stoned from a little after-dinner pot out on the balcony – my thoughts are still with Brock and I can't stop them. Not for anything. I picture his face, his arms, his hands. I roll onto my side, as far away from Logan as I can get, as if that will make the fantasies more acceptable, less guilt-inducing, and I think of Brock touching me, stroking me, talking to me, fucking me.

From the way he acted at Bar Fly, I believe that he can't stop thinking about me, either.

And here's the truth: I don't want him to.

EXT. WORK SITE

DANIKA is firmly tied to a large metal beam, her naked body shining beneath the amber lights. THE MAN admires his handiwork. His belt is holding her slim wrists together over her head. She could kick her legs out, but she doesn't. With her various jujitsu skills, she could try to defend herself, but it's obvious that she doesn't want to defend herself. She wants everything that's happening to her, everything that she has coming her way.

THE MAN comes closer to her, and then he runs his fingertips under her chin, tilting her head upwards.

THE MAN
Now, tell me what you want.

CLOSE UP:

On DANIKA'S body. We can see from the blushing hue of her cherry-coloured ass that she has recently been seriously spanked. We can see from the slick wetness on her thighs that her pussy is very, very ready.

DANIKA
Fuck me! Just fuck me.

CUT TO:

Me in bed, with the heavily slumbering Logan. My fingers make their knowledgeable circles around and around.

'Fuck me,' I beg silently to an imaginary Brock. 'Just fuck me.'

Book Two

'I don't want you to be true
I just want to make love to you.'

– Willie Dixon

9

'I like you when you're dirty.'

'Dirty how?'

'Dirty like this,' he explains, cradling my face and using his thumb to wipe a bead of sweat off my forehead. We've been hiking up in the wilds of Will Rogers Park. I'm not properly dressed for the activity. I have on a skirt and black boots with a low heel, and I'm hot and wet all over, my damp crimson T-shirt sticking to me. I self-consciously reach to smooth my hair, but he stops me.

'This,' he says. 'I'm serious. You look real. Not fake. Not all blow-dried and fancy.'

'You don't like blow-dried?'

'No, that's not what I'm saying. You always look delicious, but now you really look like you. Not a polished-up version of you. Not the way you want other people to see you, but like the real you.' He kisses me before I can say anything in my defence. Before I can make up excuses for not being pristine and clean. I believe that he's telling me the truth, the way I know that Logan is telling the truth when he says I look better with my curls ironed straight. Logan has a look that he prefers. Unfortunately, it's a look that takes a lot of time, effort and money to achieve.

Brock lifts me up suddenly and throws me over his shoulder. I pound on his back, laughing even as I beg him to put me down.

'We're not there yet,' he says, carrying me further up the trail.

'Where?'

'To the special spot.'

'Tell me where you're taking me,' I demand, breathless, my face so hot from dangling upside down with all the blood rushing to my head.

'Here,' he says, setting me carefully upright and spreading his arms out to show me a small clearing, off the hiking trail, secluded among the trees. In the centre of the space is a shady tree and, under that, he spreads his jeans jacket and motions for me to sit down.

I stare for a minute, looking at him.

'What are you waiting for?'

'I don't know.'

'Then stop waiting.'

I let myself fall into his lap, and I feel his strong legs beneath me. I think about what he'll say when he lifts my skirt and sees the scarlet panties that I've chosen for just this moment. These naughty knickers are the most expensive item of lingerie I've ever purchased, and I want him to notice the extravagance. But he doesn't comment on the colour of my panties, or the silky fabric, or the way the knickers hug my shapely ass.

Without a word, he slides the panties down my thighs and begins to spank me, slowly, steadily, until I'm squirming in his lap. He starts to go a little harder, and I realise that he's really smacking me now, and I also realise that as I press my pussy against his leg, this is going to make me come.

'Don't even try it,' Brock hisses.

'Please.'

'I'll tell you when, baby. Don't disobey me.'

With a shudder, I keep myself from rocking against the ridge of his knee, and I close my eyes tight and try to will myself not to come from the spanking. That's just when he spreads my legs wider apart and begins to let his fingers make striking contact with my pussy. I feel as if my lips have swollen to twice their normal size, feel as if every slap against my pussy is destined to make me climax. I wonder what he'll do if I disobey him, or really if my body disobeys him and comes on its own. Because I have no say at this point. I'm going to come, come hard, come fast, come –

'Now!' he says, and I do, with a grateful rush, a shivering sigh, I come as he gives my pussy those startling love-taps, and then I feel him pushing me over onto his jacket and I know that he's going to fuck me. While my cunt is still spasming recklessly, he slides his cock into me, and I greet him as if hugging him with my body, welcoming him with the after-echoes of pleasure.

'See?' he whispers into my ear as he thrusts hard. 'See? You are dirty. Only a dirty, dirty girl would come from a spanking.'

I'm too lost in the bliss to respond, but Brock wants me to talk. 'Tell me something, dirty girl.'

'What?' I ask him, a rush, a whisper.

'Tell me your other fantasies. I knew from the first time that I saw you that you wanted to be spanked. I just knew it. But tell me something else.'

'How did you know?'

He laughs. 'You had a look.'

'Tell me.'

'Guys who like spanking girls can find girls who like to be spanked. It's part of nature's great plan.'

I giggle. I like that kind of plan. But then I realise that means he's spanked girls in the past, and I can't believe the wave of jealousy that rolls through me. It's much stronger than the guilt I've felt about cheating on Logan. I narrow my eyes at Brock, and he shakes his head, as if he knows just what I'm thinking.

'Yeah, I like it. And I knew you did, too. Don't worry about the rest.'

He's fucking me as he talks to me, and I once again think about how amazing that is. He can remain present enough to hold a discussion even while engaging in the most erotic actions. 'I like it when you talk,' he says, and his voice has grown hoarse, letting me know that he's close. 'So talk to me, dirty girl.'

And there it is again – he likes me when I'm dirty, when he's dirty, when we're at our most base.

No need to hide.

No place to go.

Nothing that isn't out in the open.

'I want –' I start, but I don't have the ease that he does. Speaking while being so seriously taken is a job to me.

'Tell me what you want, dirty girl, and I just might make it come true.'

Reels of images spiral across my mind. I think of all the different flickering moments of pleasure I've had, and I try to remember the fantasies that have taken me there. Because in the past, the only way I've ever come while having sex is to think of being somewhere else, to think about having something else done to me. I rarely come with Logan, but those few times I've managed to reach the faraway gates of pleasure were while visualising being spanked while he fucks me. Or being fucked by one of our friends. Or one of our friend's girlfriends ... or both ... and this is the first fantasy I share with Brock.

'I want to be in another threesome.'

'Ever done it before the other day?'

I think of Mike and Todd and I know somehow that Brock will adore the story.

'You have,' he says, guessing correctly from my

silence. 'You didn't tell me that, did you? You conveniently left that part out.'

'Yeah.'

'And it was good the first time?'

'Oh, yeah.'

'And it was good the other day?'

'Oh, yeah.' I sigh at the memory.

'And now you want to try it again.'

'With you,' I tell him, 'and –'

'Another girl,' he says, finishing the thought for me. And he's right. I want to be with him and another girl. While we're pushing our fantasy boundaries now, that one is at the peak of mine. Me and Brock and some sexy nymphet, fucking in – not tandem, because that means two – in a trio, limbs entwined, mouths and hands working overtime. How funny that I never dreamed of confessing this sort of sexy scenario with Logan. Or maybe that's not humorous. Maybe it's just plain sad.

'Tell me about the other ménage you had,' Brock insists. 'Who was the girl? What did she look like?'

I smile. It's my first time to shock him. 'Not a girl,' I say. 'I was with two guys, just like with you,' and he groans, fucking even harder into me.

'Oh, you are dirty,' he says, and I can tell from the expression in his eyes and the gleeful quality in his voice that he is absolutely thrilled. 'Tell me. Come on, Cat. Tell me!'

'There were these boys I knew at school,' I start, and I realise that I'm being coy. Even with my body pressed against the rough denim, my hair getting tangled in the dirt and twigs, I'm being coy, and I'm enjoying being coy.

'Their names,' Brock urges.

'Mike and Todd. One was ROTC, the other was more

the intellectual type. One blond and the other dark. Slim and buffed. And we got a little tipsy –'

'Not on white-wine spritzers.'

'No,' I say, clenching down on him, my whole body teased to the point of a second orgasm. I'm reliving the moment with my two buddies while being fucked by my new lover, and the talking and action together take me higher and higher. 'Tequila,' I say, 'and I was a lightweight, but we did a lot of shots. I wanted to keep up with them. I didn't want them to think that I wasn't tough.'

'Oh, yeah,' he says, his voice taunting me. 'You're a regular tough guy.'

'We went out at some point for more drinks, and I ended up leaning on the outside of the grocery store, and then I slid down into a sitting position. Todd was inside, and Mike bent down and put his arms around me and kissed me. And I knew right then that it was going to happen. I knew, and I think that Todd knew when he came out and caught us in a clinch. We walked home, one on either side of me, and I got wetter and wetter with each step.'

'But how did you end up doing it?'

'Back at the dorm, I wound up on the floor between them. I had these button-fly jeans on and a thin white T-shirt, and the shirt rode up, showing off my flat belly, and Mike started running his fingertips up and over the buttons on my jeans. Casually, almost rhythmically, and then Todd started stroking my breasts through my T-shirt. I felt so adored by these two guys who I liked so much, and I just floated there, letting them touch me, letting the night progress in a way that it had to. It was as if we were all on this destiny-like ride. Predetermined.'

'Yeah,' Brock nuzzles against the back of my neck. 'Predetermined by a bottle of tequila and two horny frat guys.'

'Wasn't like that,' I tell him, and I try to let him

understand how it happened. 'We liked each other. They liked each other. The three of us together made something happen that was impossible in any other circumstance.'

'So tell me,' Brock says, and I know from his breathing and his motions that he's getting closer still, so close that his body trembles all over as if he's trying to hold himself back. 'Tell me the details. I want to know the slippery wet little details. Who was where? That sort of thing.'

And I tell him. What I've never told anyone. What Todd and Mike and I never talked about. How Todd pulled my shirt over my head and then unsnapped my white satin bra. How Mike finally undid the shiny row of buttons on my jeans and slid them down my thighs, pulling them completely off until all I had on was a pair of silky blue bikini-style panties. How Mike carried me to the bed and spread me out and the boys stripped down quickly and joined me, one on either side. And how I told them to blindfold me, because I didn't want to think about who was touching me where, I just wanted to fly in the feeling of those different hands on me, those different bodies, mouths, tongues.

Everything overlapping.

Brock comes as I tell him that part. The best part. The overlapping part in which they lubed me up and slid inside, one in each hole, and their fingers touched each other, and their cocks butted against each other through me, and how we all just basked in that warmth of the bed. In the glow that surrounded us. And as he comes I wonder how I lost that glow. The sense of freedom that came with that night. A freedom that had nothing really to do with sex, but everything to do with choices.

That's what I'm still thinking about when I meet Janice for drinks. It's my intention to tell her that the wedding is off. That I have to move out. That maybe I've been wrong all along about what I was looking for in a man.

'You know, you'll never have to worry about money again.' She's the practical one.

'I don't worry about money now. I'm doing fine.'

'But movie careers are so transitory. If a new studio head comes in –'

'And if a new editor takes over your 'zine –'

'We're not talking about me,' Janice snarls. 'I've got Allan. He's doing great. Between the two of us –'

'I thought we weren't talking about you.'

Her eyes flash at me, and I can tell she's offended that I've even suggested she might have financial troubles. But she's the one who brought up my circumstances in the first place. I wonder why it is that people who have no qualms at all about pointing out someone else's flaws always become extremely defensive when their own flaws are put under a bright light and inspected.

'Right,' she says, taking a deep breath. 'With Logan, you have no worries.'

'That's not true. I have plenty of worries.'

'But none about money. Not worrying about money is a huge relief. You've got to admit that.'

'Here's the thing,' I tell her, knowing that I've said this before, and also knowing what her response to my logic will be. 'Logan doesn't have lots and lots of money.'

'But his father does.'

'And if he quits his engineering job and becomes a full-time writer, his father will disinherit him.'

'Which is why he's never going to do that.'

I gaze at Janice, wondering why she seems so sure of herself. Whenever Logan and I have this talk, I'm left feeling that nothing has been finalised. Janice acts almost as if she has more information than I do. She seems to feel my inquisitive stare and she flutters her hands in an awkward gesture. 'I mean,' she says, 'he's too smart to do that. With millions at stake, he'd never do something totally nuts. He can always be a writer after hours and an engineer during the day. Especially now that he's been promoted. He won't ever leave that kind of success.'

Maybe Logan and I would get along better if he would do something crazy. Maybe if he'd do something 'out of the blue' like my favourite Bowie song suggests, the two of us would have a more common ground of communication. Way back when, Logan took his time telling me about his family's wealth. It was almost as if he were embarrassed by how much money they had. In fact, I had no idea he wasn't just an average engineer until well into our third month of dating. He drove me through Holmby Hills one night to see the new house his father and stepmother were building. Everything was dark on the construction lot, but I knew the area well enough to know the local landmarks: the Playboy Mansion was just down the street. A famous music producer lived next door and a best-selling romance author was the neighbour on the other side.

Logan watched me realise what he was telling me, and I knew he was judging my response. I had none. Not really. I'd never thought the two of us would become a serious item, so I couldn't really fathom caring about his parents.

'What do you think?' he finally asked, moving the car away from the kerb as a security truck rounded the corner.

'Big,' I said.

'Yeah,' he nodded, muttering the square-footage to me.

'Really, really big –'

'It's not my life,' he said. 'I live within my means.'

Now aside from a few expense-paid vacations we'd tagged along on, our lives couldn't have been less affected by his parents' money. Janice knows that. So I don't understand what she's trying to get at with her line of questioning.

'Security,' she says finally, summing it all up with one word. 'Can your hunk offer you that?'

'I don't know if he wants to offer me anything.'

'See?' she says. 'You could be trading in your whole life for a little bit of fleeting pleasure. You could throw away all of that security. You could throw away everything for nothing.'

It's not nothing, I want to tell her. What Brock and I do together, what we *have* together, is so far from nothing she couldn't possibly comprehend it.

'Somehow,' I tell her, 'the concept of security just doesn't seem as important to me as it used to.'

'Before your mind got all clouded with sex.'

'You said sex with a handsome stranger could be a good thing. You were all about "the fling".'

'But I didn't think you'd turn it into a relationship.'

'It's not really a relationship,' I say, 'it's a fireball of sexual energy that's too hot for me to control.'

'You sound like Marilynn,' she says sadly, and I know for a fact that she doesn't mean it as a compliment.

'I sound like me,' I tell her.

'Not the Cat I know,' she says. 'Not the Cat who always weighs the facts before making an important decision. At least think about it. What kind of a guy is your new boy toy if he's willing to see you while you're still attached to someone else.'

'Attached,' I repeat, 'like a growth.'

'You know what I mean, Cat. You're officially with another man. What sort of guy would see you on the sly? What kind of guy does that make him?'

'But what sort of girl does that make *me*?' I ask her

right back. Janice purses her lips at me in her standard disapproving manner, letting me know exactly what kind of a girl she thinks I am.

The ring comes off. The ring goes on. The ring comes off.

I think about the day Logan proposed to me. It was December 14th, which didn't mean anything to either of us. It was just a day. I knew the proposal was coming, because Logan had taken me to Tiffany's several months before – 'just to browse'. He'd asked me for my favourite, and I'd chosen a $12,000 pink tourmaline and diamond engagement ring. The clarity of the diamond was what made the ring so expensive. I never thought he'd go through with it; that was the only surprise.

He proposed on a day when I got into a car accident. I was only ten feet from our driveway, and I was about to make a right-hand turn into the underground parking lot. The woman who lives across the street from us was having a garage sale. She'd dressed for the event in a risqué tiny black bikini and thong outfit, and I'd thought earlier that morning that she was going to cause an accident, standing on the corner like that, looking for all intents and purposes like a street whore. Turns out that the seventeen-year-old boy driving the thirty-thousand-dollar banana-yellow convertible behind me paid more attention to her thong than to the stop sign on the corner and ploughed into the back end of my car.

Logan heard the crash and came running out and, after he'd calmed me down, he brought out the ring. 'To take your mind off your day,' is what he said. No, it wasn't the most romantic moment, but I never was with Logan for romance.

Now I dream about losing the ring. I panic when I can't find it, only to discover the sparkling item wedged into the bottom of the change compartment in my purse, glittering in there among the pennies and dimes and odd change from a London trip that I can never force myself to get rid of. Would you stuff $12,000 into a change purse? I chide myself. No. But the ring mocks me when I wear it. I can't bear to have it on when I'm with Brock, can hardly stand to see the thing when I'm at home. It gathers lint, and I have to brush it off, polishing the stone against the hem of my T-shirt, wondering why the sparkle seems to have faded.

I worry constantly that I'll forget to put the ring back on. That Logan will notice someday and become concerned. Would that really be such a bad thing? Am I too much of a coward not to face this whole issue head on?

And then, suddenly, a different worry assails me.

'You're mine,' Brock says one evening. We're hanging out later than usual because Logan has a town council meeting in one of LA's provinces.

'I know.'

'Prove it.'

I look at him, curious. What can he possibly mean?

'Stay the night with me.'

My heart begins pounding. I've been worried that at some point he'll want signs of a stronger commitment and, with my brain so rattled by the fact that my wedding is fast approaching, I don't know what to do.

'You won't.'

'I want to.' That's better than saying 'I can't,' isn't it?

'But you won't.'

10

'The thing is,' I say, knowing that's one of my verbal tics – the thing is. 'The thing is that there's nothing really *wrong* with Logan.'

'Wow, you make him sound so appealing. You're saying that he's not completely disgusting to you. That he doesn't make you retch on sight. That being in the same room with him isn't akin to experiencing the worst torture –'

'You know what I mean,' I tell Marilynn, shutting her up. I've finally come clean with her about the whole Logan/Brock situation, and she's taken the information in her stride. 'He's handsome. He used to be charming when we went out together. He can still tap into that roguish charm, anyway, when he wants to.'

'He's Peter Pan. Never wants to grow up. He feels as if by getting engaged, he's showing everyone that he's an adult. But he's not.'

'That's not really the problem at all,' I tell her. 'He's perfectly fine being a grown-up. Steady job. Steady pay cheque. Nice wardrobe. Good manners. But I just don't feel the spark any more.'

'You're looking for greener pastures.' Marilynn manages to say this without any sound of judgement in her voice. This is one of the reasons I love her as a friend. I can honestly tell her anything. She'll never make me feel bad or guilty. The problem is that Marilynn has no real conscience when it comes to dating. So maybe sometimes she should try to make me feel a little guilty.

'We're too comfortable. That's what it is.'

'I read about couples like you last time I was at the salon. They only stock the girliest women's magazines, all full of self-help columns and diet tips to make you look good for your tenth high-school reunion. There wasn't anything interesting for me, so I read all about couplehood and couple troubles. And you fit this one section, one particular type of rut that people can fall into. There's even a name for what you are: PJs.'

'PJs?'

'Like Yuppies or Gen-Xers, or whatever you want. PJs are so relaxed with one another they can wear their rattiest sweats all the time, never do their hair or make-up, crash with a video and take-out food. You know. Just hang out. There's no romance left, but there's plenty of comfort.'

'We're not that slovenly,' I tell her. 'Not yet, anyway.'

'But that's what you're dealing with,' Marilynn insists. 'The comfort factor. You want him to swoon when he sees you. You want him to do all the things that Brock does. Aren't I right?'

I think about it. She sounds right. Makes sense. The only problem is I don't think that's what I want. I just want Brock to be doing all those things he does. Every last kinky one of them.

'So tell me,' Marilynn says now, her voice lowered. 'Exactly what *are* those things that Brock does?'

I blush, and she squeals with delight.

'He's good, isn't he, Cat? He really knows how to turn you on.'

'Yeah.'

'So tell me.'

'I've never been any good at that kind of thing,' I say. 'I'm not like you in that way.' I think about the times she's detailed her experiences with Declan, with Marco, with Johnny . . .

'I know. But that's because you've never really had anything to share.'

'I can't –' I start, and then quickly correct myself. 'It's strange, but I just don't know how.'

And suddenly, when I say that, I do know my problem. I know it because the thought pops up in my head when I don't want it to, but when I'm too tired to keep it from hounding me. What if Brock is just playing with me? What if he doesn't really want me. What if he only wants a toy?

Could I uproot my whole life for that? For a possibility?

'He wants me to go away with him. Logan's going out of town on a business trip on Friday, and Brock wants me to go to Palm Beach with him, to take a little vacation and see what we've got together.'

'Of course you should go,' Marilynn says emphatically. 'Why the fuck wouldn't you?' She lights a fresh Marlboro with the butt of her still-lit one, then snuffs out the old fag and continues puffing without a break. The smoke surrounds her dark hair in a silvery haze. You're no longer allowed to smoke in most LA bars, but we're at Ye Olde Rustic Inn, one of the throwbacks to the days when vice was a virtue. Heavy glass ashtrays line the scuffed wooden bar. Nobody would think of complaining to the health inspector, so the Inn hasn't been busted yet.

I shake my left hand in front of my face. The jewels catch the light, even in the grey, smoke-filled room. They twinkle as if they're trying to make me feel guilty by their presence alone. I'm reminded of one of my favourite Grimms' fairy tales. In the story, three drops of a mother's blood tucked into a handkerchief speak to her princess daughter whenever she strays: *If your mother only knew, it would break her heart in two.*

'So?' Marilynn asks again since I haven't responded. 'You're getting married. You're not being crucified, for Christ sake.' Marilynn does not respect the marriage institution. Or rather, since her own devastating divorce several years back she considers marriage just that: an institution. She doesn't understand why anyone would willingly be locked into one.

'What if Logan finds out?'

'You're trying to get this guy out of your system. If it works, then Logan will win you forever, right? No big deal. It's not like you're fucking his best friend.'

This is the reason why Marilynn is no longer married. She has difficulty with the concept of monogamy, a difficulty her ex-husband couldn't get used to when he found her in bed with his golf buddy. Marilynn lives her life as if she were the star in a 1930s black-and-white movie. Her dialogue is brief and cutting. Her relationships are all about quick wit, raunchy repartee and the most fierce love scenes of all time. Unfortunately, she has yet to find a lover who can make that intensity last.

'Do you want to go?' Marilynn asks, making direct eye contact with me.

I nod.

'Will you always wonder what might have happened if you don't go?'

I nod again.

'There's your answer,' she says, taking a sip of her fresh drink. 'Now let's move on to something slightly more pressing.'

I raise my eyebrows, waiting.

'Do you think we can get those two studs at the end of the bar to buy us drinks?'

I know what's going to happen when we go. He's already told me, spelled it out in great detail. He's going to be my master for the weekend, and my body will be his to use as he desires. Yes, he's going to spank me, and tie me up, and fuck me, and he's going to leave marks, but he'll make sure they'll be gone by the time Logan gets home. That's another of his promises.

I'm going to have a truly punished ass, and when I'm red and raw he will stand me up in the corner and let me think about what a bad girl I really am. And that will be the most delicious torture of all.

And I can't wait. I really can't.

This is how I will absolve myself with Brock for not being able to stay with him the other night. By giving myself entirely to him for four days, even though in a couple of weeks I'm supposed to be giving myself eternally to somebody else.

Mentally, I say goodbye to Logan when Brock picks me up. Logan's out of town for a conference, and I tell myself that I shouldn't do this. I should stay home. I should be good. And then I see Brock's truck, and I selfishly forget everything else. I climb inside and let myself go, let my fears go. Let everything go.

Brock doesn't say a word to me when I get into the truck. He tilts his sunglasses down to check out what I'm wearing, and whether I obeyed his requirements of a skirt and no jeans as he'd told me in an email the night before. I did just as he said. For a moment, he smiles. Then he puts one hand on my thigh, feeling my hose. He wanted naked legs, but mine are not naked. I couldn't go without stockings today. Not for the meetings I had. Yes, California is known for casual dress codes, but when you're called in by the bosses of a studio, you have to dress professionally. Brock lets his breath hiss between his teeth as he admonishes me.

'What are my rules, Cat?'

'Obey.'

'What didn't you do?'

Fresh tears well in my eyes.

'What didn't you do, Cat?'

I start to explain. 'We had a meeting –'

'What didn't you do, Cat?'

'I wore nylons.'

'I thought you said you were a smart girl.'

Guess I wasn't. Or maybe I was. Who knows? If being disobedient is the thing that's going to get his belt to land on my naked, upturned ass, then I guess I'm ready for my honorary Harvard diploma.

'Take off your hose.'

I do so with shaking fingers, first kicking off my heels, then slipping the pantyhose all the way down my long legs. Beneath the pantihose, I have on a sleek pair of hip-hugger panties. Brock can see them easily.

'Jesus, Cat. What are you doing to me?'

He demanded a thong. I know it. I ignored the email, going in favour of comfort for work. We both know I could have changed in the ladies' room before seeing him – that I would have done so had he not changed the plans and upped the time of our meeting to earlier in the day. And that's even worse than being disobedient, I realise suddenly. Being sneaky and sly – getting what I want and what he wants.

'You're in for it, baby doll,' he assures me. 'But I'm not going to give it to you. Not yet.'

Then he smiles and starts the truck, and we're off. I realise that I have no idea precisely where he's taking me, that it didn't occur to me to leave a contact number with either Marilynn or Janice of my exact location. But maybe that's part of this whole adventure: not knowing. Maybe that's the most important lesson for me to learn. That I don't have to have control over every situation. That lack of control can be a major experience, free-falling into not-knowing.

Brock turns on the radio while we drive, and I feel myself start to relax. I watch Los Angeles disappear as we head along the highway. I start to wonder whether he's taking me to some spa, some so-Cal resort, and then I remind myself that thinking *is* the box; that I'm supposed to be working on *not* thinking. Only obeying.

I close my eyes, planning on listening to the music without the visual stimulation, and don't even realise that I've fallen asleep until I wake up. The sky is a dark, deep blue. I'm being lifted from the truck and I gaze into Brock's eyes, but he just looks down at me and says, 'Sh, sleeping beauty. Go back to your dreams.' I close my eyes again and melt into the warmth of his chest as he carries me ... Where? I don't know. I don't care. I don't think.

The next time I wake up it's morning, that early hazy-light of dawn illuminating the thin curtains of the bedroom. We're in a large, spare, whitewashed room, and I am bound firmly to the centre of the bed. I turn my head and see Brock, standing there, watching me, waiting for me to wake. He smiles, and then comes closer, and he kisses my lips, then works slowly down my body, touching every part of me with his hands or lips or tongue, every single part until he reaches the V-intersection of my thighs, and then he slows down – then he starts to dine.

I moan and arch, realising from the hoarse quality of my voice that I haven't said a word in hours. The sound is startling.

'You like that?' he murmurs into my skin.

'Oh, God, yes.'

'I'm going to keep it up until you come.'

I say, 'Thank you,' as if he's promised me a special treat. 'Oh, Brock, thank you.'

'But you have to do something for me.'

'Anything.'

'I want you to make a list.'

I'm confused. 'What do you mean?'

'Of your fantasies.' He loves for me to talk about what turns me on. It's as if knowing what arouses me is his own number-one arousal. 'Can you do that?'

I grin at him. I've been making lists like this all my life.

'So tell me about them. I want to see what's going on in that sweet head of yours.'

I think about registering for gifts with Logan, two months ago. It was a nightmare for him. He couldn't focus on the different kitchen utensils, and he had no opinion to offer from one place setting to the next. I ended up doing almost all the work, which mostly meant blocking Bernie from getting her way.

Now, with my new lover, I'm about to register for fantasies. The concept is much more appealing than choosing one design of flatware over another.

'Start with the first thing that comes into your mind.'

I am silent for a moment, considering my range of options, but that's not what he wants.

'Don't think,' he admonishes me. 'Just talk.'

I sigh as he continues to trick his tongue along the spread lips of my pussy. He connects with my clit almost accidentally, and I squirm and sigh, loving that tiny burst of pleasure that throbs through me. Brock continues to lick between my lips for several seconds. Then he says again, his voice much more stern, 'The first thing, Cat. The very first thing that comes to your mind when you think about what turns you on.'

So I start. 'Number one,' I say self-consciously.

'Number one,' he prompts.

'I'd like to play with sex toys.'

'What kind of toys?'

'Don't know, really. Anything. Everything.'

'Greedy thing.'

'I just don't have a lot of experience with that type of thing.'

'Do you have *any* experience?'

'Well, one time I was accidentally sent this catalogue that showed pictures of anal beads and synthetic cocks, and I couldn't believe how excited I got as I flipped through the pages. But then Logan found it in the drawer of my bedside table, and he tossed it out, horrified.'

'But what would you really like?'

I hesitate for another moment, before realising that there really isn't anything I can't tell Brock. And if I *do* tell him what I really want, then there's a good chance that he'll make my fantasy come true.

'The dildos,' I say finally.

'Dildos,' he repeats, stressing the fact that I've used the plural form of the word.

'You know.' And I pause again, searching for the nerve to say it. 'One for each hole.'

'Oh, yeah,' he says grinning. 'I like that.'

'And then your cock in my mouth,' I continue, and his smile broadens. 'To finish everything off.'

'I like that a lot,' he says. 'Next one,' and now he uses his fingertips to spread my lips open wide and I groan and arch my hips skywards. I love the feeling of being handled like that. Brock knows all about what I like. He is a master.

'Number two,' I say, clearing my throat. 'I want you to fuck me at a restaurant.'

'Which restaurant?'

'I don't care.'

'Why at a restaurant?'

'Because it seems impossible.'

'Nothing's impossible,' Brock says, and now he opens his mouth wide and lets me feel the wetness full on against my own slippery self.

'Three,' I groan, lifting my hips again to press firmly to his lips. I need the strongest connection now. 'I want you to spank me in public.'

'Bad girl,' he says against my skin. 'You need a spanking everywhere we go. I ought to have given you one at Bar Fly. You know that. You really deserved it. As soon as I saw you there, I wanted to lift that pretty dress of yours, bend you over one of the bar stools, and give you a proper hiding. I would have made you so wet, baby.'

'I know.'

'So wet that you wouldn't have known what you wanted next. For me to fuck your pussy or your mouth or your ass.'

'Oh, God,' I sigh. I'm getting closer now. Whenever Brock talks like that to me, I end up coming.

'Go on,' he says. 'Keep talking.'

I feel dizzy with the proximity of my orgasm, but I know that I must play by his rules if he's going to take me to the end. 'Number four,' I say, trying not to stutter. 'Number four . . .' my mind searches for another fantasy. I've had so many about Brock, but I never thought I'd have to rank them, never even really expected that I'd share them with him at all. 'I want you to dress me up.'

'How?' he asks.

'What do you mean?'

'How do you want me to dress you up?'

'Anyway you'd like,' I say. 'Anyway you'd see fit. The turn-on would be being dressed by you.'

'Give me some examples.'

Now I'm being asked to tap into my fantasy costume designer. Images come to mind, and I try to tell him the first one that catches my fancy: being dressed as some frilly, flirty flapper from the 1920s in a dress made entirely of fringes that tickle my naked skin when I walk. Music plays in my head, and I can see Brock shaking my dress out so that the fringes fall correctly. Then I see him bending me over and pushing the fringed hem aside, revealing my nude body beneath. 'Like a flapper girl,' I say, my voice a whisper. 'In fancy fringes with nothing at all underneath.'

'Sounds so sexy,' he says, 'And five?' he asks.

'I want *you* to dress up.'

'Like what?'

I close my eyes, embarrassed.

'Tell me.'

'Someone in uniform,' I confess. 'Like a cop.'

He laughs, but he doesn't make fun of my choice. 'Six.'

I have that ready, at the forefront of my mind. 'I want you to fuck my ass.'

'Say that again.'

'I want you to slick up your cock and slide it inside my ass.'

He's the one to sigh now. 'Seven,' he says, as if that's a dirty word. 'Seven.'

'Seven,' I repeat, 'I want you to fuck me.'

'What do you mean?'

'Now,' I say. 'Oh God, Brock. Fuck me now. Please.'

He smiles at me. 'I'd be glad,' he says, 'to make your fantasies come true.'

I've read about men who like to dress up as women. Some favour old-fashioned housecoats in gaudy floral prints and beg dominatrices to force them to iron or mop or clean. Others go for frilly baby-doll dresses and ruffly panties in a twisted game of age play. But Brock isn't this type of man. He doesn't want to slide on the nylons or wear my sexy panties. This doesn't mean he is fetish-free. Not by a long shot. When I make my way into the living room after our morning marathon fuck-session, I see the outfit he's laid out for me. And, honestly, I can't believe it.

'You said you wanted to play dress-up,' he reminds me.

But I only told him about that fantasy today. How can he have gotten a costume together so quickly?

'It happens to be one of my fantasies, as well.'

I nod, examining the various items he's laid out for me. This is not a flapper girl costume at all. Not even close. I can feel my eyebrows raise in surprise, but that doesn't mean I'm not aroused at the idea, because I am. I just don't know if I can actually go through with this.

'We won't fool anyone,' I tell him.

'You work in movies. You should know all about costuming.'

'But there's no way.'

'Come on, Cat. Try.'

I shake my head and, as soon as I do, I feel his fist wrapped in my long, dark hair. He holds me steady. 'What are my rules?'

'Obey,' I whisper. The word comes quickly and easily to my lips. If I can't do the job he requests, then trying my best counts. Failure is only acceptable if I push myself to my limits. Being a nonstarter isn't even an option. This sort of rule system reminds me of the work-outs I've occasionally gone in for at the hip Hollywood gym most of the people at my office belong to. A former Navy Seal pushes us through gruelling one-and-a-half-hour workouts. No resting. No bathroom breaks. Red buckets at the front in case you feel that you're going to be sick. Failure is only acceptable if you pass out while trying.

I gaze down at the faded Levis, the heavy scuffed workboots, the bright reflective vest, the hard hat.

Everything is quite obviously too small for Brock, but apparently just my size.

'I won't be able to pass for a workman.'

'Not with that attitude,' he agrees, and now he leads me by my hair over to the sofa, then gives me a shove so that I'm face down on it, ass in the air, awaiting his belt already. How well I know him. How well he knows me. But this time is different. This time, Logan is out of town for three more days, and I'm not going to feel the sweet light sting of leather on my skin, I'm going to feel the bite. This time, my tears aren't going to streak my cheeks in anticipation of a raging orgasm, they're going to come from pain. These are the promises I tell myself – promises that Brock has made to me. I know he won't let me down.

The belt hisses in the air and lands on my silk nightgown. I tremble, but not from fear. He strikes me five times through the expensive fabric before telling me to lift the gown by the hem, slowly, and reveal my naked legs to him. I lift the gauzy fabric all the way up to my hips so that he can see my panties.

'Pull them down,' he demands. 'Down to your ankles.'

Quickly, my fingers follow his instructions.

'You're going to count for me.'

I nod.

'Respond correctly.'

'Yes, Sir.'

'You're going to count for me, and you're not going to beg me to stop. You're not going to tell me you've had enough. Believe me. I'll know when you've had enough.'

For some reason, this makes me think of Logan. Of me watching him drink at Paul's and asking, haven't you had enough? And of him sneering at me and saying, 'Believe me, *I'll* know when I've had enough.' Not a sexy concept then. But now. Oh, now everything is different. Now, when Brock lays his hand on my bare skin and rests his palm there for a moment, this is the sexiest encounter I've ever had. Now, when Brock says, 'Don't worry if you cry. Don't stop it. Don't hold back. I want to hear you cry.'

That makes everything OK with me. I don't disgust him. Isn't that a new concept? I want him to spank me until I feel it at my core – he wants to do the same – and the idea of him hurting me in this X-rated way has me on the verge of climax already. Reminds me of when I was a teenager and one of my friends told me that oral sex was 'talking about it'. And I guess 'aural sex' would be listening to other people do it. But what kind of sex do Brock and I have?

The belt connects with my upraised buttocks and my worries melt away. I am focused intensely on every sensation. My racing thoughts have finally slowed down to let me process what is going on. To let me contemplate each vibration of my breath through my chest. Each blink of my eyelashes. Each minute bit of moisture that builds within my tear ducts.

Brock lets the belt slap against my skin over and over, but I know that he's not going as hard as he could, as hard as he might someday. Even though we have a couple more days together, he can't leave marks that will last. Because of this, he's only starting, giving me a very small taste, and even this is enough to make my bottom sting and make that familiar wetness begin between my legs. And then, just as I start to squirm under the blows, he lifts me upright and pushes the outfit at me. He stands, with his arms crossed, with the leather belt still dangling in his hand, and nods at me to follow his orders.

With shaking hands, I pull my nightgown all the

way off and drop the frilly garment to the floor. Then I slide the tight white sports bra over my breasts, flattening them close to my body. Next on is the wife-beater-style T-shirt. Then the plastic-coated vest, the faded 501s, the heavy boots. Brock comes forward and wraps my hair into a knot, then fastens it with an elastic band. He sets the hard hat on top of my head, and then he tells me to stay exactly where I am. I do, my hip cocked forward, my jaw set tight. I feel different in these clothes. I know I look nothing like a real construction worker, but that doesn't matter. My attitude has changed, and this is what Brock wants, I can tell that from the way he's looking at me.

'You think you're tough, don't you?'

I can't keep the smirk off my face. Deep down inside, I know I'm not tough at all. But in this outfit I find a cocky strength, and I push my shoulders back and stare at him.

'Show me what you've got.'

I fold my arms in front of me, mimicking his recent stance, and I find that I'm flexing my muscles unconsciously, trying to puff myself up.

'Pretty good,' he says, walking around me in a slow circle, checking me out from all angles. 'Pretty fucking good.'

He takes a step closer, and then he pulls the vest off my body. 'I like you better without,' he says, removing my hard hat next. My body is still in a tensed position, and being in these kick-ass boots adds to my confidence. But then Brock grips on to me, lifting me easily in his arms, and he carries me like that back to the bedroom. He throws me onto the mattress, face down, and he rips my jeans open and slides them just past my hips. I have no underwear on and my ass is still red from the lashing he gave me minutes earlier.

I hear Brock rummaging for something in his suitcase and, when he comes back, he has a bottle of lube in one hand. I close my eyes when I see it, and I feel the confident aura slip away.

'You're not so tough, are you?' he asks softly.

I shake my head. He presses his body into mine on the bed, so that I can feel his jeans on my naked skin, and then he bites his way along the ridge of my shoulder. 'Not so tough now.'

'No,' I say again, feeling him work his way down my body. He parts the cheeks of my ass and I feel his tongue between them, wetting me, and then he lifts the bottle of lube and drizzles several drops along my crack.

We haven't done this yet, but I want to. I'm scared, because it's been years since I had sex like this, and still I want to. He hurries to kick out of his jeans, and then I feel the rounded head of his cock as it probes my back door. I think of Marilynn regaling me with her tales of anal sex, of how good it can feel if a lover takes it slowly. I remember being with Todd and Mike, being caught between them. I think about being with Brock and the nameless man he invited to our threesome, and being relieved when they didn't take me in two ways at once, but let me suck on one while the other fucked me.

Then I stop thinking of anything else as Brock presses forward and I hear myself cry out, the sound surprising me.

'Relax, baby,' he says.

He reaches one hand beneath my body, his fingers pressed between the mattress and my pussy, and he strums his fingertips along my clit as he pushes his cock in deeper. I am filled in a startling way. Brock's cock is so large that I feel impossibly stretched as he pushes in even deeper. Then suddenly we are sealed together, he's in as far as he can go, and I relax onto the bed, still half-clothed in my workman's costume, and I start to say his name over and over as he continues to stroke my throbbing clit.

'Brock,' I say softly. 'Oh God, oh Brock,' and the climax builds higher as he begins to move back and forth inside me. 'Oh God, oh Brock, oh yes.'

All I can manage to say. All that I need to say.

'Yes.'

11

'You were caught up in the heat of the moment,' Janice says, when I confess that I've just come back from a weekend spent nearly entirely in bed with Brock. 'You wouldn't have been so super-turned on if you and Logan were having sex more. That's the situation you really ought to be addressing.'

'You said we'd be bunnies on our honeymoon.'

'Maybe you need to be bunnies before,' Janice decides. 'In order to *get* to the honeymoon.'

As usual, I don't tell Janice all of the facts. For instance, I don't tell her that Logan and I have *never* been bunnies. At our best times, we were snails. According to a fairly disgusting nature movie I saw one time, snails don't have sex very often but, when they do, they can make love for twelve hours at a time. Tantric snail love, I suppose. Now there's an image I'm not sure I need to own forever. In our defence, Logan and I have almost always been sporadic sexual partners, but we used to do it Tantrically, for long periods, our bodies close together, feeling the climax build between us, the power of it shaking us both for hours afterwards. During our down times, between sexual escapades, we'd cuddle in bed together. We'd kiss each other in passing. Now we rarely even do that.

'Talk to him,' Janice says. She takes a sip of her espresso, swallows it, then rips open one of those paper packages of cream. 'Just talk to Logan. It can't hurt, Cat. It can only help.'

But Bernie gets to me first.

* * *

'The bride wore gold,' Bernie says with a flourish, holding out a metallic balloon-like gown and making the panels rustle with a shake of her hands. I can't imagine wearing this dress, not even for a costume party. Not even on Hallowe'en. It's a huge, bloated creation that has no business being in a dress shop, and yet this is what Bernie wants me to change into after the ceremony.

'I'd look like a water-retentive Oscar,' I tell her, referring to the award, not the grouch. I try to get her to smile, but she doesn't.

'It's in,' she insists, giving me her latest mantra. 'It's the rage.' She stands next to me at the three-way mirror, laying the dress against my body so that I can see the shimmering effects. The thing does shine. I'll give it that.

'You really think this is the style?' I ask her.

'It's like money,' Bernie continues. 'Gold is always in.' She flashes her rings at me, as if to finish her point. The lustrous jewellery gleams as brightly as the metallic dress. I'm starting to think that she knows I'm having second, third, and fourth thoughts about marrying her son, that she's on a trip to see how far she can push me before I scream out the truth, before I break down before her and cry, 'I've been fucking a man from the road crew. I can't go through with this charade any longer!'

'What do *you* like, honey?' she asks, indicating the racks of dresses. At first, compared to the shimmering wonder she has in her hands, the rest of the dresses appear fairly tame. On closer inspection, the beads and baubles begin to catch the light, pearlescent sequins sewn in swan shapes on one skirt. A train made entirely of glittering silver stars pinned onto a heavy netting of silver mesh on another. She has taken me, in all probability, to the mafia-princess wedding store. I've never seen creations like this in any bridal magazine. Of course, Bernie still favours jumpsuits with epaulettes and dresses with thin gold chains dangling across the front. If she could, she would drape herself all the time like an extra on *Dynasty*. The only thing stopping her is the difficulty in finding the hideous fashions she craves.

'I have to tell you something,' I say, but then stop. Can you tell the mother-in-law that the wedding's off before you tell the groom? Are there rules about how to break an engagement? Where's Miss Manners when you need her?

'Yes, Cat?' Bernie asks, looking positively aglow as she spies a hideous chartreuse number created, apparently, of fish scales dipped in acid and then embedded in some form of charred plastic. If she makes me try this on, I will confess. I will fall on my knees, cling to her ridiculously tight beige jodhpurs (which she adores although she's never been anywhere near a stable) and sob out how sorry I am.

Instead, she passes on the dress for a satin checkerboard number complete with a matching black-and-white pashmina. It's Las Vegas style. The lower portion of the dress is imprinted with the suits of cards – diamonds, clubs, spades, hearts – and all of the designs are outlined in sequins, of course.

'Nothing,' I mumble, deciding that Logan and I will have *the* talk tonight. It's been months since we last had sex. Maybe Janice is right in her assessment. Maybe my Brock fixation is simply a case of misplaced hormones mixed with wanderlust. Once I talk to Logan, he'll help make things better. It won't come as a surprise to him. He has to know that something is wrong.

Something is really, very wrong.

'Nothing's wrong,' Logan says over dinner. 'Sex just isn't that important to me.' He effortlessly swirls the fettucini around his fork, takes a bite and chews slowly, obviously considering his words. 'I love you like a sister.'

I have nothing positive to say to that. I know his sister.

'Look, Cat,' he continues, ignoring my horrified expression, 'about two months ago, when you had your last little hormonal freak-out about our sex life, I polled my family.'

'You what?' I can't believe I'm hearing this, can't believe he's telling me the truth. This has to be something he's culled from his latest screenplay.

'I called up my siblings and asked them how often they do it.'

Before he can tell me the rest, I hold up my hand to stop him. I catch a glimpse of my reflection in the mirror over the mantle, and I look like a traffic cop, but I can't help myself. 'You talked to your brothers about what we do in bed?' I instantly picture the three Riley boys lined up in a row: the lawyer, the doctor, and the engineer-slash-writer, all talking about sex. It makes me want to hide my face in my hands. No, that's not quite the feeling I'm having. The thought that Logan has talked to his siblings about our sex life makes me want to move to another state. 'You didn't. Not really, did you?'

Logan doesn't answer this question, as if it's simply not important enough for him to bother taking seriously. He continues with his story, starting with his eldest brother first. 'Jack and his wife make love twice a week, but only since Viagra came on the market. Joseph and Hilary are twice-a-monthers since the birth of the twins. My father is a little more active since he went on the Pritikin diet, but even he confirmed what I always thought.'

'Which is?' I prompt, watching him spin another

mouthful of pasta around his fork, getting it wet in the cream sauce.

'It fades. The sex drive fades. Companionship's far more important.'

Companionship, I wonder. *What* companionship? We're never together. Since he discovered the wonders of pot, he hardly ever leaves his office when he's home. I don't say that. It's a subject that will cause more of a battle than I am prepared for. Instead, I say, 'I'm twenty-eight, Logan. Companionship shouldn't be kicking in for another fifty years.' I visualise the two us sitting side by side in matching wicker-backed rockers. Is this what Janice meant when she said Logan and I were made for each other?

Logan leans back in his chair. His eyes are glazed. I should have had this conversation with him in the morning, before he started smoking.

'What do you want from me, Cat?' he asks now. He looks genuinely perplexed, but I don't know if it's honest confusion or the drugs.

'Romance,' I say softly, not even knowing if it's the truth. It sounds plausible. But even I don't believe me.

Logan shrugs. 'Romance isn't that important to me. It never was,' he says, shrugging again.

It's difficult for me to accept how different Logan and I are. Once, when we were on vacation in Paris, I kissed a bit of chocolate off his lips while we were seated at an outdoor café on the Boulevard Saint Germain. No, this wasn't the most normal thing for me to do. Generally, Logan eats his food and I eat mine. We're not like those cutesy couples who dine off each other's plates, who share forks, or ice-cream cones, or even French fries. But on this day, I was feeling relaxed and amorous from the atmosphere of a Parisian summertime and two glasses of chilled white wine and, in the late periwinkle-blue twilight, I leaned over and kissed the chocolate off his mouth. He pulled back as if I'd bitten him.

'What're you doing?'

'Just –'

'Just eating off of my mouth?' The disgust was evident in his voice. 'What do you think you are? One of those birds who cleans the teeth of an alligator?'

My mind was heavy from the wine. His response confused my senses. I'd been going against nature by licking chocolate from his skin, but the action had been done in a spontaneous moment of romance. Shocked by his anger, all I could think was that I'd rather be a bird than an alligator and be able to fly away from him.

When we got home from the trip I didn't bother telling this story to Janice, because I knew she'd take Logan's side. But now I tell Marilynn, and she understands. Strange how I've spent so many years judging her, silently, but judging nonetheless. Of the three of us, she has always appeared the least together to me. Janice has everything figured out with her husband, her career, her house. Up until recently, I was on my way to sorting everything out with Logan. And then there was Marilynn. Chaotic. Occasionally ditzy. Sometimes so hard at work that she actually forgets to eat. Now she's the one I turn to for advice, and I find that I trust her. Even when I don't want to hear what she has to say, I trust her.

'You want someone who loves you no matter what,' she says simply when I share the Parisian café scenario.

'Go on.'

'When you're clean from a shower, it's easy to have sex. But when you've been camping for four days, then let's see who's going to want to fuck you. Right?'

I think about Logan and the way he criticises Marilynn sometimes. The three of us girls have been out to brunch some mornings when Logan decides he's hungry enough to hang out with 'the hens'. It's always Marilynn that he picks on. Logan and Janice get along fine – they have the same sensibilities on a lot of topics, and they laugh at the same jokes. But Marilynn always annoys Logan. Certain mornings, it's obvious from her appearance that she's unshowered, and it's also obvious she fucked her bartender, or her roommate, or whoever she wound up in bed with the night before – and maybe the morning, too – prior to meeting us. And afterwards, Logan will say, 'Jesus, Cat, can't your friend ever take a bath? Or a shower? Or something?'

But I'll see Marilynn with that golden glow of good sex, and that sheen to her skin of a night spent romping, and I'll be envious of her life.

At least, I've been envious before. Not any more. Because Brock likes me when I'm dirty. God, I have to say that again. He likes me when I'm not fresh from the shower, not blow-dried, not in clean panties and a matching bra. He likes me after we roll around on the rough army blanket, and there are twigs in my hair, and my knees are scuffed and raw from the equivalent of an all-natural rug burn. He likes the smell of sex on my skin, and he has me put on a pair of my panties after we fuck, and wear them until it's time to split, and then he takes them with him. And I know that later, much later, he jacks off with those sticky panties around his cock, and the smell of us all around him. The dirty smell of really good sex. Something Logan will never, ever understand.

Because good sex – really good sex – doesn't smell like toothpaste or mouthwash or floral douche. It smells like ... like ... God, like Brock and me, and the salt taste of his skin, that place I like to lick at the hollow of his neck.

'Like Elvis,' Marilynn suggests into my dazed silence.

'Excuse me?'

'You know, that concert he did on TV back in the sixties. They show it on VH-1 all the time, clips of it, anyway, and he's singing in that black leather suit under those hot studio lights. And he's back, big time, and everyone knows it. But it's hot, so he's sweaty. Not bad sweaty, but a drop of sweat shines on his cheek. He's smiling even when he's singing that sad, sappy song, "Love Me Tender". And all I ever want to do when I see that shot is lick the sweat off his neck.'

'You're disgusting.'

'No.' She shakes her head forcefully. 'I'm honest. There's a big fucking difference. And you know,' she says, getting ready to insert one of our favourite quotes, 'I'd fuck Elvis. And so would you.'

'Maybe,' I say, 'but maybe Logan just doesn't get it because nobody's explained it to him.'

'So try.' She snorts. Marilynn has made snorting an art form. 'See how far that gets you.'

'What do you mean?'

'He's going to know.'

I look down into my wine.

'Come on, Cat. You know he's going to know. Remember that time with Miles and me? And I wanted it to work out so badly with him, because he was a good person, and I thought it was about time I hooked up with a really nice man for once, but there wasn't any spark there. And I liked that other guy.'

'Harrison,' I say, nodding. Oh, do I remember Harrison. So good looking. So rebellious. Almost clichéd in his attire. Black jeans. Black leather jacket. I smile thinking about him, and Marilynn does, too. Even Janice had to admit that Harrison knew how to enter a room. It was as if he'd channelled Marlon Brando's spirit from his early days as an actor. He radiated danger.

'And he wore those silver rings on his fingers and those jeans that just hugged his ass.'

I nod again. I won't admit this to Marilynn but, occasionally, I've 'remembered' Harrison during private, solo sessions between me and the shower massager.

'And so I bought Miles some rings when I was out at Venice, just silver trinkets I found at a jewellery stand at the beach. What was I thinking? As if that was going to solve all of our problems, right? And he knew immediately that I liked someone else. And that was that.'

So rather than go to Logan, I try the argument on Brock instead.

'Do you really like me when I'm dirty?' I ask, my voice so soft even I can hardly hear it. 'I mean, it seems like you do. And I know that you said you did, before. But I was just wondering if you really meant it.'

He eyes me carefully as if this might be some sort of psycho woman's test and that I'm quite possibly setting him up for failure, as if any answer he'll give me will be wrong.

'Just tell me the truth,' I say. 'This isn't a quiz. I want to know if you like me like this.'

'You look plenty clean.'

'But I'm not,' I say. 'You just fucked me. You know –'

'I know what?' As always, he's going to make me say it. Brock doesn't let me get away with anything. Is that why I like being with him so much? He won't allow me to put on a false front, to cloud the issues with fancy arguments.

'That your come is inside me.'

'And that makes you dirty? *My* come.'

I shake my head. He's not getting my point. At least, I think he's not. I'm not explaining myself well enough. But then, with actions rather than words, he proves that he understands. He pushes himself down my body and he starts to lick my pussy. Slowly, softly, because I've already come once, and so has he. I can't take it. The way he tongues me feels too good. I grip into his thick dark hair and hold him against me, and then he slides two fingers inside me, where I'm so warm and wet and sticky, and he rotates his fingers in the combination of our juices, and I think I'm going to swoon.

Slowly, he starts to fuck me with his fingers overlapped, still keeping his mouth busy on my clit, so busy, and I start to come, knowing that he's answered my question without any words, knowing that there really weren't any words needed to start with.

As soon as I climax, he is in instant motion, moving so that my legs are over his thighs and his cock is inside me. He presses in deep, and my muscles are still in their tight connection of pleasure, so I squeeze him and he sighs. Looking down at me, he proves my point – or his point – I can't think clearly any longer. Who was making the point, after all?

'Dirty?' he asks me, teasing me. 'Is *this* dirty? Do you think so?'

How did he get to be so good at the game, twisting my thoughts and fears into his own little lessons in our lifestyle together? He's making his own point out of my insecurities.

'Is it, Cat? Do you feel dirty, baby?'

I can't answer. Not now. But I shake my head, and my curls go wild over my face, and I feel him brush them out of my eyes so he can watch my face the whole time.

God, does he like to watch.

Now he tricks his fingers against my clit, so that his thumbs take turns stroking me, first one, then the other. I feel weightless as I fall into the bliss of a third ferocious climax. It's almost as if it happens unexpectedly, because even though I'm growing accustomed to multiple orgasms with Brock, I haven't learned yet to take them for granted. So as his thumbs play their gentle rhythm, I gaze into his bottle-green eyes, and come again. The bed starts to shake with the impact of my contractions. I don't know if I scream out when I come this time. I'm so far away in Brock's gaze that I don't even know exactly where I am. But I hear him talk to me, as if speaking from a long distance away.

'Dirty girl,' he says. 'Of course it's dirty. But it's real. That's why I like fucking you when you've got that just-been-fucked glow to you. That's why I like getting in deep when I've already come inside you, when you're slippery wet and full of me. That's the best time, Cat. Don't you get that? Licking your skin and tasting that salt-sweet taste at the back of your neck. Drinking you in. The flavour of you. The real scent of you. That's the very best part of all.'

I hear him. I listen. And I think that if I were to lick chocolate away from Brock's lips, he'd stay still and let me, and then he'd get more chocolate and spread it over my body and lick every bit of it clean.

And even then, I'd still be dirty.

'So what are you up to tonight?' Brock asks softly. He's tracing invisible designs up and over my curves, and I am lost in the way he effortlessly touches my body. I've already come three times this afternoon. How could I possibly come again? I don't know – but the concept seems distinctly possible, especially as his fingers make their way down the flat of my belly, dancing their way ever closer to my clit.

'Do you know?' he teases, and I'm sure that I look like a wanton hussy, desperate for even more pleasure. I don't deserve this, do I? Brock apparently thinks that I do. 'If you don't talk, I'll stop,' he assures me.

'Going out,' I say quickly, so quickly that he laughs.

'You and –'

I don't like saying Logan's name when I'm with Brock. It feels like I'm cheating on him. *Brock*, I mean. It feels as if Brock is my partner and Logan is some random guy I see on the side. How distorted is that? I can't truly fathom. But that's what my life has become. Brock doesn't seem to care that when he mentions Logan's name it makes me feel evil suddenly, like one of the bad girls in the movies that I am always working on. One of the girls that the audience hates from the start. One of the girls who generally ends up in a bad way, and everyone is glad.

'You *know*,' I say.

'So tell me.'

'We're going out with friends. A fortieth birthday bash.' I try to pull away from him; talking schedules isn't sexy in the slightest. But Brock doesn't let me get away. He anchors me in place with one firm arm over my waist, and now he moves so that his mouth is so close to my pussy lips I can feel just how hot his breath is on my warm, wet skin. This is one of my all-time favourite sensations, and Brock knows this full well.

'A party,' he says. 'Whose party?'

It's amazing to me that he can keep on a conversation so automatically, while at the same time pleasuring me with his fingertips and tongue and breath and lips.

'An old friend.' The words come out in a rush.

'Wish it were yours,' he tells me.

My mind isn't working well enough to make sense of his statement. I guess teetering on the verge of climax makes me stupid. 'Why?' I ask.

'Then I could give you a birthday spanking, obviously.'

I shiver as he speaks, because I know what it would

feel like. Of course I do. I know all about what a spanking feels like delivered from Brock. But now I think about a birthday spanking, and it would be different, somehow, from a real over-the-knee everyday spanking. I see myself in a party dress, something white and frilly with a wide satin trim in pink. This sort of dress would call for ruffly panties beneath – something I would never wear. Never would have, anyway, before I started cheating. But with Brock, I just might. With Brock I can see the combination of sexiness and irony a pair of good-girl panties would bring to a scenario.

'You have a look in your eyes,' he says.

'Just thinking about what you said.'

'But you're thinking more. I know you are. Tell me, Cat.'

I shake my head. 'What are you doing tonight?'

'After this?' he asks, and now for what must be the hundredth time this afternoon, his tongue meets my clit, and yet I still forget all else. When Brock eats my pussy, nothing else matters. I forget about Kim and Paul. About a pretty ruffly dress and having my bottom seriously spanked until I cry real tears. About anything but Brock's magic tongue making those endless – please, God, I silently pray, please let them be endless – circles and spirals and ovals around my clit.

'Talk to me,' he warns.

'Yes,' I say, breathless now. 'Yes, after this.'

'I've got a dinner engagement tonight, too,' he says, his words partially blurred against my skin.

I try to be polite. I know that I should be polite. He is dining on my pussy, after all. He's making those deliciously decadent circles up and over my clit, treating that little pearl of pleasure exactly how I most crave. I should give him what I know that he wants, which is this conversation. Yes, I find it torturous to talk when he's making me feel so good, but I work hard. Besides, now I'm genuinely curious.

'With who?' I ask.

'Jealous girl.' As soon as he says the words, he half-rolls me onto my side and gives my ass a stinging smack. I draw in a deep gasp of breath, waiting to see if the spanking will continue, but no, he's quick to push me back down and continue making those tantalising designs with his dreamy tongue. There is no better feeling than this. Except maybe being fucked by Brock. Or spanked. Or tied up and taken. Or –

'Ow!' I squeal as he rolls me back over and spanks me a second time.

'Be careful,' he warns, 'or I'll give you a serious hiding.'

'I want to know who you're going out with.'

'Then you'll have to do something for me.'

'Come on, you have to tell me!' My interest is more than piqued. I am exactly the definition of a jealous girlfriend, which is crazy considering my place in Brock's life. But now I push up on my elbows and gaze at him.

'Your call,' he says. 'Make me a trade. What will you give me?'

I think about it. And suddenly I know what he wants.

'You can do that thing you like so much,' I say.

'Do what?'

We're at that old game again, where he will pretend he doesn't understand me unless I spell something out in great detail.

'You can fuck my –' my voice becomes a whisper '– you can fuck my ass.'

'I can do that anyway.'

I nod. He's right. He can.

'But I like it best when you ask for it.'

'Please, Brock,' I say, 'please fuck my ass.'

'I'm going out with James,' he says, 'an old friend. We're going out with a few people I know from work. This one guy I'm moonlighting for out in Holmby Hills. He's a contractor, and he's always good about throwing extra work my way. Hate the fact that I have to socialise with him, as well, but you gotta do what you gotta do.' Now he grins at me, and I see how shiny wet his chin is from my heady juices. 'And do you know what you have to do?'

I shake my head.

'Roll over. Because that was only a taste.'

'What?'

'That little love slap. Now I'm going to give you a quick spanking before making you come. And once you come, I'm going to lube myself up and take your asshole.'

All thoughts really do stop, and I obey immediately, feeling Brock shift on the bed so that he can pull me over his lap. His hand lands repeatedly on my naked ass, and I buck a bit over his knees to gain the contact that I crave. I want my pussy pressed firmly against his lap so I can come while he spanks me. Brock has other plans entirely, and his plans override my own, as always. He gives me about ten good, solid spanks before moving back on the bed again, this time positioning me with my knees bent under me, my hips up, belly to the bed, so he can lick from my exposed clit to my pussy and back again, over and over until I come. The very second I do, he enters me in this modified doggy-style position, thrusting his rocklike rod in deep.

I cry out forcefully as he fucks me, but he remains totally silent, gripping my hips in his large hands and moving me to his own inner rhythm. When his cock is dripping wet from being inside me, he pulls back and starts to press against my asshole. The position and the way he holds me all feel so good that I don't even think about the party tonight. Don't think about the fact that Logan and I have been invited to take our friend Kim out for her birthday. Don't wish that I were going out with Brock and James instead, and what that situation might mean. Oh, but I can see it, even in a flickering thought: me between Brock and James, the two of them fucking me together, one in front and one in back, with me as the creamy filling between. And then I simply come. For the fifth time in one day. A world record for me.

An Olympic feat.

From the very start, it's an odd evening. I'm unhappy to be where I am. I feel trapped and confused, and I want to be anywhere that Brock is and, as he's nowhere around, I don't want to be around either. This attitude is fully unfair to my oblivious boyfriend. I know that, and that only makes me feel more like a bitch. But Logan doesn't seem to pick up on my mood at all because he is stoned.

As usual.

In fact, when I think about it, I realise that stoned is his general mood these days. Is it because of extra pressure from work, or the fact that I'm not as warm as I used to be? Could he be worried about the wedding, or worried that he's losing me? I pause in my pouting, trying to figure out just when Logan became the full-on stoner that he is, but I can't place a date.

So that's the atmosphere from the get-go, and that's only our scene. With our friends, things become even more complicated. Kim has been at the bottle all day long, in her words 'celebrating'. Her boyfriend is unaware of Kim's emotional state, as Logan is to mine, but for a different reason entirely. Paul is always in the dark. That's his style. He is a player and a slick cat, and he is as shallow as a wading pool. He's also Logan's best friend.

The four of us meet at an upscale Chinese/Fijian restaurant on La Brea called Chi-Fi. The bar is crowded, but we squeeze into a corner booth while our table is being prepared. I realise immediately how drunk Kim is, and I steel myself for a roller-coaster evening. She's tough to take when sober. After a few drinks, she can be impossible. Logan orders a beer, his standard. Paul has a Cosmo, because Paul always goes for frilly, girlish drinks. It's his thing, same as the way he dresses up as a woman every year on Hallowe'en. It's one of Paul's quaint character traits. Logan loves him for them. He feels that Paul is relaxed in a way that he will never be. At least, not without marijuana.

When the waiter reaches me, I ask for a white-wine spritzer and Kim glares at me. Her glare intensifies when the waiter asks me for identification. I realise from Kim's expression that this is a bad thing. As her brow furrows, I think that this may be the worst thing that could possibly have happened. Kim has been drinking for most of the day. Apparently, fortieth birthdays will do that to you.

'Safe drink,' she spits at me before ordering a Mai Tai. 'You always drink the safe drinks.' We're waiting for one more couple, someone Paul and Logan know from work. When Kim criticises me I suddenly wish I'd ordered smarter: something like Jim Beam straight up. Still, I attempt to be diplomatic. I shouldn't be a bitch to Kim on her birthday, even if she is caustic.

'It's my standard,' I say, trying to be light-hearted.

'Baby drink,' she sneers. 'You couldn't do a grown-up drink if you tried.'

I think about Brock and his Martinis. But that's a bad road to take. I shouldn't be thinking about him at all. Not here. Not now. But I can't help myself. Which is why it's strange that I don't pick up on the situation in a more timely manner. Maybe I'm still in a sex-dazed high. Maybe I'm slow. I *should* know. I deal with scripts like these every day. I should know far in advance that the other couple will be Brock and some date who I will immediately despise from the moment I lay eyes on her.

It's true. I do.

Paul waves to Brock and I turn to see him clad in a black suit and a cobalt-blue dress shirt, heading our way with a tall, leggy blonde in an ice-blue dress. The material caresses her body so subtly that I know this is a very expensive dress. The simplicity is all a show. The dress was made for her. I immediately think of Brock's hands on her, and I want to kill her.

'You remember Brock,' Logan says when the couple reaches our table, 'don't you, Cat? You met at my promotion party. He's been doing some side-work for Paul. In fact, he's going to be helping my mom with the remodel. You do remember him, right?'

'Sure,' I say, nodding. 'Yeah, I remember Brock.'

I am intensely aware that I am still wet from our encounter, only hours before. I'm aware of more than that. He knew that he would see me tonight and didn't tell me. This makes me part furious, part curious. He must have plans for the evening. I realise that instantly. He must be up to something, or he would have clued me into our mutually unintentional rendezvous. Maybe this is why he asked me all those questions while we were fucking this afternoon. Or maybe he was just taunting me, wondering if I'd pick up on the situation quicker, giving me clues and waiting to see when I would understand the farcical nature of our social calendar.

Already I know Brock well enough to understand that this is going to be a carefully scripted evening. The only problem is that I am without script in hand, and nobody delivered the changed pages to me in vibrant rainbow colours. Not today.

The gorgeous girl drapes herself dramatically in a chair across from me, and I realise that she looks familiar. Brock introduces us and I hear her name, but I immediately forget it. She has what Marilynn and I have always called a stripper name: Tiffani, Barbi, Stormi, Laci. Something like that. Every time she speaks, I mentally give her a different name, and when the waiter comes back and leads us to our table, I switch my drinks to a Martini. Kim shoots me a look, but I ignore her, focused in a masochistic daze on a conversation with Brock's *femme fatale*.

'You work at CC Studios, right?' Ginger asks.

'Yes,' I tell her, and it hits me in a rush that she's an actress. Sure, I should have known from her beauty, but there are so many beautiful people in Los Angeles that it's hard to keep the actual stars straight. She has a small but recurring role on a sitcom that films in one of the studios at my lot. *And* she's with Brock. No worries about his stature in life, the fact that he's a worker not a thinker. In fact, her attitude makes it clear to me that she's not worried about anything. She places one hand on his throughout the drinks portion of the meal, and she gazes in his direction with big doe eyes whenever he says anything. She has a face that will most likely be up on billboards someday, heralding new movies to any potential ticket-buyers, while I'll always be the unseen script doctor, who toils in piles of paper far behind the scenes. Dresses will not be cut specially for my body. Men will not drool when they see me walk by in my power suits, or even in my California-casual hip styles of dress. It's hard to compete sometimes when everyone around you is model-gorgeous.

Logan and Paul are equally taken with the eye-candy.

Paul has always had a thing for blondes, especially white-blondes of the Pamela Anderson variety. This piques Kim's temper constantly, since she keeps her dark hair close-cropped in a no-nonsense style, perfect for her job as an entertainment lawyer. There is nothing entertaining at all about Kim tonight. Everything in her being is focused on the way her boyfriend is eyeing Bambi. But then, my beau is pretty captivated, as well.

Logan asks what it's like to work on a sitcom, and Emerald handles herself extremely well. Fuck, I think. She's not a total airhead. It's actually difficult to despise her because she doesn't seem to possess any of the movie-star ego I run into on a daily basis. In truth, she's very nice, sweet and unassuming. There's no reason for her to be treating us all so kindly, as if she's genuinely interested in celebrating Kim's birthday, but she does.

But how did she meet Brock? That question is answered quickly enough when Logan voices the same query to Nikki.

'Oh,' she sighs. 'You know, it's the funniest thing. Brock and I knew each other a long time ago, before we were even LA'd.' She says the word like a verb, and I hear 'laid'. I can't help but look at Brock, and he grins at me, as if he knows exactly what I'm thinking – and of course, he does. I'm thinking that he just finished laying her before coming to dinner, that the two of them have been romping together for the last hour, playing beneath the same sheets that he and I mussed up earlier in the day.

His expression does nothing to dispel my fears that he and this girl are a hot-ticket item. 'Then one day,' the bubbly blonde continues, 'I was walking across the studio lot and there he was – like out of a movie. He was working on the same lot that I was, doing road work for the County right there on the lot, so it really was a "cute meet".' She says this with a flourish and, once again, I just want to demolish her. Brock and I had a cute meet. That's what I want to tell her and the whole table – the whole world, even. Why would he bring her here if he knew that I was coming? To rub it in my face? Is this his way of ending things with me, or of letting me know that he's not going to wait forever. Or that he's not even waiting right now.

'Cat works on the same lot,' Logan says, not tearing his eyes off the girl long enough to glance in my direction, so captivated is he by the starlet. 'I guess I'm lucky that you spotted Brock first, huh?'

Everyone at the table laughs at this, including Brock, and I want to crawl under the tablecloth and hide. Brock gives me a silent head-shake, which I take to mean that I should pull myself together. I glare back at him.

Whatever the message he's trying to impart, the upshot is this: I feel like an idiot. Worse than that, I'm embarrassed by Logan. That doesn't make much sense, does it? I shouldn't care what Brock thinks about my boyfriend – fiancé! – but when Logan takes his time studying the menu, I'm mortified. He is doing this because he's so baked. I know that. It's one of his things. The more pot he has, the slower he is able to make a decision. Any decision. Especially when food is involved. When he tells the waitress that he can't order yet because he's still 'composing' I want to scream. Brock doesn't say anything. He looks at me, and he raises his eyebrows slightly, but he leaves the punch line to the waitress, who stifles a giggle as she says, 'Then maybe you should have the composed salad.'

Logan glares at her. He doesn't like being the butt of anyone's joke. The waitress immediately realises that her tip may suffer, and she says, 'I don't know why they call it that. I always thought they should have a hysterical salad nearby, just to balance things out.'

Logan likes that. He feels the girl is on his side after all, and he shoots her a patient smile that makes her blush. For some reason, this evening has left me feeling as if I'm out of my body, watching everything without being personally tied to the events. So when I look at Logan, I see him from the waitress's point of view – as a handsome, intellectual man, who is slightly soft around the edges. Nothing wrong with soft in a city where everyone else is hard-edged and sharp. Then I see him from Brock's viewpoint, and I see the soft part as a downside. As a blow, really. Can't trust a guy who is too soft. Can't respect him, and I find myself repelled by my judgement.

What about me? What do I look like to other people? A cheating girlfriend who is actually able to dine with both her future husband and her lover, without actually collapsing in a puddle of guilt right in the centre of the table – right here in front of God and everyone.

'Cake!' Paul announces gleefully. The frilly drinks have gone to his head. 'I'm ready for cake!'

'Be right back,' I say, before the dessert arrives.

'Where are you going?' It's Logan who's asking but Brock's eyes are on me. Don't, I think. Don't follow me to the bathroom here. Don't confiscate my panties now. Not when I'm wallowing in my ill feelings to myself. Don't threaten to spank me or fuck me or tie me down until I can control myself. Because I'm long past being able to control myself right now.

'Just to the ladies',' I say, directly to Logan, ignoring Brock's openly questioning gaze. Well, fuck it, I think. If he wants to follow, let him. Just let him. That thought actually makes me excited. That's what a bad girl I am. Even though I've been sitting here, feeling guilty, the thought that my lover might fuck me, or touch me, or make me suck him, mere feet away from my boyfriend, well, that's gotten my panties all drippy wet. So I guess I'm a dirty girl after all.

To my dismay, it's Kim who follows after me. I don't have the slightest desire to talk to her right now, and I can sense from her drunken stature that she has something she's going to get off her chest. Inside the tiny space, she lays into me immediately.

'I thought you weren't going to register.'

I don't have the faintest idea what she's talking about.

'Register,' she repeats. 'Write down all the things you want –'

'How do you know about that?' I ask, mortified. Can Brock have given her a list of my fantasies? That doesn't make any sense.

'For the gifts,' she hisses. 'For your *wedding*.'

'Bernie convinced me to do it.' I think about my fantasy list that I created with Brock, the one in which I registered for things that I actually care about, different fantasies for me and Brock to play. An X-rated registry of toys and games and activities for my lover's pleasure. How would that go over with the guests invited to my wedding with Logan?

'So you *are* in this for the prizes. That's what this whole thing is about.'

'What are you talking about?'

'All that goddamn fluff about how you thought marriage was a melding of the minds.'

'I never said that,' I assure her, surprised at the open animosity in her voice. 'Really,' I say, 'that wasn't me.' This is true. There's no way I'd say anything so contrived. It sounds suspiciously like a quote from Master Logan.

'You think you're so great,' she says next, throwing me completely off balance. At this precise moment, I don't feel so great at all. Brandi, or whatever her name is, seems pretty great. I feel like a cheating girlfriend whose lover has just trumped her at dinner, showing up at a dinner party with Miss America. No, with Miss Fucking Universe. I look in the mirror. God, while I'm dressed in one of my severe power suits, no cleavage, no –

'You do,' she says, interrupting my inner rant.

'Do what?' Exactly what is it that I do? This is what I want to ask her. Exactly what, Kim, is it that I do that bothers you so fucking much?

'You're getting married. You wave that goddamn rock around as if it were a magic wand.'

I don't know what to say. If I told her that I carried the engagement ring around in my change purse half the time, would that make her feel better? If I told her I stay up at night and stare into the ocean wondering if I should jump, that I have dark circles under my eyes because I'm afraid I'm engaged to the wrong person, would she respond in a positive manner? I don't think so. 'Caustic Kim', as I've named her in privacy to Logan, would never be satisfied by anything I'd have to say. That's her personality.

'You're twenty-eight and you have it all planned out.'

'Planned?' I ask, because I simply can't help myself. I'm spinning out of control, and this girl thinks I have answers to all the questions.

'Your real life is starting. You know what I'm talking about.'

'Real life?' I wish I could stop repeating all of her words. I wish I could tell her that she's got it all wrong, that my *real* life is with Brock, who has just stunned me by bringing the most gorgeous girl to a dinner party with me and my loaded boyfriend. 'Real life?' I repeat, but Kim doesn't catch my anger. She's far too busy being angry on her own.

'You know. Getting married. Getting a house. Having babies. Real life.' She pronounces both words carefully, as if they hold some magic, some power that could recreate the world around us. A power that she can't have because Paul won't ask her. And he won't ask her, because he's so shallow that he's always waiting for the best offer. How can he commit to Kim if he has a minute shot of getting someone better? Someone blonde, most likely. Someone with dizzying beauty and an amazing affinity for making him happy. Kim can't see it. She's too close. But I can.

Instead of responding to Kim, I close myself into one of the two minuscule stalls and wait for her to leave. Do I have it all planned out? If so, then I've planned pretty poorly because nothing is going according to schedule. I'm supposed to be glowing, shining, even basking in this period of my life. Instead, I feel ill all the time, except when I think about Brock. And now, here he is, with some other cookie, and I don't know what to do about it.

Maybe this is why I let him fuck me in the parking lot, or how I end up in a sexy threesome while Paul, Kim, and Logan go around the corner for an after-dinner drink at Key Largo. Out in the parking lot, Brock doesn't say a word about what Brittney means to him. He just lifts me up in his arms and anchors me with my back against his shiny yellow truck. I grip his body with my thighs and feel him enter me. I'm still wet inside from our afternoon exertions, and this turns me on even more. The fact that his cock has only been absent from my body for mere hours, that I'm still warm and dripping inside from our previous encounter.

'You look so hot when you're all dressed up like a teacher.'

'I thought you liked me dirty.'

'I like you any way I can get you,' he says. 'I like you any way at all.' He pushes aside my hair and bites first lightly against my neck, then not so lightly, but I don't squirm away. I know he won't bite hard enough to leave lasting marks on my skin. But I wish he would. Tonight, I wish he'd brand me as his own, so that all my silly mind-game worries would be over. That he'd drive me to the tattoo parlour up on the Strip and have his name emblazoned in golden ink on my ass. That he'd take me to The Parlor on Santa Monica and have me pierced for him – my nipples, my pussy lips, anywhere. That he'd do something – anything – to make me his own once and for all.

Crazy, isn't it? If I have these desires, that should answer all my questions. But I can't keep the chaos out of my head, the people who give me their constant advice and opinions. Like Kim, who says I should jump into my real life. Like Bernie, who assumes that marriage equals happiness (so I suppose since she's been married five times then she is five times as happy as the rest of us). But most importantly I have my own real fears that Brock isn't in this for the long haul. That I'm a fling to him and he should be the same for me. One last fling before diving into adulthood. If that's the case, then I ought to jump now. Before it's too late.

I grip into his arms and hold on as he bounces me up and down against him. I know that this is risky, the riskiest thing we've done up to this point. Truth is that I don't care. I want him to come inside me again. I want him to make me come over and over. Until I can't think or speak. Until all the lying fades away and I'm stripped back down to nothing.

'You smell so good,' he says, again with his mouth near my neck. 'I could eat you up.'

Now he sets me back down on the ground, and bends me over, entering me from behind. We are in a secluded area in the parking lot. But it's not *that* secluded. I think about Logan, and I wonder what he would do if he saw us. Then I think about Kim and how happy she'd be. She'd burst with glee to find out that my 'perfect' life isn't so entirely perfect. But neither of them are the ones to see.

It's Lu-Lu with the pale-blue dress and gorgeous mane of blonde hair who emerges from the glistening inky-black darkness and then sits in the back of the truck to watch.

As I said before, I'm a fan of movies that time-jump. In fact, I wish I had the ability to time-jump myself. To flip the pages to the end of the script (the script of my current life) and find out who I end up with. Brock? Logan? No one? Now, would that be a depressing switch. I remember my conversation with Janice in which she tried to decipher the genre of my current status: comedy, tragedy or farce. I still don't know the answer to that one. But let me explain for a moment how we got to this point.

CUT TO:

Interior of fancy restaurant. The fortune cookies have arrived. CAT reaches for hers and breaks it open. As a way for the restaurant to appear endlessly hip, the fortune is written in French. BROCK's DATE reaches for the slip of paper and easily translates, making CAT dislike her even more.

BROCK'S DATE
It's a cliché, even in French. 'Be careful what you wish for, it might come true ...'

FLASHBACK:
After returning to the table, and hearing the guys' plans for the rest of the evening, I decide to back out. I know

I shouldn't. I know I'll piss Logan off for no good reason, and that this isn't something to draw a battle line about. But I can't help it. I'm feeling selfish, and I want to go home.

'I'm just not up to it,' I say, and I shoot Kim a fierce look as I speak, to let her think it was her conversation that's turned me off her celebration. She doesn't respond, keeps her eyes down on her empty cake plate, but I know she's as angry as I am, and I also know that somewhere deep inside herself she understands I'm not the one to blame for her unhappy stature in life.

Logan tries for a moment to convince me otherwise. 'Come on,' he urges. 'We'll have fun.' But he knows that when I don't want to go somewhere, I won't. Especially where Kim is concerned. I'm stubborn that way. Logan and Paul are best buddies. I don't expect him to give up their relationship for me. I'd refuse to give up Marilynn or Janice for him. But I'm so tired of Kim that I have a difficult time going out with them. So when I shake my head again, Logan says, 'No problem, hon. See you back at home. Don't wait up, OK?'

I tell him fine, and then grab my coat and purse. Since we drove from work – or, at least, he drove from work and I drove from my ferocious fuck-session with Brock – we each have our own cars. No logistical problems there. Brock seems to know exactly what I'm thinking, because he makes excuses for himself and Sapphire, and all of us part company. I end up in my car, waiting to see what will happen, not at all surprised when Bambi takes off on foot down the street, and Brock raps softly on the window.

And that leads us to fucking at his truck. Brock undresses me and gazes at my body before undoing his fly and letting me see his cock. I had it inside of me only hours before, but now I want it again. In fact, I am so desperate that I make a voracious sound of urgency to let him know how turned on and ready I already am. He grins at me and says, 'I wanted to do this from the moment I walked into the restaurant.'

'Tell me.'

'Wanted to throw you up on the table, rip your panties aside, and just fuck you.'

And that's what he does, fucking me so rock-hard raucously that when Amber, or whatever the hell her sexy stripper name is, starts to watch, I can do nothing except let her and enjoy the audience. I have nothing in me to tell her to go away. I don't want her to go away. That's the truth. Even though I was envious of her from the start, I don't need her to leave now. Because suddenly I sense something in her eyes, in her very attitude, that lets me know she isn't a foe at all. She's a friend. Or a potential friend. She's everything I've ever wanted. When she comes forward and starts to kiss me while Brock continues to fuck me, well, that just about makes me come.

I should confess something else here. I don't only like *Mulholland Drive* for the time-warp effect. I like the girl–girl action, as well. Writers often slip a little bi-sex into movies, or at least imply a bit beyond girlish flirtation, in order to titillate the crowd. I know this, and yet it still works for me.

12

'Who'd ever have thought?'

'Tell me about Ruby.'

'You can be so nasty,' Brock says, pushing a lock of my dark hair out of my eyes and looking directly into my face.

'I like "dirty" better.'

'No, I mean you've got a mean streak in you. Never would have thought that before. You have such a sweetness to you.'

'Why do you think I'm mean?'

'Her name is Sterling James, and you know that perfectly well. You're just being a petty little girl by constantly calling her by other names.'

'Can't help it with those stripper names,' I insist. 'It's too difficult to keep those straight in my head: Brandy, Ginger, Amber, Amity –'

'You're jealous.'

'So tell me.'

'Tell you what?' He's playing innocent, now. He does it much better than I do.

'Tell me who she is.'

'Just a friend,' he says.

'You tend to fuck friends like that?'

'I wasn't the one fucking her.'

'You know what I mean,' I insist, but even as I say the words, I can't help but blush. He's right. *I* was the one fucking her, not him. I was the one with my mouth on her pussy, my fingers in her hair, while all Brock did was stand by and watch.

'I knew your fantasy, and I knew you'd never do anything about it yourself. There's no way you'd have let yourself get involved with a woman, is there?'

I think about this, then shake my head.

'So I wanted the daydream to come true for you. I told her all about you and she was game.'

This doesn't compute for me. I don't live in a world where a phone call gets you an easy, no-strings-attached three-way. I consider my engagement ring and think of the safety and security it means. Can I trade all that for the sexy underworld life of being with someone like Brock?

'Is that all you wanted?'

'No, baby,' he says, and now he bites my bottom lip hard, until I squirm away from him. 'No, baby. I wanted to watch, too. Didn't you know that? Your fantasy and mine blended together perfectly. You wanted to be intimate with another girl – and I wanted to see you with another girl. See you fuck another girl and eat another girl and come because of another girl.'

I can't help but smile back at him. I'm getting all wet again at the way he's talking to me.

'Did it meet your expectations?'

'Oh, yes,' I sigh, honestly. 'All of them and more.'

'So tell me about it.'

'I can't.'

'You have to. If you don't, things will be worse for you.'

'Worse how?'

'Or better, I guess, knowing how much you like to be spanked. But I'll tell you this.'

'Yeah?'

'If I spank you tonight, I'm using my belt. Ten times. Harder than you've ever felt it. The stripes will be lined up neatly on your bare, naked skin. You'll have a bit of trouble explaining the brand-new decorations on your ass when you go and get your wedding dress sized, won't you?'

'I didn't know what a woman's pussy would be like,' I say hurriedly.

'But you have one. Christ, you've got a beautiful cunt.'

'It's different. Kissing a girl down there is different. She was sweet and musky and I couldn't get enough.'

'I know you couldn't, dirty girl. That's why she's coming over to my place tomorrow night.'

I shake my head.

'Yes,' he says.

'No,' I say out loud.

'Don't say "no" to me.'

'I can't –'

'What are the rules, Cat? Do you need a crash course in life with me? *Cliff Notes* or something? I thought you were such a quick study.'

'Not tomorrow night.' My mind races through the different meetings filling my electronic organiser. There are various wedding duties I have to take care of and then, in two days, the costume party at the studio that Logan says he has no time to attend.

'She wants to return the favour.'

I feel my pussy tightening at the thought of her pretty lips kissing me down there. I can't imagine how good that would feel. That's not true. I can imagine. Of course I can. And I bet it will feel even better than I think it might.

I don't know why the concept of a girl going down on me is so different from the thought of Brock doing the exact same action, but for some reason it is, and for some other inexplicable reason, I say yes. But maybe it's not *so* inexplicable. People have done crazier things for lust, haven't they?

I know I have. Many crazier things than this.

Lust makes people do interesting things. It makes me shop for Brock's brand of shaving cream, shop as if on a mission, shaving cream the only item on my list. In the pharmacy, I lose myself in the action of picking up the different cans and lifting the caps, smelling each manufactured fragrance. Suddenly, I find myself starting to flush.

Crazy, I tell myself. You're going crazy.

But just the thought of his scent, a scent he uses, makes me ache. I buy the shaving cream as if I'm purchasing pornography, something illicit and explicit that I ought to be embarrassed to own. Something that ties into a secret fetishistic fantasy, because it really does. My goal isn't simply to use his brand, to be close to him as a comparative consumer, sharing in his world of pharmaceutical supplies so that our medicine cabinets look the same. I want to smell the way he does.

The drive home from the pharmacy is a short one, yet I've never been so impatient on this tiny trip before. When I miss the light near our house, I actually swear at the glowing red light. I fumble with the paper bag and pull out the can again, smelling the scent while I wait impatiently for the light to turn green. I wonder if people in cars around me are watching, and that thought gives me a rush of pleasure.

I force myself not to run from the garage to the elevator, but by the time I reach the front door to the condo, I have lost all sense of decorum. I strip on the way to the bathroom, flicking on both knobs of the tub to full blast while I rummage around the drawers for a fresh razor.

Finally, soaking in the tub, I spread the scented

cream over my legs, shave them smooth, and I catch a whiff of Brock and get pulled back into a memory of kissing him, his smooth cheek against mine, the scent of his shaving cream.

It turns me on, just that slightly mentholated fragrance. Manly, clean, and all him. I smell like him. I lean back in the tub, looking at the blue and white can, looking at my razor. Then I push myself out of the water to sit on the edge of the tub. I spread the shaving cream all over the skin of my sex and shave there. Not just the normal clean-up job to make sure no stray hairs find their way free of my orange bikini bottom between now and my next wax job. But bare, completely nude, until I look nubile. The skin here is soft and pale and, when I dry myself after the bath, I smell like him down there, too.

What would he say if he were to kiss me there? Would he smell himself? Would he know what I've done? Would it seem sexy to him, or slightly insane? Every day I find myself slipping away just a little bit more. This evening, I find myself slipping over to Brock's place, exactly as he demanded that I do yesterday, but I cover myself first – making a phone call to Janice for an excuse.

'I don't like to get involved,' she says. 'It doesn't feel right. I mean, I know Logan, Cat. He's a friend, too.'

'Just do me this one favour,' I beg, and I know she will.

She has to.

She owes me.

When Janice was with her first husband, she cheated. That's the hypocritical thing about her responses to my latest series of actions. She cheated in a huge way with her new husband, Allan, and she used me to cover. Randolph wasn't an imbecile. He guessed something was up, and I had to play this odd role of covering for

Janice, saying that she'd just left, and then calling her cellphone to let her know she had to run home with a manufactured excuse that she'd decided to go to a step aerobics class. When Randolph called I'd say anything to keep her options open, and I was filled with relief when she finally made the decision to leave.

So now, Janice has to do the same for me. She has to. No questions asked.

But there *is* one question I do keep repeating to myself: how did we all get in this mess in the first place? Everyone I know has cheated at some point. Literally, everyone. Even Trini has had the occasional fling, which I know about only because of her occasional changes in attitude. She'll suddenly begin to take longer lunches, or have closed-door phone calls, or ask me to page her if her husband calls, but not to put him through to her private cellphone – a number so private even he doesn't have it. Then, after a few months, she'll return to normal, and I'll know that whatever was going on is now over.

Maybe, like Janice suggested, humans really weren't meant to be monogamous in the first place. At least, maybe not in Los Angeles, where divorce rates are higher than those in the rest of the country.

And maybe I shouldn't waste my time thinking about all that, because here I am . . . already at Brock's.

There they are, waiting for me. Sterling is all in white, clad in one of those trendy expensive cashmere tracksuits that fits her curves in a way that makes me long to cut it off of her and see the expensive fabric hang in tatters and shreds from her gorgeous figure. When she stands and goes over to the picture window, I see that the hoodie says 'Porn Queen' on the back. Brock is in jeans and a T-shirt and he's as comfortable as I am ill at ease.

'I got you something,' Sterling says, handing over a pretty paper bag filled with petal-pink tissue paper. Stunned and excited at the thought that she bought something for me, I reach inside to pull out a fuchsia tracksuit that matches hers. On the back of this one it says 'Sex Kitten'.

'Brock told me all about you,' she says. 'So you don't have to worry.'

'What did he tell you?' I'm dying to hear. Did he tell her that I like being spanked? Did he tell her that one of my top-ten fantasies was to share him with another girl, something I'd never thought was sexy before meeting him? Or did he tell her something about the two of us, some information he has yet to share with me, such as his feelings for me, or what he thinks our chances are at having a relationship in the future?

'He told me that he –'

Brock puts up his hand, and Sterling seems to bite down on her words.

'That he's *with* you,' she says, obviously amending whatever she was going to say to appease him. 'So relax. I know you guys are together. I'm not the type of person who interferes in relationships, despite what the latest *National Enquirer* said. And the truth is, I'm not really into men at all.'

My eyes widen. Sterling continues speaking without any prompting from me. She has got to be the most relaxed person I've ever met when it comes to discussing sex. 'Brock is fun, every once in a while.'

Now Brock smacks her ass with one of his large hands, and she squeals but doesn't back down. 'Yeah,' she says, 'you're fun in a pinch, but I tend to have my steady relationships with girls.'

'Girls can't do for you what I can do.'

'You can't do for me what *they* can do,' she shoots back. 'You're good with your tongue, but you have no breasts to play with. Not like Cat, here. Don't you think women's breasts are sexy?' She smiles at me.

I nod, but only because I have nothing to say. This girl is so open about her sexuality that I'm floored. I always thought that Marilynn was open but, compared to Sterling, she is only ajar. *She* should be Danika, I think. Because here is a real-life person who talks honestly, no holds barred about things that are important, while I spend my entire life pussyfooting around so that nobody will be disgusted with my desires.

'I do have a steady girlfriend,' Sterling continues, flushing slightly, 'but she has a normal life that holds no place for me, so we always meet on the sly. So I guess that makes me feel a bit freer about exploring other fantasies every now and then, and I've had a crush on you ever since I first caught sight of you on the lot.'

'You're kidding,' I say, absolutely shocked.

'I like the way you walk, as if you're always en route to somewhere important. I like how focused you look when you talk to people, from the security guards to the ladies in the cafeteria. And I like the way you look.'

Now I'm the one to blush.

'You have a bit of that repressed librarian quality, with your suits and your little spectacles that you slide on when you read. And I've always gone for that smart-dyke look. Even before it became all the rage. But there's more to you than that. I guess that's what I like. Because one time I saw you driving off in your sports car and that surprised me. I'd have pegged you as a Volvo girl, or at the very hippest an Audi. So I thought you might have a sexy side as well.'

As she talks, she strips me of my clothes, then helps me into the new outfit. I love the way it feels. So soft. But even more than that, I love her fingertips on me, caring for me, the way she gently slides the zipper up to the top. The way she circles my waist with her hands, nodding to herself as if she likes the way I look. I can't see myself, and I know I'd never have chosen this type of outfit, but I somehow know I look sexy.

'Thank you,' I say somewhat lamely when she's done.

'Twins,' Brock declares, admiring the two of us. But we're not fully twins, not with her white-blonde hair and my brunette tresses. We're more like a striking set of mismatched *objets d'art*. Brock doesn't care for specifics. He comes towards us and slowly undoes both of the zippers – the one that runs down the front of her hoodie and the one that runs down the front of mine. I tremble even more as he reveals me, and then I let myself collapse into her arms as she embraces me, more for support than in a sexual grip.

'This way,' she murmurs. 'The bedroom.'

'Oh, yes,' I say, agreeing automatically. 'The bedroom.'

We walk there with our arms entwined about each other's waists. In moments, the two of us are on Brock's large mattress, while he stands across the room and watches. And this is what he sees:

Sterling on top of me. Straddling my body high up. She places two fingers against my bottom lip, and I lick them with a wild pleasure, as if they were dipped in honey, then I suck on them instinctively, warming them with the motions of my mouth. My tongue presses them up against the roof of my mouth and then gently taps against them. I imagine that I'm sucking on Brock's cock when I do this. I think about him in the same position, thrusting forward so that his large, hard cock reaches the back of my throat. I love to suck him off, and I'm sure that as he's watching me suckle on Sterling's fingers, he's imagining me bestowing that same generous thrill on his own hard member.

Then I gaze at Sterling as she slowly slips her body

backwards, moving towards my feet, and for a moment I forget all about Brock.

When she reaches the space between my legs, she settles there, looking up at me. More than anything else, I want her mouth on my pussy. I will her to part her lips, and to part my nether lips, and then to lock her pretty pouting mouth around my throbbing clit.

Just like Brock when he's in a teasing mood, Sterling takes her time. She uses her well-manicured fingertips to spread my lips apart, exactly as I fantasised she would, and then she regards me again, as if staring at a picture, one that she wants to memorise. Right when I think I can't wait any longer, she gives in. I feel her perfect mouth against my pussy, feel the tip of her tongue flick out several times in a row to tap firmly right on my clit.

'Oh, God,' I whisper, thinking that I'm going to come right away, in a rush, embarrassing myself for not being able to hold out. But then Sterling changes her actions, so that she's cresting her tongue on either side of my clit, first along the left side, then the right, and I know that she's going to make me teeter for a while in this neverland place of not quite reaching it.

The shivers that work through my body are testimony to the fact that this girl knows how to eat pussy. I guess she should, if she really does spend most of her time in relationships with women. That thought turns me on even more, as I fantasise about how Sterling might have learned to do the sweetly nasty things that she's doing right now between my legs. I feel the way she uses her tongue softly, then fast, slowly, then hard. I feel her fingertips part the juicy coated lips of my pussy as she spreads me open wide. The pleasure building within me is powerful. I start to stroke her hair away from her face, wanting to watch as she continues to press her lips and tongue against me.

'You let yourself go,' she instructs.

I'm trying, I think, but I don't say a word.

'When you come, I'm going to fuck you.'

I know that my eyes open wide at that statement, but I remain silent still. I've learned over the years that if you don't speak when you don't know what's going on, you'll appear smarter than if you try to fill every gap in a conversation with useless words. However, I've never used this theory in bed before.

Sterling grins at me, her lips glossy and so fucking sexy coated with my juices. I feel as if my European art-house movie has taken a groovy detour into a 70s girl–girl porn flick. And that's OK with me.

'I always pack,' she says. I think I know what she means. I think that she means she has a strap-on nearby, but again I wait for her to fill in the blanks.

'Just come,' she says, as if sensing how close I am. 'And then you'll understand everything.'

I do just what she says because I couldn't disobey if I tried. I close my eyes and come, the climax flowing through me and, as the waves are still cresting and retreating, Sterling moves off the mattress and reaches for her purse. I was right. 'Packing' means a dildo. She's got a harness and a tool that attaches inside, and she slides into the contraption and starts to grease up her synthetic cock with a handful of lube. I realise that Brock hasn't said a word since we started fucking. He's been totally silent, sitting on the edge of his large, leather armchair, regarding us with what I can only categorise as a boldly encouraging expression.

Maybe he believes that if he says something or does something, this vision before him will vanish. Somehow, I don't think that's the case. I feel more as if he has taken the role of a king and we are the mere players putting on a show for his pleasure. And I like that thought. I really do.

Sterling tells me exactly how she wants me, on my back with my legs up in the air. Then she moves forward and slowly, gently, presses the head of her synthetic cock into my still-spasming pussy. My legs automatically go over her shoulders. When she starts to slide in deeper, I close my eyes, but she won't have that. Just like Brock, she's the dominant one in any bedroom situation. I wonder how it is that I've found two tops in short order when all my life I've been either with equals or men even more submissive than I am. How lucky I am to have been so successful this time around. Then I wonder what she and Brock do in bed together if both of them are fighting for an upper hand. Sterling must give in, I decide. There's no way that Brock would submit to her.

'Look at me,' she demands, and I lock on to her beautiful eyes as she fucks me. 'Forget everything else,' she instructs, and I try to see only her, not to think about other men in my past or Brock so close by, but to think only of her. As she fucks me, she caresses my clit with her nimble fingers, rubbing me softly yet firmly as if polishing a precious stone to shimmering heights.

My breath begins to come faster, but I continue to obey her desires, never closing my eyes, never looking away. I feel completely open to her, and totally in tune with her desires. When I come, the sensation is washed over with the feeling of her eyes on me, of her own body clenching tight and then releasing, coming with me. Coming so hard that it's as if we become one being. For a single moment we're entwined, and for that moment all my worries vanish.

And then all those worries come back as Brock comes close to the bed and starts to stroke us.

'There's that party tomorrow night,' he says, reminding me once again about my duties – in work, for the wedding, and in my life. 'Which one of you is going to be my date?'

13

When you're on a lot with movie stars all day, you can actually forget what real life is. Why on earth would you fuck a real-life workman with his dirty hands and his scuffed boots, with his five o'clock shadow and his uncouth style of drinking long-necked beers by the beach with his buddies, when you can fuck a handsome, clean actor who is *playing* a workman? A man who knows where to shop for his designer suits, where to get his hair cut, how to order fancy wine in a restaurant, how to treat a woman right. That's not my original sentiment. I overheard a girl say it in the bathroom one time: why fuck a fireman, when you can fuck Colin Farrell playing a fireman? Why indeed!

And fucking movie stars isn't that difficult. Not as difficult as a lay person might believe. Not when you're in Hollywood. Getting close to stars on a set is easy, if you're pretty, that is. Celebs have no problem engaging in trysts with the help, as long as they trust that you won't reveal the details. There are several professional girls around here, ones who work in the front office or in accounting or in costumes, who are famous for that speciality – or a combination of specialities, really. They're known to be good with their mouths in bed, but able to keep their lips zipped off the set.

All around the movie lot, reality and fantasy blend together, until sometimes people actually have a difficult time telling the difference. Is this a real street, or a *faux* movie set decorated to look like a real street? And, honestly, who actually cares? If you're walking down the cobbled road on your way from the office to the cafeteria, then it serves the necessary purpose, right? It's a road and you're walking on it.

But every once in a while the fantasy hits you with a striking blow that actually manages to wake you up. While in a meeting with a well-known director, you look out of a window at the lovely grove of trees to find – bam, all you see is a photograph and some spindly stand-ins with paper leaves. Take a deep breath to smell the flowers – got you again. They're all handcrafted in China from colourful silk, so that they look fresh every day of the year.

Same with Brock.

Real versus fantasy. Have the past few weeks been only an illusion? Or is he one of those what-you-see-is-what-you-get types? As far as I can tell, the reality of Brock's way of life is better than any fabrication. The dirt and the grime. The smell of his skin. The roughness of his hands.

Oh, God, I think, I'm going to lose it. Here I am at work, and I'm actually going to lose it.

I take several deep breaths and try to forget the way he looks at me, the way he touches me. I focus on breathing with my diaphragm, pretend that I'm in one of my power-Yoga classes, and that my body is limp and relaxed. Unfortunately, my mental games don't totally work. When Brock enters my brain, I can hardly see straight. My breathing speeds up again, and I fan myself like some southern belle on a hot day.

It's not too crazy that I've fallen in lust with someone like him, at least, not when you know all the facts. I've always had a thing for reality when it comes to guys. I don't want someone who pretends to be something he's not. Sure this may seem like a strange philosophy for someone who lives and works in a world of dreams, who actually makes a living by writing fantasies on a studio lot where *everyone* is someone else. Where you can't trust your eyes at all. You might think that you just saw a police officer walk by, but in fact he was an actor on an antacid commercial. You might think that beer looks good enough to drink, when in reality it's yellow water with a healthy shot of milk foam on the top. Not my idea of a good cold one.

So maybe even this intense sexual connection I'm having with Brock isn't real. Maybe what I think I see in his eyes is simply a reflection of my own hazy, sexy daydreams. That's what I need to tell myself, anyway. That's what I need to remember.

But all those thoughts subside when he shows up at the studio's annual costume party and discovers me there. I should have known what he'd choose to go as. And I should have known he'd attend, since he knew that I had to. That he wasn't kidding last night with Sterling. I should have known that Brock would reach a point where he was no longer content to remain in the background as an understudy, but ready to claim the leading role.

'God,' I tell Marilynn. 'Just look at him.'

'How could I not?' Marilynn murmurs. 'You know me and cops.'

Yeah, I know all about Marilynn and cops. I know about her little speeding fetish, and how she hooked up with a police officer in his speed trap. But this isn't Marilynn's X-rated Dating Diary. This is my life.

He's here with Sterling, and they make a pretty duo indeed – both in full cop regalia, most likely purloined from Sterling's set. Brock looks amazing tricked out as an officer of the law. I'm not the only one in the room drooling over his attire. Yet he seems equally captivated by mine. The couple make their way to my side, and I realise that I'm not jealous at all about Sterling. Not any more. But like Pavlov's dog, I have developed a certain response to seeing her – I'm wet already.

'Got you out of your uptight working-girl clothes, it looks like,' Sterling croons at me. When she runs her fingers through my ringlets, I hear Marilynn suck in her breath. Ah. I've managed to keep a dirty secret from my bad-girl best friend. It's very evident to Marilynn that I know Sterling in an up-close-and-personal type of manner. From the way my buddy is eyeing me now, I realise that she knows all. And she knows I know.

'You look better out of the suit,' Sterling continues. 'But, of course, I already knew that.'

She gives Marilynn a conspirator's glance, as if Marilynn and I are a couple, and Marilynn sucks in her breath again. Wow, twice in two minutes I've managed to upstage my racy friend. I watch Marilynn watch Sterling, and then I turn to follow the blonde's travel through the crowd. She looks unbelievably sexy in her cop gear, and people instinctively move out of the way, as if she really does possess an officer's power. While Sterling stalks across the room, after a different prey entirely, Brock comes closer. I find that I can't make up my mind what to do. Play coy? Play cocky? Brock takes over for me, answering all my questions with an easy one of his own.

'What do we have here?' he asks, glancing up and down.

'What do you mean?'

'I'd say you were impersonating a tart. Am I right?'

'She's a flapper,' Marilynn says quickly in my defence. Brock gives her a look, as if to say, *'Did I ask you a question?'*

Marilynn purses her lips at him. Brock remains silent, and it's obvious that he wants Marilynn to leave us alone. Marilynn gives me a look. 'Too bad Logan couldn't be here,' she says, reminding me for a moment of Janice.

'Stop it,' I hiss at her.

'You're at work,' she says back, her eyes scanning the room and then meeting mine again. I know that she's only trying to protect me, but I find that I don't care any more. Besides, with everyone partying and in costume, the evening feels deliciously free.

'You're sure you're OK?' she asks and, when I nod, she just shrugs and then flounces off towards the bar. Declan's working behind the counter. This is a gig that Marilynn got for him. She perches herself on a stool and then gazes in my direction. It's clear to me that she can't decide whether she's going to be happy for me or not. Maybe she's worried I've taken over her calling – slut on command. Perhaps she's fearful that all of her advice has finally taken root in my brain. What will she do if I usurp her power?

'So what are you really?' Brock asks, mouth to my ear. '*Are* you a flapper girl?'

I shake my head.

'Didn't think so.'

He runs his fingers along the rise of my cheekbones, and I'm dreamily aware that others are watching. 'You can't do that here,' I tell him, but I don't sound like I mean it. Not even to me.

'Your man going to stop me?'

I shake my head. Logan won't be attending tonight.

'Are *you* going to stop me?'

I shake my head again.

'Then what are you telling me you want?'

'Everything you want,' I say quickly. 'But not here.'

'Name the place.'

And now, for once, it's up to me. So what do I do? What do I suggest?

'My office,' I tell him. 'Do you know where that is?'

'Won't people wonder where you went?'

I shake my head. The room is filled with partiers. Nobody will notice if we disappear. I'm sure of this – and even if I weren't, I realise, I wouldn't care. Have I gotten to that point, then? Am I already on the edge?

Or have I gone over it?

In my office, Brock sits on the edge of my desk and stares at me. 'Nice outfit,' he says.

I thank him politely, confused by how out of character this all feels. Here we are, in my office, at my job. Who is this person pretending to be me, parading around in an outfit that I'd never wear, walking with such confidence and power?

Brock continues, 'But I'd much rather see it in a puddle of silk on the floor,' he says. As soon as he speaks the words, I slip the straps off my shoulders and let the dress ripple off my body. Beneath, I'm wearing a bra and panty set that Brock bought for me during our mini–vacation, and I'm fully aware of how turned on I am, being on display for him.

'Come closer.'

I shake my head.

'Come closer.' His voice is menacing now.

'No.'

'Don't play games with me, Cat. Don't play games you can't win.'

'I can win.' Is it the one glass of wine that's making me so bold? I don't think so. Is it the fact that I'm desperate for another spanking? Maybe. Or maybe I just want to see if Brock can hold up. Is this a world we could live in 24/7? Would he want to?

I watch as he pulls the handcuffs from his belt and dangles them in front of his body. 'If I have to come get you, I'll bring you back over here wearing these.'

Now, I give him my best bratty smile, and I don't

move an inch. Brock's on me in a blink, crossing the room with his big stride and capturing my wrists in one of his large hands. He has my wrists cuffed behind my back immediately, then half-drags, half-carries me over to my desk.

'It's never going to work out the way you think,' he tells me as he slides my panties down my thighs.

I actually giggle. It must be nerves. I'm sure laughter won't help me now, but I can't stop myself.

'Really, baby,' he says. 'You must be testing me. Never test me.'

That laugh again bubbles up inside me and makes me shake. I stand awkwardly and turn around, trying to kiss him, licking his neck. I'm so wet now I can hardly handle my arousal. 'Fuck me,' I say.

'Did I tell you to move?'

I shake my head. 'Just fuck me,' I repeat.

'Oh, we're not even close to that,' Brock tells me. 'We're nowhere near close to fucking you. Now, assume the position,' he says, 'and don't move again without my permission.'

I do my best to follow his command, turning back around and leaning over the desk slowly, so as not to lose my balance. Brock shoves me the rest of the way, so that I'm falling, but he grabs my shoulders at the last second and lays me down on the desk. The wood is cool under my cheek. I'm aware of my breasts pressed flat against the hard surface. I'm aware that I'm sticking my ass up high in the air, that I want desperately to feel Brock's hand connecting with my naked skin. He doesn't start that way. Instead, I feel his cock head pressing between my cheeks, pressing firmly against my asshole, and all urges to giggle leave me in a flash.

'No,' I start. Not like this, I'm thinking. Not here, in my office, where I won't be able to run to a shower afterwards. Not without lube, without gentle coaxing. 'No,' I say again, trying to roll over to face him.

'Don't tell me "no",' he says, but he pulls back slightly, and I feel myself starting to relax again. He leans over me, pressing his whole weight into me. Then he brings one hand to my mouth and says, 'Suck.'

I feel his thumb part my lips, and I start to trick my tongue along it, as if I were playing with his cock. I think about the fact that I've never done anything like this with Logan. I know that if I started to kiss his fingertips, to lick them and suck on them, he would pull away from me in alarm. I used to believe that deep down, all men liked raunchy sex, but after six years with Logan, that belief has faded. Now, Brock brings it back to the forefront of my mind.

'Don't give it a blow job,' he says sternly. 'Suck the tip like a lollipop.'

I do exactly as he describes. I get his thumb all wet and, for some reason, having his big hand pressed against my mouth makes me even hotter than I was before. I suck for all I'm worth until he suddenly pulls his hand away from me. I make a little yelping sound, trying to tell him what I so urgently want, but he ignores me. Suddenly, I feel a slippery wetness around my asshole as he brings his thumb between my cheeks. He rubs his fingertips in circles around my hole, then slowly eases his thumb inside me. I squeeze down on him automatically, and my pussy clenches along with my asshole.

He wants me, I think. He wants me so bad – as bad as I want him. I can tell just from the way he touches me. Gentle and rough at the same time, which I find so sexy I can hardly stand it. But more than that. The way he touches me is necessary. This is how the scene has to happen, and it could happen in no other way than it does.

Characters behaving characteristically. That thought comes into my mind again. Nobody would think that this behaviour was characteristic for me. Not Logan. Not Janice. Not Marilynn. But I guess I've changed. Being with Sterling, being on a trip with Brock, being happy and sexually fulfilled – all those things have managed to change me from being scared to being a screamer, from scurrying silently to savouring every moment.

I close my eyes tightly, and reality sets in again. I know that this is wrong, and for a moment I think I should tell him 'No'. He'll stop if I ask him. I know that he will. But the truth is that I don't really want to say no. I want him to do whatever he wants to. I want him to make me want everything he does. I'm his. I realise that in a rush. I'm his to use. To take. To devour.

I'm all his.

Book Three

'The symptoms are so deep
It is much too late to turn away.'

– Terence Trent D'Arby

14

Brock won't make promises.

Logan will.

Brock won't say that he'll love me forever. I don't ask
him to say this, I simply wait to see if he'll offer up the
sentiment on his own, but he doesn't. Somehow I
understand how things work in his head. With Brock,
the only thing he demands is that I must trust him. If I
put my faith in him, everything will work out. If I
believe, he'll take me everywhere I need to go. He'll
give me everything I've ever wanted.

That all sounds fine when we're together, but at
night, when I lay there in bed next to Logan, I think
that maybe being given everything I want just isn't
enough. I'm not a twenty-year-old any more. I don't
have all the time in the world. Ultimately, I want
someone who will say that he'll be with me forever and
mean those words. Logan has said that. But he doesn't
always show it. What can I expect, anyway? I'm
unfaithful. I deserve nothing.

But I want – oh, do I want – I want *everything*.

I think of one of my favourite fairy tales from child-
hood, one called *White Snake*. A young woman married
a man she could never look at. That was the agreement.
She lived in a palace and all of her needs were cared
for, but her husband remained a lovely mystery to her.
Her sisters were jealous of her extravagant wealth and
told her to peek at him one night in bed. She refused,
but they wore her down with their constant pressure.
When she finally held the candle near his face, she saw

how handsome he was, and then watched in horror as he changed to a snake in front of her eyes. He'd been spellbound by a witch, and now he would be a snake forever because of her mistrustful nature. In order to get him back, the girl had to walk through seven pairs of iron shoes, break seven iron staffs, and dissolve seven iron loaves of bread in her mouth.

What do I have to do to prove my faith to Brock? Only trust him. And how can he trust me when my feelings fluctuate daily? When I know deep down that if Logan changed, even slightly, I might be willing to believe that we could make things work. If he surprised me with flowers even one time. If he told me he thought I looked beautiful. If he kissed me unexpectedly, or joined me in the shower for a sexy, soapy embrace. If he did any one of a number of sappy things that people do in made-for-television movies all the time, I might consider falling on my knees and begging him for his forgiveness. Of telling him that I had cold feet, that I needed one last tryst with another man in order to see what I might be losing. Of putting my cards out on the table and taking my chances.

Instead, Logan grows ever more distant. When I go to teach my Wednesday night class, he hardly bothers to say goodbye to me. We're like strangers, or aloof roommates, who live together but prefer not to share in one another's lives. And the problem with that is our wedding day is almost here.

When I first got engaged, I spoke to Trini about my plans. She works hard at her job, but she doesn't have to. She was born into Beverly Hills wealth, as was her husband. Trini's parents drive matching silver Bentleys. That's the level of wealth that is legendary in this town. Somehow, Trini escaped relatively unscathed by her upbringing. She talks and acts like a fairly normal person. That's why I was so surprised when she took me aside and said she had some marriage advice for me. It wasn't the action of taking me aside, but what her actual advice turned out to be.

'Make sure to talk finances before you tie the knot.'

I shrugged. Money isn't high on the list of the problems Logan and I have. Never was.

'Clear things up fast,' she suggested. 'When Liam and I got together, he pledged to deposit fourteen thousand dollars a month into my account. Half for business. Half for personal expenses. I wasn't working yet, so that really helped me out. I never had to go to him for money.'

I looked at her, shocked. Trini always seems to know what's going on in script development. The thought that she'd be so out of it when it came to her staff's finances was astounding. I nodded, helplessly, thinking that Logan would die laughing when I told him I wanted him to fund a $14,000-a-month lifestyle. I was sure the two of us would get a huge laugh out of the concept. He didn't think it was funny at all. He said, 'That sounds a lot like my father's second wife's allowance,' and that was that. As someone who didn't grow up in Bel Air, I was more surprised, I guess, than the rest of the rich kids.

But now Trini finds me one day under my desk, crying. I don't know how I got to this place – this mental state and the physical state of regarding my office from knee-level – but here I am.

'What's wrong, Cat?' Trini asks me, her voice soothing.

'The caterers are giving Bernie a hard time,' I start, helpless. 'The tuxedo that Logan ordered is missing from the exclusive men's store in Beverly Hills. And everyone is calling me for advice, but I don't have the faintest notion about what I'm doing. I don't even have an opinion any more.'

'Stress,' Trini nods. 'Don't worry, hon. When you get to your honeymoon, all will be well. You only have to make it through the wedding.'

Tears streak my face. Trini takes another look at me, noting what must be the raccoon-like circles of mascara ringing my eyes, and then hurries to her office. She comes back with a bottle of pills.

'Xanax,' she says. 'It will calm anything. I take two on hard days.' She breaks one in half for me. 'Don't want to put you in a coma. Just relax you a little bit.' The pill is like magic. I take it with a swig of Diet Coke, and almost instantly I start to relax. I can't imagine working, however, and now I look at Trini differently. She takes *two* of these? Christ, how can she manage to walk a straight line?

Trini stands up and closes my door. Then she comes back and looks at me. I've crawled out from under my desk, but I'm still sitting on the floor, legs splayed in a most unladylike position. When I look over at my desk, I can think only of Brock fucking me on it. Of him lubing my asshole with my own spit and driving his cock hard inside me until I cried out.

'You don't have to go through with this,' Trini says.

'I don't know.'

'You don't,' Trini insists.

'Everyone wants me to –'

'Sh,' she says, 'just be quiet for a minute and listen, OK?'

I take another sip of the soda and wait.

'I was nineteen. I'd had one semester of college. I knew nothing about the real world. I'd been sheltered my whole life in my parents' house. Never allowed out without a chaperone. Never allowed even to have my own thoughts. They were all given to me. As he was. Liam was the perfect man. Everyone said so. But I wasn't sure. For the first time in my life I had an original thought. And what I thought was that maybe this was too soon. Maybe he wasn't the perfect man for me after all.'

'What did you do?'

Trini shrugs. 'I did what anyone would do in my position. I had a fling right before the wedding with the most unsuitable person on earth. Max worked odd jobs in our neighbourhood, drove a motorcycle and dressed in a James Dean style. I told my mom to call it off. That was the mistake. I told her to. I should have done it myself.'

I look at her, shocked. Trini doesn't voluntarily share this level of deeply personal information. Not ever.

She shrugs again. 'My mother told me that it was far too late to call off the wedding. The invites were already in the mail. The caterer had been booked.'

It's as if she's telling me my whole life. Only I'm older than she was. And I didn't lead the sheltered life Trini did. I should be able to look out for myself, shouldn't I? And then I realise exactly what Trini is telling me. She didn't want to marry her husband. She didn't want the life she has, a life so many people are envious of.

'We get along,' she says, as if understanding exactly what I'm thinking. 'We made it work. Everything's fine now. I was just young. Too young. But you're young, too.'

'I'm not nineteen,' I tell her.

'Ages are different now. Sixty is considered middle-aged, as if people live to a hundred and twenty! You do what you need to do. Don't worry so much about what people think about you. Why should you care?'

Because everybody does, I think. In this tiny community of wealth and prestige, everyone is always paying attention to everyone else. I recall a T-shirt I saw in Westwood a few weeks ago. It said: 'It doesn't matter who you are, it's what you wear. Because when it all comes down to it, nobody cares who you are.'

That summed up the sickening LA mentality in only a few words.

Trini pets my hair while I'm thinking this. 'You'll make a beautiful bride,' she says, sounding for an instant like Bernie. 'But make sure you marry the right groom.'

With that final piece of advice, her best yet, she says, 'Now, why don't you take another pass on the script. The Xanax will give your mind a whole different vision of the words on the page. And by the way,' she adds, 'everyone has been very impressed with your latest rewrites. They're sexier than anything I've ever read from you.' She winks at me, then stands and leaves the office. I lay back against the rug on my office floor, contemplating the underside of my desk as if it were the most interesting thing I've ever seen.

Xanax. The wonder drug.

When I leave the office, I have the Danika script on a zip disk in my briefcase. I've been worried about the character's arc. There doesn't seem to be one. In *La Femme Nikita*, my favourite of the female action genre, in fact of all action films, Nikita experiences a definite arc – she undergoes a total mental and physical transformation. Danika, unfortunately, is the same person from page 1 to page 120. I suppose, in that way, she's like James Bond. He doesn't change from film to film. The only transformation occurs in the actors who portray him.

And what about *my* arc?

I've definitely changed since meeting Brock, since giving into my basest fantasies and living out X-rated activities I thought would never happen to me. But is being perfectly fucked a transforming experience?

I don't have the answer to that.

If I get into that wedding dress and march down the aisle, I will definitely have undergone a transformation of one kind. But I don't even know if I'll be a beautiful bride, as Trini said. I won't according to the experts at *Beautiful Bride* magazine, in which a poll revealed that honesty is the most important quality for any relationship to succeed. And without honesty, you can't have a perfect marriage. Without a perfect marriage, how can you be a beautiful bride?

I haven't got a clue.

What I do know is this:

I lie. Every single day, I lie. Somehow, the more lies I tell, the easier they get to say. I get so good at forgoing the truth that I find myself lying about things that don't matter. For no reason at all, I tell fibs. Logan asks if I picked up his prescription at the pharmacy, and I say 'yes' even though I haven't, without a thought to what that might lead to. It's as if I want to get caught at something, at one small thing, and then I would be able to come clean about it all. I envision the dam of my heart breaking, and all those hidden secrets flooding out.

It never happens. I am invincible.

There are moments when I am sure he knows. When we stare at each other and words don't come and I think: he hates me. Finally. Perfect. He hates me. He'll ask for his ring back. We can end this farce and move on with our lives. But the accusations never come.

What a coward I am. Normal, strong, mentally balanced people would have gotten past it and gotten over it. Instead, I slide through the days in a guilty haze, feeling bad about what I am doing to him and despising him for making me do it. When I tell this to Janice, she disagrees entirely.

'Nobody is making you do anything,' Janice says in

her matter-of-fact tone. 'If you don't tell him soon, someone else will do it for you. Cat, you're sick if you think that this won't hurt him more in the long run.' She takes a sip of her wheat-grass smoothie. I grimace. Why would anyone ever drink that without a gun to their head? 'No one is making you do this except you.'

But how about my father, saying, 'He's the right one for you, Cat. Everyone has cold feet. You'll get over it.' Or my mother, adding, 'You'll regret it for the rest of your life if you let him go. This is your one chance for happiness.' How can someone say that to a person? Who knows what I will or will not regret?

How about his mother, Bernie, planning each step of the marriage ceremony. Choreographing it. Sending invitations out to more people than I could have gathered without paying cash by the head.

She calls me at night, tells me that she wants me to know that she'll always be there to listen to me. Says that her boys' wives are like the daughters she never had, aside that is from the one daughter she does have who was a great disappointment to her. She claims to be an impartial observer, and she says that I can tell her anything.

'Anything,' she repeats forcefully.

I'd like to try that out. I'd like to prove her wrong. For instance, I'd love to tell her that on the other line, Brock is waiting for me to come back to him. That we'd been having phone sex until she interrupted. I can just imagine it. I'd been in the middle of describing a scenario in drastically kinky detail, fucking him on my balcony, looking out over the Santa Monica beach, the silver-tipped waves crashing below, his body slamming into me above. The foam from the waves like white cream lapping at the glittering sand. Or perhaps I could tell her that on our first date, standing face to face at that dive bar, he told me that he was going to spank my bottom until I couldn't sit down. I don't think so. I keep secrets to myself until I feel that I am going to burst, rupture, explode.

'You know, I'd love to chat, but I'm on the other line with Marilynn,' I tell Bernie. 'She thinks she's finally gotten fitted for the bridesmaid dress you chose,' and Bernie lets me go immediately.

Brock says, 'Who was that?'

'You don't want to know.'

'I do.'

There they are. The two words I'm supposed to say in a few days. I feel as if my biological clock has become a wedding clock. Tick-tock! I do! Tick-tock! I do!

'Future mother-in-law,' I say.

'Oh, baby,' Brock mocks me. 'Talk to me about your in-laws. I find that indescribably sexy.'

'Give me a break,' I say, shortly. If he wants to be with me, then he can see my bitchy side. Brock won't fall for it.

'What were we doing before she beeped in?'

'Fucking,' I say.

'But we shouldn't have been,' he tells me, and I feel the panic wash through me that he's going to tell me it's over. We shouldn't have been because I'm taken. I'm so taken that in the midst of us having phone sex, my future mother-in-law is calling me with wedding updates. Instead, he says, 'We started getting into it too soon.'

'What do you mean?'

'If I were really at your condo, and we were really out on your balcony, I wouldn't fuck you right away. Not at all.'

'What would you do?'

'First, I'd bind you to the railing with Logan's best ties.'

'You're evil,' I say.

'And you love it, don't you?'

'Yes.'

'I'd tie you down,' he continues smoothly, 'so that you couldn't get away, no matter how you squirmed around, and then I'd get one of his leather belts and whip you with it.'

'So evil,' I say, but my voice is wavering now.

'And that would make you come, wouldn't it, baby?'

He's right; it would. Even though this all feels so wrong. Still I radiate. Heat. Lust. Life. Later that night, when I hurry to the grocery store for a bottle of gin to make a Martini at home, the man behind the check-out counter says, 'There's something different about you.' A pause. 'You look happier. That's it. Happier.'

I'm miserable. I feel sick all the time.

Except when I'm with Brock.

'Don't think,' Brock says as he leads me into his front room.

'What do you mean?'

He explains carefully. 'I'm not telling you to think outside of the box,' he says, 'I'm saying that thinking *is* the box. I don't want you to think. I want you to let me do everything, and I want you to relax.'

I try. I take a deep breath and let Brock position me exactly how he wants me, dead in the centre of his living room. I can't keep my eyes from taking in the various sex toys that are displayed before me, but I try not to worry about what he might use the toys for, or how they might make me feel.

'Relax,' he says again, 'and trust me.'

There has been no conversation with him about the fact that my wedding is this weekend. He knows this, yet he says nothing. Unfortunately, it's all I can think about. The fact that Logan and Janice and Bernie and my parents and my friends are all pushing me forwards. The fact that in my court, all I have are Marilynn and Trini and me. And Brock.

'Sh, baby,' Brock says, even though I haven't uttered a word. It's as if he can read my thoughts. 'Don't worry. Relax.'

Now he brings a pair of slim-fitting steel handcuffs and places them on my wrists, so that my hands are chained in front of me. Next up is a dog collar, a thick black leather band that he fastens around my throat. I gaze at the array of items still waiting for his attention. There is a harness-like contraption made of black leather, something I've never seen before. It's similar to the one Sterling wore, but there are more parts to the device. When Brock realises that I'm starring at it, he grins.

'That's right,' he says, 'you're going into that now.'

He patiently buckles me into the odd-looking contraption. The leather fastens around my waist and between my legs, leaving open holes in the front and rear. Dangling in front of the holes are odd, triangular shapes of leather with snaps that fit over the holes to close them. Finally, he shows me two phallic-shaped dildos, one a deep cornflower blue, the other a vibrant hot pink. I can't help but smile when I see them, because I can easily envision Brock going into a sex-toy store and looking around for something pretty to buy me amidst all the tacky merchandise. There's that place on Melrose that I've been in with Marilynn. People walk in, averting their eyes, pretending that they accidentally wandered into this store, and – oh, my goodness, just look at these butt plugs! Who would ever have thought? – but Brock wouldn't be like that. He'd have in mind something ahead of time, and he'd be straightforward about his purchases. I try to imagine Logan going into a sex-toy palace, but my mind comes up blank. He wouldn't go in looking for purchases for me, that's for certain. Would he ever go after something he might want for himself? That's a more interesting question.

'One for each hole,' Brock says, and the smile fades from my lips immediately. I take a step back from him, but he won't allow any unapproved movement. He pushes me right back to my starting mark, and he says, 'Watch me closely, baby.'

My eyes focused intently on his actions, I watch as he first lubes up the pink toy, then he bends on his knees in front of me. I swallow hard as he forcefully parts my pussy lips.

'Just look at that,' he says, 'you're already so shiny wet I hardly needed the lube. It's like icing on a pornographic cake.'

He's right. I can feel how slippery I am, and I watch as Brock works to keep my pussy lips spread apart. Then he grips the base of the toy and slides the dildo deep into my cunt. I suck in my breath at the sensation, watching him as he flips over the triangular flap of the harness, then snaps the leather holder into place, effectively holding the toy in place inside of me. I sigh even harder when he reaches for the blue toy, because I know exactly where this is going now. I understand everything. Brock is making another fantasy of mine come true. He is going to fill all of my holes: my pussy and my asshole with the freshly purchased toys, and my mouth with his hard and ready cock. He is going to use me for his pleasure, and this is what will ultimately make me come.

I realise as he lubes up the blue toy in front of my eyes that he has done the impossible – made me stop worrying about my impending wedding. Because now all I can think is that the blue phallus looks awfully large. How is that going to fit inside me? How on earth?

'Ready, baby?' he asks.

I shake my head no. I'm not ready. Not in the slightest. Brock laughs and the sound is rich with humour and a bit of sensitivity. 'Never ready for your fantasy to come true. Is that right?'

I shake my head again. I'm just not ready for that toy. My whole body tightens in expectation of the intrusion, but Brock takes his time. He wants to make sure that I'm relaxed. That seems to be the theme of the evening.

'Bend over,' he says, but my wrists are cuffed, so I'm scared that I'll fall.

'I won't let you,' he assures me. 'Bend towards me.'

I slowly lean my body forwards, and Brock supports me against his shoulder as he reaches back to part my asscheeks. His fingers are smeared with lube and he rubs the greasy tips up and down the crack between my cheeks. My pussy is pressed hard against his shoulder, and this pushes the base of the dildo even deeper inside me. I'm so well filled by this one synthetic cock that, when he starts to slide the second one inside me, I feel that I won't be able to accept it. There's too much already. But Brock is patient and gentle. He won't be dissuaded. Slowly, easily, he slides the knobby head of the second dildo into my asshole.

I realise in a hot flash as he slips the toy deeper inside me that I like it. I guess I knew I would. I had to, I suppose, in order to have confessed this as a fantasy to Brock. What I didn't know was how *much* I'd like it. My breath is coming faster now, and I begin to shift my hips against Brock's shoulder, slowly working myself up to a steady rhythm in which I'm actually fucking the dildo deeper inside of me with each press of my hips against his body.

But then he slips the dildo further into me and I gasp out loud. I feel so filled already. How much more can there be?

'Relax, baby,' he says again. 'This is what you want. Remember that. This is exactly what you wished for.'

And I think as he says it that he's repeating my fortune, the one I got when I was with him and Logan and Sterling: be careful what you wish for ... it might come true. Again and again and again.

'You're a sensualist,' Janice says over coffee at our favourite café the next morning. 'Any outsider looking into your world could tell in a minute that's your main problem.'

'That's a problem?' I ask, looking around at the other diners. We're situated in the front window overlooking Montana Avenue. As far as I can tell, all of the people around us are sensualists, digging into colourful fruit salads, devouring stacks of blueberry and banana pancakes, demolishing French toast cooked crispy on the outside and coated with powdered sugar. Outdoors, more sensualists stroll the streets, wearing sunhats, admiring the flowers in pots along the sidewalk, taking in the golden-hot rays of glorious California sunshine.

Maybe all of the citizens who live in Santa Monica are sensualists. My neighbours choose to reside next to the beach, beneath year-round sun and near-tropical temperatures. Californians are all about the weather. That's probably why that bumper sticker has such appeal in this area: 'The weather is here. Wish you were beautiful.' (Although few people outside of pick-up truck owners seem willing to emblazon their vehicles with stickers of any kind.) My fellow Santa Monicans come outdoors in sheer sundresses, brightly hued shorts and tank tops. They wear straw sunhats with ribbons trailing down the back, or baseball caps and Wayfarer shades. Nowadays, they slather on 45 SPF suntan lotion, gaining their actual tans in a salon in Beverly Hills, the type of salon that airbrushes the tanning lotion on. No tanning beds any more. Nothing that could cause real harm. But *faux* tans are still the rage. They always will be in California: home of the beach-blanket bunny in the itsy-bitsy thong bikini.

'Sure it's a problem,' Janice says. 'When you think everything is supposed to be erotic, when you expect every day to be pleasant for you, that is a real problem. You're setting yourself up for instant depression when things don't go the way you want.'

I don't agree with her statement at all. Sensualists don't think every day is pleasant. In fact, I don't think 'pleasant' is a word that sensualists appreciate. It conjures images of 'good enough', 'satisfactory', 'complacent', 'compliant'. Sensualists want to be drenched in a feeling, whether it's the joy of climbing under ironed white 200-thread Egyptian cotton sheets, or wallowing in absolute misery over the last glass of very good, very old, double-blended Scotch. It's making the absolute most of a moment, good or bad. And with that thought I think of yesterday with Brock. Of being filled by those two dildos. Of having him uncuff my wrists and push me down onto my hands and knees, of using my mouth, thrusting his cock deep into my throat, and then reaching behind me to flick on the motor of the vibrating dildo filling my ass. I didn't know it was motorised until the vibrations welled through me.

And then ... oh, then.

How am I going to describe the fact that although Logan can be pleasant, he isn't ever hot or cold. He doesn't give me the feeling that I am alive. That's what Brock does for me. Makes every single moment scream. The brush of his fingers on my inner wrist awakens more sensations in me than when Logan actually makes love to me. Not that we do that any more. Not that we ever did much of that at all. It's what I thought being a grown-up was. Isn't that ridiculous? Isn't it sad?

'You're bored, that's all,' Janice said, summing up my problems. 'And you know what, kiddo? You'll be bored with Brock before too long, and then what will happen?'

'You tell me,' I say. 'You seem to know the answers to everything.'

'You'll have given up your life, your whole plan, without anything to fall back on. Just memories of a good f–' she whispers the rest '– u–c–k with a handsome guy.'

'Was the plan to get married?'

'That's everybody's plan,' she says simply.

Suddenly, that plan seems much less exciting than before.

'Trust me,' she says, 'you'll wind up like Paul, always looking for the best offer, and at some point you'll realise that it's already passed you by.'

I say nothing, but I don't agree.

So why don't I just leave Logan? That's the big question, isn't it? I mean, if I'm so gaga over Brock, then why don't I just pack my bags and get out? Cut my losses while I can still – potentially – recover?

The answer is as plain as the seven crisp white envelopes waiting in our mailbox when I get back from brunch with Janice. These latecomers prove to me once again that we're in motion. The wedding is in motion. Everything is already moving forwards at an unmanageable speed. We're going 95 in a 25mph zone. How do you stop something careening out of control?

I take a walk around the block to think things over. The walk leads me to one of Marilynn and my favourite bars. One that's housed in an old firehouse just blocks from the beach. I order a glass of white wine – safe drink – and contemplate my life. How do I get out? How indeed?

Should be simple enough, right? Confess to being

unfaithful. That ought to do it. Even someone as stud-less as Logan will be unable to forgive such a transgression. So what's wrong with me? Am I too much of a coward? Afraid of Logan? It's not like he's going to kill someone. We're not starring in that god-awful Richard Gere movie.

This is real life.

But here's the truth. I need something that I'm missing. Guts, I guess. And after three glasses of white wine, I find them somewhere deep inside myself and call Logan at work. On his voice mail, I tell him we're through; that I can't do this any more. I don't mention Brock, of course. I only say that things haven't been good for a long time. That he must know it as well as I do, and then I order my fourth glass of wine and get ready for the battle of my life.

Doesn't happen.

Logan immediately calls me back on my cellphone. His voice is angry but even, and I think about him trying to remain calm-sounding while at his job. I can tell that he doesn't want his co-workers to hear him sounding upset. To Logan, illusions can equal reality if you believe in them hard enough. Everything has always been about surface appearances – I'm starting to realise that now. How my hair looks, how I dress, what food I eat, what scents I wear. I thought only Brock had rules, but now I realise I was wrong. Logan has them, too. Plenty of them. They just don't deal with sex, or pleasure, or fun.

'You can't break up on an answering machine.'

'I don't know.' I'm slurring now.

'You can't. Not after six years. Not after all the planning my mom has put into the wedding. For God's sake, Cat, the wedding's this weekend.'

This is the most animated he's sounded in months.

But what he doesn't say is what I'd need to hear to stay with him. And what is that? God, just about anything. He should say anything except what he actually does say, which is this:

'You can't fucking do it.'

And I remember the rule. Can't is not an option. But that is Brock's rule, not Logan's.

'We have to talk,' he tells me.

'I don't want to talk.'

He's insistent. 'Where do you want to meet?'

I'm glad he doesn't say at home. Maybe he knows that our condo is too loaded a place to get together. But I can't think of anywhere that I'd want to see Logan. Not anywhere.

'My mom's house,' he suggests, and everything in me feels as if it's falling down. Last place on earth I want to go is anywhere Bernie is.

'At six,' he says into my silence. 'We'll work this out, Catherine. You know we will.'

Six o'clock. Three hours away. So what do I do? I call Brock. *Of course*, I call Brock. He'll know how to fix this. He'll know how to fix me. He'll tell me what to do, how to proceed, who to trust. Or he'll invite me over, break out the dildos, and let me forget all of my current medley of problems. All I need is the pink one in my pussy and the blue one in my ass and his cock in my mouth and all of the problems of the world immediately subside.

But he's not there, and I'm left contemplating who else to talk to. I try Marilynn, but her answering machine is filled with the sexy giggling sound of her and Declan drunkenly making a recording together. When did they get so chummy? I wonder. Must have been while I've been out fucking Brock.

Finally, I settle once again on Janice.

'You're not a very sympathetic character,' Janice says, ordering me a monster cup of coffee and handing over two aspirins. 'Most people are looking for love from one person, searching for it, desperate for it. They take out ads in the personals. They go on blind date after blind date until they go blind about love themselves. You have two men who want to be with you, and you want me to feel sorry for you.'

'No, not sorry. I just want you to listen.' I'm drinking the coffee even though I still feel drunk, and the combination of the two vices is sickening. My head pounds. The floor looks unstable, the wooden boards waver when I look at them too hard. But I force myself to push onwards. I need Janice to understand. The whole time, all I've given her is bits and pieces. Now I try to explain everything.

Janice isn't a great listener. She likes to solve problems and move on. I'm different. I attack them from all angles, turn and twist and observe each side before I make up my mind. Still, I jumped into Brock's truck bed without much thought to what it meant to my life, what it honestly meant in the grand scale, the larger picture.

'Dump Logan. Date Brock. Revamp you're entire fucking life. Get it over with.' She sounds decidedly bitter. When Janice swears, she's reached her limits of decorum. I think that she really did want me to join her in the club of marrieds.

It sounds easy. But it isn't easy. I live with Logan, am engaged to Logan. Would anyone believe me if I said I didn't want to hurt him?

'You're really in over your head,' Janice said. 'Way, way over. Get out while you're still mentally balanced . . . and alive.'

'What's that supposed to mean?'

She pauses, as if she's not sure she should tell me.

'You know that lots of people who cheat get killed, don't you?'

Now she's trying to scare me. 'I'm balanced,' I say. My diamond catches the light in the bar and twinkles. It seems to sparkle wherever I go. 'Besides, weren't you the one who advocated cheating in the first place?'

'A fling,' she reminds me. 'You were supposed to have a brief fling in order to come to your senses about loving Logan.'

'That's just not what happened,' I tell her.

'I think it's funny,' Janice adds coldly in a voice that has absolutely no humour at all.

'What?'

'You were an anthropology major. You studied man for four years. And look what happened.'

'What are you talking about?'

'You're studying two men at once. It's like research.' She snaps her fingers. 'That's what you can tell Logan when he finds out that you've been unfaithful.' She says this with a certain kind of glee that's impossible to ignore and difficult to forgive.

'When he *what*?'

'Finds out. He'll find out, Cat. They always find out.'

'I know what this is about,' Bernie says when I arrive at her house.

'How can you possibly?'

'I told him, but he wouldn't listen. He said that you'd never know, and what you didn't know wouldn't hurt you. But I knew that you'd find out.'

What can she be talking about?

'The ring,' Bernie says emphatically. 'That's it, right? You brought it in to Tiffany's to be sized, and they told you.'

I continue to stare at her, and maybe she thinks I'm acknowledging that she's right with my silence. In truth, I have no idea what she's talking about. The ring to me means honesty, of which I'm completely lacking, and it usually resides in my change purse so that I don't feel the guilt of wearing it. But now I have a thing or two to learn about reality versus fantasy, and I listen in silence as Bernie explains.

I live in a world of make-believe. Fantasy always wins. So the story of my ring is a lesson in the power of fact over fiction. Logan paid $500 for my $12,000 ring. He got a knock-off at a place in West Los Angeles, and then bought something small – a sterling silver trinket – from Tiffany and put my ring in the box. Should it make a difference to me? Who am I to talk about fakery?

'He has the money,' Bernie says. 'But he didn't want to spend it. He said rings were ridiculous. Not a good investment. He doesn't understand about women and jewellery. He'll get you the real thing if you insist. I'm sure he will.'

I shake my head. 'It's not the ring,' I say, but now as I look at it I wonder if we were mismatched from the start. 'Not really,' I say.

Logan arrives then, right as I make my way to the door.

'I have to go,' I tell him. 'We can talk later.'

'She *knows*,' Bernie hisses at him, pointing to her own jewel-encrusted ring finger, but I don't stop to listen to them battle about it. I'm out the door. On my way to Brock.

'Do you want to be with me?' I ask Brock. I'm standing nude in his bedroom, my wrists cuffed to a black spreader, my legs bound at the ankles. I have to work hard to keep my balance. Brock reclines on his bed, watching me, admiring my naked form. He always has such a pleased look when he stares at my naked body.

'Why do you ask that?'

'I mean, do you want to be *with* me. Not just here, like this, but all the time?'

'You shouldn't have to ask that.'

'Then tell me what to do.'

'I can't.'

'Can't is not an acceptable answer.'

He cracks a smile at the same time as he reaches over to the night table and hefts a ping-pong paddle. 'Don't put words in my mouth,' he says, and although the smile is still on his face, his tone has changed. He takes me and spreads me out on his bed, still leaving me attached to the bondage devices, and then he delivers fifteen smarting spanks to my naked ass, until I am crying out from the pain and squirming uselessly to get away from the blows.

'Don't talk for me,' he says again, unchaining me and then placing me face up in the centre of the bed. 'You don't know what I'm thinking about. You don't know at all.'

I can't say I'm sorry, because I already know he hates it. But I don't know what to do. There is a turmoil within me that I can't dissolve. Pressure from all sides to go forward with Logan. Desire on one side – the side that counts – to stay with Brock. But can I do that? Do people actually live like this? The way we are? Won't we burn out, *9½ Weeks*-style, so that I end up in an institution and he goes off in search of his next stranger in the night? The next woman to tie down and fuck, to tie up and fuck with, to destroy in a halo of fire and heat.

'This is your life,' he tells me, and now he moves to straddle my chest, placing his cock right at the bottom of my lip. I flick my tongue out immediately to taste him, relishing the way his skin is warm and soft even on this most hard protrusion. I forget everything when

I suck him, the way I realise that I've forgotten to take off my ring. And that's what ends this scene.

For so long, I've worried that I'll forget to put the engagement ring back on when I return to Logan. Now I've forgotten to remove it when I'm with Brock.

'Make up your mind,' he says, pulling away from me, and his eyes are so sad and cold that I want to cry. He stares at my hand rather than at my face, and it feels as if the ring is burning into my finger. 'Then you get back to me.'

I don't want to get back to him. I want to fall into his arms right now. This very second. I want him to spank me and cuff me and bind me and fuck me. But he won't play my game any more. The rules have changed. He doesn't have to tell me that, he doesn't have to explain a thing. The answer is clear in his eyes: as long as I have any bindings to a man other than himself, Brock is off limits. He looks at me for one more moment, then turns and walks away.

Logan isn't there when I get back to the apartment. A note rests on the kitchen table. 'I've gone to Paul's to stay. I'll be ready to meet you at the altar. I hope you will be too.'

I don't sleep all night.

15

'You read it in the paper every day,' Janice says. 'I mean, just last week there was that celebrity thing in Hollywood.'

'Logan's not a celebrity. He's just a guy.'

'That was the exception,' Janice says. 'Usually, celebrities don't kill each other, normal people do. Logan's normal, right?'

'He's harmless. He's quiet.'

'It's the quiet ones that surprise you.'

'You're suggesting that I stay with him forever, live a miserable existence, because if I don't he might kill me?'

Janice shrugs. 'Which would you rather have: life with Logan, or death with Brock?'

Are those really my options? I stare at her, concerned. Finally, I say, 'What about C – none of the above choices at all?' And Janice simply gives me her G-rated lip-pucker and waits for me to calm down.

'Besides,' Janice says, 'your wedding is tomorrow. It's too late now. Go through with it, forget Brock, and see what happens. If you really do think you made a mistake, you can always get a divorce or an annulment.'

'I'm not Catholic.'

'You know what I mean. So many people have been married before. Even me. You remember how jittery I was before my first.'

'Yeah, and you were right. You said so yourself. That turned out to be a nightmare.'

'I would never have found Allan if I hadn't married Randolph.'

'You're confusing the issue,' I tell her. 'And you're confusing me. I need to get out of this.'

'It's too late,' Janice says, and she waves her hand for the check.

Is it too late? Is she right?

EXT. BERNIE'S HOUSE: HOLMBY HILLS

The mansion is decorated to look like a fairy-tale castle. White-and-silver streamers dangle from the trees. the front walk is lined with iced-silver irises – specially spray-painted for the festivities. The help has been colour co-ordinated to match the decor: men are in tuxes that look as if they were crafted from tinfoil. The girls are all dressed in spangled outfits that barely cover their thighs. Their garters show jauntily beneath the crinoline skirts. They look like something from a space-age stripper movie. Bernie says they're 'in'. She hired them all from the hip diner Swingles and asked that they spray-paint the combat boots they wear as part of their daily uniforms. They did so gladly, for an extra fee, of course.

JANICE
(softly)
Nervous?

CAT
Actually, no.

JANICE
Really? I'm not sure that's a good sign.

CAT
(smiling)
I'm not going through with this. I choose C – none of the above.

241

DISSOLVE TO:

Cat, waking up in bed. It's all been a bad dream. A nightmare. She looks around the room, relieved, only to spot her wedding dress hanging on the back of the closet door right next to Logan's tuxedo.

CUT TO:

Ceremony setting.

CLOSE ON:

Wedding cake. Plastic bride and groom.

CUT TO:

LOGAN and CAT hold a knife together as they cut the first piece of the cake.

> CAT
> (voice-over)
> So I did as Janice suggested. I went for it.
> Maybe what Brock and I had was just a fling.
> A sexy one, for sure. A hot moment in my life
> that I'll never forget. But sometimes in life,
> you have to put fantasy behind you and act
> like a grown-up.

CUT TO:

Audience walking out of a theatre, echoing BOOS and HISSES as they pour onto Santa Monica Boulevard.

> AUDIENCE MEMBER 1
> God, that really was a total downer.

> AUDIENCE MEMBER 2
> She should have gone with Brock.

AUDIENCE MEMBER 1
Brock should have showed up last-minute like in *The Graduate*.

AUDIENCE MEMBER 2
But remember the end of *The Graduate* when they're on the bus together? Neither one looks very happy at all, as if they both realise that they might have made a huge mistake.

CAT
(voice-over)
So let's try it a different way . . .

16

Bernie's mansion in Holmby Hills is decorated more thoroughly than many sets I've been on. Not one detail has gone unnoticed, as far as I can tell in my dizzy state. Bernie might be a good film designer, I think to myself. She's got a way with balancing all parts of the process, while never seeming flustered.

I, on the other hand, am beyond flustered. This is why I'm so pleased when I peek out the upstairs window and see a Harley pull up. It's Marilynn, arriving with Declan and a smile. I hurry down the stairs to greet her, despite the fact that I'm all dolled up in my wedding dress, veil fluttering behind me. I don't care if guests see me. I need to talk to my friend.

I watch as Declan gently helps Marilynn off the bike. Along with his tux today, he's got on black motorcycle boots. His dyed-black hair shines in the light, and I can tell somehow that he hasn't gotten a lot of sleep.

'What are you doing?' Marilynn asks, hurrying me back into the house. 'You're not supposed to be out where people can see you!'

'Then come with me,' I tell her, pulling her after me up one of the twisting staircases to Bernie's dressing room. This is where I'm supposed to be sequestered until the ceremony. Many of Bernie's friends have twittered in to check on me, but I've waved off their help. I'm beyond help, I think. Yet even in my self-obsessed state, I notice that Marilynn appears more at ease than I've ever seen her before. In fact, aside from emanating that great-sex glow, she looks positively happy. I'm shocked when she says that she and Declan are moving in together. Yes, I always thought they'd be good together, but I never believed they'd realise that fact themselves.

'You know,' she tells me, 'I can't keep living this playboy lifestyle forever.'

'But what about him? What about the dreaded ex?'

'I'm not worried,' she says, looking over the brides-maid dress that has been laid out for her. 'We're beyond that. She only had power when he gave her power. Now he doesn't even answer the phone when her number shows up in the caller ID box.'

'But how do you know this is right?' I ask. 'You've been wavering for so long.'

'Sometimes you just do. It's not as if I've transformed him into something that he's not. He's still hardcore.' From the way she talks, I understand that the two will never transform into Ozzie and Harriet. Marilynn proves this with her next statement: after the ceremony, they're going to the Sunset Strip Tattoo Parlor to get matching inked designs. So maybe they're more like Ozzy and Sharon, but that's OK, too.

'You really *are* sure,' I decide.

'As sure as I'll ever be,' she tells me. 'As sure as you are.'

And now I turn away from her. Because I'm not sure at all.

I want Brock. I don't know if he'll have me back. I don't know if he's even interested in hearing anything I have to say. But I have to find out.

'I have to talk to Logan,' I say.

'Bad luck. He shouldn't see you in the dress.' Who would have thought Marilynn would be superstitious?

'I have to,' I insist, and I push past her and streak out of Bernie's dressing room to the main part of the house, searching to find Logan. I know that he'll be somewhere with his groomsmen, but I don't know his exact location and I don't have a map. Bernie's mansion is gigantic. Even though I've been here many times, it's easy to get lost in the labyrinth-like maze of hallways, libraries, and living rooms, of which there are three aside from the grand room where the wedding will take place.

The groomsmen, I discover, are in the 'entertainment centre' waiting for the ceremony to start. The guys are giving Logan a difficult time, ribbing him about his upcoming nuptials. Trying to get close to him, I push my way through the boisterous crowd of his friends, but every time I arrive at the spot where he was, he is standing somewhere else. He's like a bead of mercury that I'm trying to trap. The journey to reach him makes me feel light-headed. I give up for a moment and sit down on the edge of the immense fireplace. As if he's interested, Bernie's fifth husband sits at my side.

'Having fun?' he asks. He's a lech, and I know he's only there to look down my dress.

'Tons,' I say, and then the path to Logan miraculously parts. I excuse myself from Bernie's soon-to-be-ex-husband and walk over, pulling off the ring on my way. I look around, making sure there are people close by to help me if I need assistance. I don't want to be killed, and if Janice has anything right, Logan is going to try to throttle me.

'It's off,' I say, handing over the ring.

'What's off?'

'The wedding,' I tell him. 'I can't go through with it.'

Never say 'can't'. Never.

'I won't,' I say quickly, editing myself.

'Why not?'

'I don't love you any more,' I say. I make sure to be a step away from him, just in case he flips out and tries to hurt me.

'That's what all this is about?' he asks.

I nod.

'The craziness. The distance.'

I nod again.

'And love is very important to you?' he asks quietly. His blue eyes focus on me for once. I can tell that he's actually paying attention to what I'm saying.

'Yeah.' He's taking this better than I thought.

'You must love someone else then,' he says, brilliantly deducing the situation. 'Otherwise, how would you know what you were missing?'

'I do,' I tell him. I want to add that I'm sorry, but sorry is not acceptable, especially because it's not the truth. I'm not sorry that I'm in love with Brock. The only thing I'm actually sorry for is disappointing Logan. But haven't I always been a disappointment to him on one level or another?

'You're sure about this, Cat?'

'I didn't mean to hurt you.' There, that's a direct line from at least seven screenplays I've rewritten in my life, and I have no better way to put the words. They're true, on some level, even if they are dangerously clichéd. What Logan says back to me is not.

'No problem,' he says. 'More fodder for the screenplay.'

'What do you mean?' The statement doesn't compute.

'All great writers go through pain and suffering.'

He doesn't look like he's suffering at all. In fact, as I lean closer, he smells of his familiar fragrant pot smoke, such a different scentsation than Brock's deliciously male shaving cream.

'No hard feelings?' I ask.

He puts the $500 ring in his pocket. Then he takes my hand in his and shakes it, as if we've just completed an important business transaction that was a letdown to both parties. Or maybe as if we're dissolving a partnership in an adult, nonemotional manner.

'None,' he says. 'I wish you all the best.'

I wonder if Bernie's going to take this as well.

'What do you mean there's not going to be a wedding?' Each word is bitten off separately, as if her incisors are being sharpened on the question.

'I can't marry your son,' I say, as forcefully as possible, but I take a step back from her, as well. She's standing in the giant kitchen, quite close to the rack of expensive restaurant-quality knives, and I stay as far away as possible, across the marble-topped island from her. If anyone might completely lose control, it's her. Christ, Bernie lives for weddings. She's had five of her own and has planned all of her nieces' and nephews' celebrations. If she could attend a wedding every day, she'd be in heaven.

'Well, why can't you?'

'Can't' is not an appropriate response, I remind myself. Haven't I learned that yet? Haven't I learned anything? I *can* do whatever I want. I don't want to marry Logan. I hear that in my head, crystal clear for the very first time, and then I say it out loud. 'I don't want to marry Logan,' I tell Bernie, hearing the force of the words. This is truth. She won't be able to argue with the truth. Turns out, she doesn't even try. For a script doctor, I sure don't know my characters very well, do I? Maybe I've been too introspective to pay attention to the motivations of the supporting cast.

'Who do you want to marry?'

I hesitate.

'Someone, right? You're talking to the wedding queen, kiddo. Who's on the shortlist if it's not my son?'

'Things just are not right between me and Logan.

They haven't been for quite some time.' This sounds like dialogue from a movie I worked on years ago. Who says 'quite some time' in real life? Guess I do.

'Apparently,' she says, and her forehead tries to wrinkle. Nothing happens. That's the effect of too much Botox. 'I guess that's what you were saying the other night, but I didn't want to hear you.' She hesitates, looking me up and down. 'But, sweetheart, here's the thing . . . you have a glow. A blissful glow. That's what threw me off. I'm usually so good at spotting trouble on lovers' lane. Remember when my friend Marcella left her husband? I saw that coming even before she did! You've got that "in love" halo around you. You must want to marry someone.' She's quiet, staring at me. It's obvious she's going to wait me out.

'Brock,' I finally say.

'Paul's Brock?'

I somehow manage to nod, even though I don't think of him precisely as 'Paul's' Brock.

'How convenient,' Bernie says, reaching for her cellphone and dialing in a number.

'Who are you calling?'

'The baker. They're running late, which is lucky for us. I'll have them change the groom on the cake. We'll need a dark-haired one instead of a blond.'

'What on earth are you talking about?'

'He's on the guest list.'

I just stare.

'Oh, honey, when I throw a wedding, I invite everybody. My manicurist, hairdresser, gardener and, in this case, contractor. He RSVP'd that he'd attend.' She looks at the clock. 'He'll be here in twenty minutes. It's perfect. We have plenty of time.'

'But I'm not marrying Logan.' I wonder if she may have actually lost her mind.

'Didn't I tell you that I love all my daughters-in-law

equally. We'll still have the wedding. You're still flesh and blood.'

'I'm not,' I say, thinking that I never was. 'I'm not marrying your son.' How many times will I have to say this before the facts sink in? Has Botox managed to atrophy her brain as well as the muscles in her eerily smooth forehead?

'But you're getting *married*,' Bernie says, as if talking to someone brand-new to her soap-opera lifestyle. She touches the edge of my dress, positively beaming at me. Into the phone, she says, 'We need to change the groom. You had a blond up on the top with the bride. Do you have a brunette?' She looks at me and winks.

'I love a good wedding,' she says, wiping away a tear.

You'd think that was enough chaos for one day. But it's not. When Janice hears the news, spread to her by Marilynn, she stalks over to me. I note that my friends have optimistically changed into the hideous eggplant bridesmaid gowns chosen by Bernie. I'll have to tell them to put their street clothes back on.

'Now, I have to tell you –' Janice begins.

'That you think I'm making a huge mistake. You've already said so. Repeatedly.' I'm expecting a tirade; what I get is something else entirely.

'No, that *I* made one.'

'What do you mean?'

'I left Allan.'

'Oh, God,' I sigh. I didn't see that coming at all.

'And I've been seeing someone else.'

'The trainer.'

She shakes her head. 'On Wednesday nights. Every Wednesday night, for the past year and a half.' I sit down on the nearest gold-brocade sofa as I begin to fully understand her confession. Then I look over at Logan. He looks away. I can't be angry with him. Not me. Not after all I've been through. But still, I find this information difficult to hear.

'Why on earth would you have pushed me so hard to stay with him?' This doesn't make sense. Not in my movie. Maybe this is more of a composite, after all. Maybe there isn't one real star. In life, everyone has a supporting role, right?

'Guilt, I guess. If it worked out between you, I would have backed off. Really,' she squeezes my hand. 'You have to know that. But we're good together. That's why I couldn't stop. I tried to. Every time you made a commitment to get back with him, I tried to leave him, but it just didn't work. We have a lot in common, it turns out.'

I think about the times when Janice called just as I was leaving for somewhere else. She must have been calling to talk to Logan, not me. Then something else occurs to me.

'You don't even smoke.' Whenever Marilynn and I have asked her to join us for a bit of pot and a stupid movie, she refuses.

She grins. 'Sometimes. With him it's fun.'

Logan and Janice always laugh at the same jokes, I remember. I picture different scenarios, like snapshots in my mind, and I recall how her eyes seem to light up when he's around. Why hadn't I noticed that before on a deeper level?

'So,' she says, 'you know, I was wrong.'

'You said that.'

'No, about the genre.'

'Meaning?'

'This wasn't a farce at all. But a comedy.'

'A romantic comedy,' I say, nodding. 'Thought you hated those.'

'The edgy ones can be good,' she says, and she seems shy for a minute, before I put my arms around her and give her a hug. What else can I do? She and Logan are perfect together. He and I are not. Now, the only thing missing is –

Brock.

And there he is, as if some director has given him the cue to enter. He walks to my side and looks down at me, a silent question in his eyes. I nod, flashing my bare hands before him, wiggling my naked fingers. Smiling, he joins me on the love seat, sliding closer until our bodies are hip to hip. 'So you made your decision.'

I nod.

'You answer when I speak to you.' My stomach clenches when he says these words, and I realise that I will always have this reaction to him. A combination of immediate star-bursts of desire and a wavering flitter of a delicious urge to submit. Together, the two feelings make me more aroused than anything I can think of.

'Yes, Sir,' I say, and then, 'Yes, Brock.'

He reaches for my hand. Just the brush of his finger-tips against mine makes me shiver.

'You ready for all of this, then?'

I start to nod, then catch myself. From the corner of my eye I see that Trini is watching us both through her sparkling glasses. She's standing with her date, and I suck in my breath when I realise she's with Sterling. I think about the fling Trini told me she had before her wedding, and I wonder if it was with a girl instead of a guy. My boss gives me an enthusiastic thumbs-up sign, as she continues to appraise Brock from the rear.

'Yes,' I say, and I feel the heat welling up in the centre of my chest and radiating outwards. 'Yes, Sir,' I say.

He reaches into his pocket and pulls out a small box. Inside is a simple platinum band. He slides it on my finger as he mouths just one word: 'Mine'.

It's all I ever wanted to be. All that and more.

Through the huge picture window, I can see his truck, with cans tied to the bumper. So he knew all along that ultimately I'd make the right decision. I've learned a lot over the past few weeks, but this is the thing that's made the biggest impression – workmen will surprise you every time.

Brock surprises me once more as we leave the mansion together. He drives us back to the site of one of our secret rendezvous, the secluded area in Will Rogers Park. Although the decor doesn't begin to rival the extravagance at Bernie's, this is much more my style. There are long white streamers attached to the trees and a red-and-white checkered blanket spread on the ground. The sun has warmed the air, and when he peels my white dress off of me, I stand naked before him, staring back at him, not ashamed, not guilty, not anything but pleased.

I realise as he looks me over that I feel more at ease with my body with Brock than I have with any other man. Maybe it's because he likes me when I'm clean, but he needs me when I'm dirty. Maybe it's because he thinks my hair looks good the first thing in the morning when I get up instead of right when I leave a fancy Beverly Hills salon. And maybe it's just because we're suited for each other, like characters are supposed to be in any romantic comedy.

He takes his time with his own suit, making me wait, but letting me admire every moment. I watch the jacket come off, then the shirt, shoes, slacks and boxers. When we're naked together, he spreads me out on the blanket and fucks me. His body is hard and powerful on top of mine. His hands roam everywhere, touching my face, stroking my hair, caressing my breasts. He kisses my lips and then moves his mouth along my shoulders, biting me hard, harder than he ever has, hard enough to leave marks.

'Oh, yes,' I sigh, thinking, finally. Finally!

As our bodies come together, pushing against one another, working with each in the perfect rhythm, I realise that I probably won't ever know everything there is to know about life, love and men in general.

But I do know something about workmen.

LOOK OUT FOR THE ALL-NEW BLACK LACE BOOKS – AVAILABLE NOW!

All books priced £6.99 in the UK. Please note publication dates apply to the UK only. For other territories, please contact your retailer.

SEXUAL STRATEGY
Felice de Vere
ISBN O 352 33843 1

Heleyna is incredibly successful. She has everything a girl could possibly want – a career, independence, and a very sexy partner who keeps her well and truly occupied. Accepting an invitation from her very naughty ex-boss to a frustratingly secretive club, she begins a journey of discovery that both teases and taunts her. Before too long she realises she is not the only person in the world feigning a respectable existence. **Sexual experimentation at its naughtiest!**

ARTISTIC LICENCE
Vivienne La Fay
ISBN O 352 33210 7

In Renaissance Italy, Carla is determined to find a new life for herself where she can put her artistic talents to good use. Dressed as boy – albeit a very pretty one – she travels to Florence and finds work as an apprentice to a master craftsman. All goes well until she is expected to perform licentious favours for her employer. In an atmosphere of repressed passion, it is only a matter of time before her secret is revealed. **Historical, gender-bending fun in this delightful romp.**

PALAZZO
Jan Smith
ISBN O 352 33156 9

When Claire and Cherry take a vacation in Venice they both succumb to the seductive charms of the city and the men who inhabit it. In the famous Harry's Bar, Claire meets a half-Italian, half-Scottish art dealer who introduces her to new facets of life, both cultural and sexual. Torn between the mysterious Stuart and her estranged husband Claire is faced with an impossible dilemma while Cherry is learning all about sexual indulgence. **Sophisticated and sexy.**

Coming In November

HARD BLUE MIDNIGHT
Alaine Hood
ISBN O 352 33851 2

Lori owns an antique clothes shop in a seaside town in New England, devoting all her energies to the business at the expense of her sex life. When she meets handsome Gavin MacLellan, a transformation begins. Gavin is writing a book about Lori's great-aunt, an erotic photographer who disappeared during World War II. Lori gets so wrapped up in solving the mystery that she accompanies Gavin to Paris to trace her ancestor's past. A growing fascination with bondage and discipline leads her into a world of secrecy and danger. **A tale of dark secrets and female desire.**

THE NAME OF AN ANGEL
Laura Thornton
ISBN O 352 33205 O

Clarissa Cornwall is a respectable university lecturer who has little time for romance until she encounters the insolently sexy Nicholas St Clair in her class on erotic literature. Suddenly her position – and the age gap between them – no longer matters as she finds herself becoming obsessed with this provocative young man. She tries to fight her desire but soon finds herself involved in a secret affair with this dangerously charismatic student. **Forbidden lusts and the appeal of young men.**

Coming in December

ALWAYS THE BRIDEGROOM
Tesni Morgan
ISBN O 352 33855 5

Jody Hamilton is a landscape gardener who has returned from the States to attend her best friend's wedding. All is well until Jody finds out what a sex-crazed rotter her best friend is about to marry. With too many people involved in the preparations for the big day, bickering, back-stabbing and infidelities soon ensue. But in the middle of the mayhem, Jody thinks she may have found the man of her dreams. **An exotic pot-pourri of sexual flavours.**

DOCTOR'S ORDERS
Deanna Ashford
ISBN O 352 33453 3

Helen Dawson is a dedicated doctor who has taken a short-term assignment at an exclusive private hospital that caters for the every need of its rich and famous clientele. The matron, Sandra Pope, ensures this includes their most curious sexual fantasies. When Helen risks an affair with a famous actor, she is drawn deeper into the hedonistic lifestyle of the clinic. **Naughty nurses get busy behind the screens.**

Black Lace Booklist

Information is correct at time of printing. To avoid disappointment check availability before ordering. Go to www.blacklace-books.co.uk. All books are priced £6.99 unless another price is given.

BLACK LACE BOOKS WITH A CONTEMPORARY SETTING

☐ IN THE FLESH Emma Holly	ISBN O 352 33498 3	£5.99
☐ SHAMELESS Stella Black	ISBN O 352 33485 1	£5.99
☐ INTENSE BLUE Lyn Wood	ISBN O 352 33496 7	£5.99
☐ THE NAKED TRUTH Natasha Rostova	ISBN O 352 33497 5	£5.99
☐ A SPORTING CHANCE Susie Raymond	ISBN O 352 33501 7	£5.99
☐ TAKING LIBERTIES Susie Raymond	ISBN O 352 33357 X	£5.99
☐ A SCANDALOUS AFFAIR Holly Graham	ISBN O 352 33523 8	£5.99
☐ THE NAKED FLAME Crystalle Valentino	ISBN O 352 33528 9	£5.99
☐ ON THE EDGE Laura Hamilton	ISBN O 352 33534 3	£5.99
☐ LURED BY LUST Tania Picarda	ISBN O 352 33533 5	£5.99
☐ THE HOTTEST PLACE Tabitha Flyte	ISBN O 352 33536 X	£5.99
☐ THE NINETY DAYS OF GENEVIEVE Lucinda Carrington	ISBN O 352 33070 8	£5.99
☐ DREAMING SPIRES Juliet Hastings	ISBN O 352 33584 X	
☐ THE TRANSFORMATION Natasha Rostova	ISBN O 352 33311 1	
☐ SIN.NET Helena Ravenscroft	ISBN O 352 33598 X	
☐ TWO WEEKS IN TANGIER Annabel Lee	ISBN O 352 33599 8	
☐ HIGHLAND FLING Jane Justine	ISBN O 352 33616 1	
☐ PLAYING HARD Tina Troy	ISBN O 352 33617 X	
☐ SYMPHONY X Jasmine Stone	ISBN O 352 33629 3	
☐ SUMMER FEVER Anna Ricci	ISBN O 352 33625 0	
☐ CONTINUUM Portia Da Costa	ISBN O 352 33120 8	
☐ OPENING ACTS Suki Cunningham	ISBN O 352 33630 7	
☐ FULL STEAM AHEAD Tabitha Flyte	ISBN O 352 33637 4	
☐ A SECRET PLACE Ella Broussard	ISBN O 352 33307 3	
☐ GAME FOR ANYTHING Lyn Wood	ISBN O 352 33639 0	
☐ FORBIDDEN FRUIT Susie Raymond	ISBN O 352 33306 5	
☐ CHEAP TRICK Astrid Fox	ISBN O 352 33640 4	

BLACK LACE BOOKS WITH AN HISTORICAL SETTING

BLACK LACE ANTHOLOGIES

BLACK LACE NON-FICTION

❏ THE BLACK LACE BOOK OF WOMEN'S SEXUAL   ISBN 0 352 33793 1   £6.99
    FANTASIES Ed. Kerri Sharp

To find out the latest information about Black Lace titles, check out the
website: www.blacklace-books.co.uk or send for a booklist with
complete synopses by writing to:

Black Lace Booklist, Virgin Books Ltd
Thames Wharf Studios
Rainville Road
London W6 9HA

Please include an SAE of decent size. Please note only British stamps
are valid.

Our privacy policy
We will not disclose information you supply us to any other parties.
We will not disclose any information which identifies you personally to
any person without your express consent.

From time to time we may send out information about Black Lace
books and special offers. Please tick here if you do not wish to
receive Black Lace information.   ❏